AN ELEPHANT ON YOUR NOSE

To Antony
Best wishes,
Warren

WARREN REED

First published by For Pity Sake Publishing Pty Ltd 2018
www.forpitysake.com.au

Cover design by Carley Commens, Carley Blue Designs
Book design by Barbie Robinson, Writing with Light
Printed in Australia by IngramSpark

A catalogue record for this
book is available from the
National Library of Australia

An Elephant on Your Nose / Warren Reed
9780648283973 (paperback)
9780648283980 (ebook)

PRAISE FOR *AN ELEPHANT ON YOUR NOSE*

'Warren Reed has a lifetime's experience in Asia and knows first-hand the world of modern spy craft. He has done readers a favour by putting his knowledge to use in his fiction. This latest novel pulls off the trick of being brisk-paced and absorbing, while also conveying larger truths about the new power game in Asia. I read it straight through."

— Jim Fallows, author of *China Airborne*
and national correspondent for *The Atlantic*

"Warren Reed clearly demonstrates the worldview of a practitioner and not just an entertainer. Having said that Warren manages to do things many writers fail to do - he informs and educates whilst writing about a hidden world of intelligence practitioners that few understand. Warren Reed does understand. Try not to take this book to bed as it will be difficult to put it down and go to sleep."

— Dr Michael Kennedy, Senior Lecturer
Police and Criminal Justice, Western Sydney University

"A cross-cultural, transnational thriller written with an insider's knowledge of bureaucracy and intelligence trade craft which at the same time serves as a prop for something much larger - the attempt by China to seduce and manipulate its neighbours to create a new Beijing-led, world order in Asia."

— Richard McGregor, author of *Asia's Reckoning*

"An Elephant on Your Nose is peppered with spy craft detail and a highly nuanced understanding of Japanese and Chinese culture and tradition that can only have come from Warren's own experience in the field as a deep-cover operative. The reader comes out of a Warren Reed novel wiser and heartily entertained. This is a grown-up spy thriller for the 21st Century."

— Ross Coulthart, Australian investigative journalist
and author of *The Lost Tommies*

PRAISE FOR OTHER WARREN REED NOVELS

Hidden Scorpion

"This book certainly captures the atmosphere of espionage operations. Its plot and characters have an authenticity that you don't find in spy novels these days. It's more like it really is than even the memoirs of so-called professionals."
— Phillip Knightly AM (1929-2016) journalist, critic and author of *Australia – A Biography of a Nation*

A sample of 5 star reviews on Amazon.com:

"A gripping well-written read."
"Real James Bond material."
"John le Carré eat your heart out."
"What a great read this is! This story has a ring of truth."

Code Cicada

"If half of what Reed writes is true about the way our spooks conduct business, we have a lot to worry about."
— *Sun Herald*

"The backbiting and internecine rivalry of our intelligence services is vivid and entirely plausible."
— *The Age*

"If you want to know what really goes on in the world of secret intelligence, then you must read this novel. It's the scary, sordid, unvarnished reality."
— Phillip Knightly AM (1929-2016) journalist, critic and author of *Australia – A Biography of a Nation*

"Recommended not only as a good spy tale, but also for its thought-provoking relevance to the current criticisms being levied against various spy agencies worldwide."
— *Good Reading*

This book is dedicated to those men and women who work in secret intelligence not just to enhance their country's interests but, through understanding and empathy, to try and make the world a better place.

*He can see a louse as far away as China
but is unaware of the elephant on his nose.*

Old Malay proverb

PART 1

Chapter 1

National Police Agency Headquarters, Tokyo Sunday, 1135 hours

Bella finished reading the secret reports and placed them quietly on the table. This will leave the Japanese scratching their heads, she thought to herself.

All of those attending were shocked by the picture emerging. The intelligence contained in the reports was startling, which was why the group had been called together over the weekend. The fact that it had been unexpectedly provided by Beijing made it even more intriguing. Translation from Mandarin to Japanese had been completed just an hour before the meeting convened.

"Yes, but is this all that they know? It's in the genes of the Chinese to hold something back."

Most of the people around the boardroom table nodded. After all, Hasegawa Junichiro, head of Japan's National Police Agency, was a man of harsh views.

So this is the cynical streak I've heard about, Bella mused. It was the first time she had met him. Thankfully, she had been afforded a private briefing on his career and idiosyncrasies by her closest Japanese friend. It was hardly the sort of rundown a Google search might throw up.

Hasegawa's attitude matched the icy atmosphere

in the room on this chilly Tokyo morning. He was never one to put people at ease. In his late fifties and stocky, he was short and balding, both of which were matters of acute sensitivity to him. He was also a chain smoker. Most people who needed to spend time in his company found this obnoxious. On this occasion he had refrained from lighting up. Surely it wasn't a concession to the foreign woman present?

Bella, one of MI6's rising stars, had a different attitude to the Chinese. She casually glanced at a few of the Japanese on the other side of the table. She knew some were more balanced in their approach to Beijing officialdom. She had seen the useful results of Japan's steady cooperation with the Central Kingdom – away from the public eye – while staying in the Chinese capital recently.

Bella glanced at the reports on the table. Was Hasegawa baiting her with his provocative comments? She dismissed the thought quickly. Based on what she'd heard about him he was probably just being himself. Understandably, he wants to know how good my contacts in the Chinese system are, she thought.

At thirty-eight, Isabella Di Stefano Butterfield was not a woman to be intimidated, nor was she tolerant of fools. As the daughter of a diplomat she'd grown up mixing with a much wider range of intelligent people than most. She was tall with an olive complexion, a noticeable presence among the other faces around the table.

The counter-terrorism meeting was a half-day affair and had been put together by Hasegawa to discuss this sudden outpouring of generosity from the Chinese. No inkling of the explosive contents of the secret reports involved had come from allied intelligence services, which was odd. Understandably, that had aroused Hasegawa's suspicion. What were the Chinese up to?

I know what's running through his mind, Bella thought. He thinks Beijing may have even more information up its sleeve but has passed on only a sketchy outline. And he no doubt assumes I'll have been completely briefed in China and passed on everything to my headquarters in London. He wants me to spill.

She was right, of course. Hasegawa was hoping for exactly that. She's obviously trusted by the Chinese, he pondered, but how much faith can we have in her, even if she is equally well-connected in Tokyo?

Hasegawa was grateful that today's meeting was in his native tongue. That was one small mercy. Her Japanese was certainly outstanding. His limited faculty in English made him feel self-conscious, but there had been no time to learn it properly as he'd climbed his way to the top. He made do with the smattering he had, which was dodgy at the best of times.

Bella was considering how lucky Japan had been, and by extension, Hasegawa himself, to receive this heads-up from the Chinese.

Except for the beheading by Islamic State of two Japanese in Syria in 2015, Japan had largely avoided becoming a target for Islamic extremism.

While home-grown radicals were popping up around the globe, Japan seemed to be free of the scourge, despite the large number of Muslim workers within its borders who did the menial jobs Japanese shunned. With so many Pakistanis and Bangladeshis living in the country it was only a matter of time before an IS cell or a lone-wolf launched an attack.

The government had already been warned by friendly services that Tokyo had been mentioned occasionally in intercepted IS communications. It was seen as a plum target, and a soft one. With Tokyo hosting the 2020 Summer Olympic Games, the Chinese reports would naturally send shockwaves through the upper echelons of government, defence, bureaucracy and the country's security apparatus.

Hasegawa glanced at Bella, who was studiously observing his every move and inflection, which he found galling. He knew it was vital to have her on side. As much as he detested having to pander to a gaijin — and a woman who was far junior to him in age to boot — he needed to ascertain how high her influence reached in the Beijing system.

She might be a useful back-channel for me into the Chinese leadership, he thought. But how amenable would she be, if at all? She's obviously adept at compartmentalising her experiences in various intelligence domains. And she's clearly masterful at constructing Chinese walls. That's reassuring in one sense but vaguely worrying in another.

They'd spent barely half an hour together, but from this and the few briefing notes he had gathered on her, Hasegawa already detested one thing about Bella. Her unassuming self-confidence was repugnant to him. She had clearly made her way in life based on her talents rather than her connections. He wished so much that he'd been able to do that himself. The more one was dependent upon contacts and the influence of others, he thought, the greater the need for bluff. In so many ways, she epitomised all that he wanted to be. Her ease with his native tongue and the handful of other languages she had also mastered was a key example. He simply felt a fool whenever he spoke English.

Bella glanced down at the reports again. They had come from Beijing's own operatives in Central Asia and revealed the degree of interest IS had in creating jihadist cells across the Asian region. One report, from a reliable source in Tajikistan, highlighted an unexpected development: a three-man IS team from Uzbekistan had recently slipped unnoticed into the southern Philippines province of Mindanao aboard a fishing trawler. Their aim was to link up with the Islamic terror group, Abu Sayef, without coming to the attention of American and other allied counter-terrorist bodies operating there with the tacit consent of the Philippines government.

The Uzbeks had been successful in their mission and had, uniquely, been able to strike up contact with a local jihadist cell run by Filipino nationals who had previously worked in Tokyo and established an IS cell in Japan. They had been musicians, entertainers, waiters and chefs and all had entered Japan on false passports that designated them Christians. This allowed them to fly under the radar. All had lived in Japan, undetected, for some time. The Uzbeks were keen to discuss the nature and viability of the Islamic cell they had established in Tokyo. Prior to this report, Bella believed, Japanese intelligence had been unaware of the cell. The report went so far as to helpfully point to a handful of Pakistanis, currently employed in labouring jobs, as the cell's most fervent members.

No one had spoken in the room, absorbing the briefing, so Hasegawa drew them back to the main task at hand, the content of the reports rather than their source.

"What makes this small group in Japan highly attractive to IS," he pointed out, "is the fact that some of the Filipinos involved still regularly re-enter Japan. And they do this on short-term employment contracts with Japanese businesses. The leader of the cell in Mindanao is, of all things, a regular visiting preacher at a Christian church in central Tokyo."

Hasegawa thumped his fist on the table, as much out of frustration as for emphasis. "This is an extraordinary cover identity, which the leader has adroitly crafted and maintained for more than ten years!"

He paused, letting the reality sink in. All of this was manna from heaven for IS, everyone listening realised, whether it was a Christian heaven or an Islamic one.

Hasegawa continued, highlighting the main threats that this revelation posed to Japan. The others knew what he was doing. Even though they had all read the reports, he wanted to make sure they focused their minds on what he regarded as the salient points. Whenever someone raised an interesting dimension he tended to talk over them, which some of those present found galling.

Bella was unimpressed by his management style, though her body language deliberately led him to believe she held him in high regard. She was only too aware of the role that silence played in Northeast Asia. On the one hand, it could be used to display deference. On the other, it could wield disdain with the dexterity of a surgeon's scalpel.

To date, the Tokyo cell had managed to provide a steady flow of reporting via Pakistan to IS in Central Asia and the Middle East. Most of this material related to itinerant Japanese business people and aid workers who might be attractive targets for hostage-taking. The cell had also procured a wide variety of technology and equipment keenly sought after by IS for delivery to jihadist cells in Europe, North America, East Africa and Australia.

Hasegawa's level of frustration rose a few notches as he rapidly moved on to what worried him most. It was one thing for him to try to protect Japanese living and working abroad, but his primary obligation was to safeguard the population at home.

"These radical Pakistanis in Tokyo are eager to move beyond this limited pattern of activity," he stressed, "and start planning real attacks on Japanese soil. They've clearly devoted much time and energy to studying the goals of our own doomsday cult, Aum Shinrikyo."

He did not elaborate. And those listening

knew why: he was still acutely embarrassed by what the cult had been planning, right under the Police Agency's nose, even if what they ultimately achieved fell far short of their goal.

In 1995, Aum Shinrikyo had launched a sarin gas attack on the Tokyo subway system. Highly qualified cult members had earlier attempted to isolate and transport the Ebola virus from Africa but had found it too volatile. Instead, they had turned to sarin gas, purchasing in Japan the necessary chemicals for its production and then flying with them to Western Australia.

That scenario was already vivid in Bella's mind, for reasons the Japanese were unaware of. Her cousin, who ran sheep farms in Australia, had become indirectly involved.

The cult's load of chemicals, she recalled, had been checked in as excess baggage at Narita International Airport. The eye-popping quantity involved failed to attract the attention of officialdom in either Japan or Australia. On arrival in Perth, cult members leased a sheep farm, paying in cash. Nobody along the way, including her cousin's property agent, thought this odd. Once settled on their land, the Japanese carried out experiments on the sheep at their disposal. They returned unhindered to Tokyo with the refined chemical agents required for the production of the deadly gas.

But it was the cult's original intent that still traumatised Hasegawa and everyone knew it. The plan had been to hire helicopters and release the Sarin gas over Tokyo, killing millions. A meteorologist had worked out optimal times for the gas to be released and dispersed by air currents. The hire of the helicopters, however, had proved problematic and the Aum adherents had opted instead for the subway. The cult had members across a broad spectrum of Japanese society: bureaucrats, defence force members, scientists – even a nuclear physicist – and most embarrassingly, police.

Back then, Hasegawa had been a pushy young member of the NPA's internal security unit, which had failed dismally to detect such penetration of the Agency's ranks by radical movements like Aum. His boss, the unit's commander, had been demoted and disgraced, while Hasegawa himself had been narrowly saved by contacts elsewhere in the system.

The fact that he studiously steered clear of all this left a huge silent space in his monologue. Like the Japanese around her, Bella's erudite nodding plastered over such glaring gaps. It was a useful habit that she had mastered in both China and Japan.

But everyone knew that the Pakistani jihadists would have been fascinated by the boldness of this plan. No doubt they had come to believe that something equally as devastating, though less challenging to carry out, could be devised in the lead-up to the 2020 Games. Word of this had obviously been passed back to IS, which had promptly dispatched the three-man Uzbek team to the Philippines, travelling on false Indian papers.

"While the Japanese government," Hasegawa stated, "has remained on full alert following the ravages of 9/11, I fear that a sense of complacency has returned. This was quickly dispelled by the capture and beheading of the two Japanese nationals in Syria a few years ago. But within the government the threat is still perceived to be remote."

Hasegawa had proved yet again that his interpretation of the intelligence should be considered superior to his subordinates and colleagues around the table. His style never lent itself to teamwork. Few in the National Police Agency were bold enough to throw up alternate interpretations and that worried everyone, even Bella, who had been forewarned of his managerial style.

"Now, as a goodwill gesture to Japan," he said, "the Chinese government has decided to pass these reports on, exclusively, before sharing them with other countries' counter-terrorist agencies. We've also been provided with additional reporting by Chinese intelligence assessing the veracity of the information."

Straightening his tie, he turned to his British guest.

"Butterfield San," he said, addressing Bella directly for the first time and using a more honorific form of address than expected, "while the action of the Chinese government in this regard is something for which we are all deeply grateful, might I seek your view on a particular aspect of it that has my colleagues and I rather puzzled?"

Bella nodded, casting him her most accommodating look. The others around the table, some of whose thoughts had wandered during his lengthy discourse on the threat posed to Japan, were suddenly riveted.

"Why do you think it's been possible," he continued, "for Chinese intelligence to produce reports of this alarming nature, yet not include in them any of the detail – names, addresses, telephone numbers – that my colleagues and I so urgently require? Would you imagine that the identities of the Filipino radicals involved and their Pakistani conspirators here in Tokyo have somehow not been ascertained?"

Bella chose not to respond immediately, sensing that Hasegawa was testing her: how much more did she know and would she reveal it? A touch of silence, she thought, might draw him out, without appearing reticent or rude. It was a tactic she used with skill. What she knew, she would keep to herself.

Hasegawa glanced around the table as though garnering support for his bluntness, even if it had been couched in exquisitely polite terms the Japanese language was renowned for.

"Could anything like that be known," he persisted, "and yet, accidentally or otherwise, not be passed on to us?"

Like Bella, the others in the room were aware that his use of the term accidentally was plainly sarcastic.

"No, not really," she responded, her tone contemplative and open. "Of course anything's possible, but I shouldn't imagine your counterparts in Beijing would hold back on a matter as significant as this. After all, why would they make such a gesture in the first place, but leave it incomplete? You and your colleagues, Hasegawa San, may be conscious of factors I have no knowledge of, but my view would be that the Chinese are reaching out to you. It's a gesture I believe should, perhaps, be taken at face value."

Hasegawa nodded, as did the others. It was a valid point and one nicely articulated in Japanese. What Bella said had effectively closed off the issue for further discussion. It was clear that she had no intention of portraying herself as an emissary of the Chinese, or even as a go-between. After all, everyone knew that Bella's arrival in Japan had nothing whatsoever to do with China. It was for a vastly different reason, and one that would distract Hasegawa's attention from the urgent task of tracking down the Pakistani jihadists in Tokyo.

More than anything else, Hasegawa was terrified that they might launch an attack before he had a chance to arrest and expose them. Such a failure on his part to protect the nation's capital would not only be ignominiously terminal for his professional career, but might also oblige him to commit suicide.

Chapter 2

Lobby, Imperial Hotel, Tokyo
Sunday, 1500 hours

Bella had not waited long in the plush lobby for her closest Japanese friend to show up. A gaggle of German tourists were taking selfies in front of a massive floral arrangement on a table, which was customarily the first thing that greeted anyone entering the hotel. It was an impressive statement of the essential role that nature played in Japanese culture.

As was her friend's habit, he approached quietly from behind and tapped her on the shoulder. She had already raised her hand to greet him, having noticed the giveaway smile on the face of an elderly Japanese man sitting in front of her, who'd spotted someone sneaking up.

Sakamoto Masataka – lean, athletic and wearing a permanent tan – and Bella were like brother and sister. Some would say twins. The fact that neither had siblings seemed to have made the relationship even stronger. They had spent years together in international schools when their fathers were on diplomatic postings.

They moved across to an area where coffee and snacks were served. Masataka hugged her warmly before they were seated. Having been brought up overseas, he was more demonstrative than most

Japanese men, a dimension of his personality that served him well. He was a member of the House of Representatives - Shūgiin - and was one of the best-known and respected politicians in the country, which was no mean achievement for a man in his late-thirties. He was frequently on TV panel discussions and his popularity crossed all party lines, due largely to his common-sense approach on issues of national and international importance. Some government members, however, found him uncomfortably outspoken on matters they far preferred to avoid.

"So, Bella Chan," he said, using an intimate form of Japanese reserved for close friends and family, "what did you think of Hasegawa? I have a particular reason for asking."

His expression was stern, which suggested there was even more to the National Police Chief than met the eye, though this in no way surprised her.

"Masa, I have to be frank. I didn't like his manner at all. The meeting was supposed to be a free-ranging exchange of ideas on home-grown terrorism, with no official note-takers scribbling away at the back of the room. Instead, it was tense and the few people brave enough to cast something into the arena, did so with such trepidation − it was like Vatican functionaries briefing the Pope on child abuse in the Catholic Church!"

Masataka laughed. He'd always loved Bella's analogies. Not that they were always suitable for polite company, but they were unfailingly relevant as well as evocative.

"I don't think anybody in the room really wanted

to be there," she continued, "no matter how great our interest was in the topics on the agenda. I suppose all of Hasegawa's meetings are stage-managed like that."

"So I've heard," Masataka said, leaning across the small table between them. "In fact, a few Cabinet colleagues I was talking to the other day told me he has a reputation for dampening down debate on political issues that might frighten the horses."

"Perhaps that's his most notable skill," Bella said, "along with being a control freak."

Masataka smiled in a way that told his British friend there was too much about Japan, like Hasegawa, that wasn't changing in this day and age.

"I gather he was trying to curry favour with you," he added.

"Yes, indeed. But I don't think it came naturally to him, what with me being a gaijin and a female."

Now it was Bella leaning across the table.

"But tell me, what's going on with him that I need to know? I assume it's something I'd rather not hear."

"Well, he's closely aligned to that wise monkey, Nakamura Keita. He's the toughest of the anti-China hawks in the government, which is one reason he's close to Hasegawa. As far as they're all concerned, no good can ever come out of gestures we make to Beijing, nor from any they make to us."

Bella had a fair idea where this was going.

"They're determined to install him as head of the new set-up you're here to help establish. Which means that any intelligence on China, from whatever source, would pass across his desk first. Everything going to Cabinet, and even briefings for members of parliament, especially those on key committees, will pass through his filter."

Bella shook her head. "This is precisely what my bosses in London feared might happen. They want to see a far more outward-oriented Japan, one that can make a more extensive and useful contribution to the allied intelligence community. If people of this ilk have their way, they'll emasculate the new agency before it's even up and running."

It had taken a lot of subtle persuasion on MI6's part, bolstered by the heads of other allied services, to be invited to help establish a Japanese equivalent of Britain's Secret Intelligence Service. To date, Japan had made do with an odd sort of body – the Cabinet Intelligence Research Office – that coordinated intelligence of all kinds from a wide variety of sources. The system was fragmented and well overdue for a major shake-up.

"I can't say I'm pleased to hear any of this," Bella said, "though from the very start I never expected your system here to adopt MI6's blueprint lock-stock-and-barrel. Of course, it would end up having distinctly Japanese characteristics. But any attempt to adulterate intelligence on key global issues will simply render a new spy service untrustworthy on practically everything. I mean, the essence of all intelligence gathering is to get a fix on what reality is rather than what someone else wants it to be!"

This unfortunate disposition would also impact on Bella's input to the process of setting up a virtual carbon copy of the legendary MI6, as the Japanese Prime Minister had told both his British counterpart and the head of her Service. A team of MI6 officers, which included Bella, would soon assemble in Tokyo to get things under way.

"With the goalposts already moving at this early stage," she observed, "I'm worried about what sort of hybrid agency we'll end up with. It might be even worse than the dog's breakfast you already have."

As she watched Masataka now, she knew what was going through his mind. Deep-seated disappointment showed on his face. Where will all this end up? she thought. And what did Masataka mean when he suggested Hasegawa might have an agenda even grander than simply controlling Japan's new spy service?

Law Faculty, University of Tokyo
Monday, 0912 hours

"I'd like to make just one point about China," Bella said, "and it comes from a vastly different angle to what you might expect. In fact, it was a story told to me by my father when I was a child in London that spurred my interest in the Central Kingdom. The tale had originated, of all places, in Palermo on the island of Sicily. And why Palermo? Because that's where my Italian mother's family hails from. My father met her on his first posting with the Foreign Office to Rome where, as they tell me, it was love at first sight. She was a budding microbiologist at the time."

The Japanese law students were intrigued.

Masataka knew Bella's story well, as he did the reaction it customarily drew from people who had never heard about China's obscure influence on the European world.

Her gift, he was thinking, is to always start off on a human note. And she does it so instinctively and naturally that people are immediately drawn in. Whenever Masataka had tried this approach he felt he'd come across stilted before he had even finished making the point. On TV he'd been told he presented more like Bella, but he couldn't understand how she managed to be so consistent no matter who she was addressing.

Bella had immediately accepted Masataka's offer to address a group of thirty PhD students in international law. While she was waiting for her MI6 colleagues to arrive in Japan she had some free time on her hands, which was something that rarely happened, plus she could run a two-hour briefing off the top of her head. It was right up her alley to do this favour for Masataka. The topic was how she had first become interested in China and in which direction did she think that country was now heading.

Masataka was on a standing brief from his old university to come up with interesting speakers for this monthly event, chaired by the Dean, a crusty academic of the traditional Confucian school. Masataka was ever keen to keep him on side. One critical word from the Dean in public of some government policy that Masataka was promoting would be like the kiss of death. If you can charm the old man for me, Masataka had told Bella, I'll be indebted to you for life.

"On my father's first trip to Palermo to meet the parents of his wife-to-be, an elderly scholar in the family told him something of enormous significance. Surprisingly, my father was unaware of it, despite his deep interest in history. The Norman Empire, which covered most of Europe and beyond in the tenth and eleventh centuries was centred in Palermo and it had a powerful link with China."

None of the students in the room, nor the Dean, had any idea what this revelation might be. Bella knew she had their full attention. This was the moment Masataka always savoured. Bella was a master of timing. When she had an audience in the palm of her hand she knew just how long to keep them in suspense before delivering her punch line. He so often wished he had her gift, for timing was everything in politics. Bella sometimes joked with him that if they were to cut each other in half and create two new people they might stand a better chance of attaining perfection.

"An American scholar by the name of Creel," she said, "in a major work called *The Origins of Statecraft in China* in 1971, looked at the extensive flow of knowledge on China that came into Europe via the Silk Road. And it came mainly via the court of the Norman king, Roger II in Sicily who lived between 1093 and 1154. He ran what was probably then the world's greatest translation unit."

The Dean caught Masataka's eye and smiled, which meant even he didn't know this. That was quite a gesture.

"Creel," Bella continued, "noted that the most startling and perhaps the most illuminating similarities between China and the West appear when comparing China's government as it existed two-thousand years ago and the highly centralised bureaucratic administration of modern Western nations. He quotes a European thinker who said that almost to the end of the 18th century, the Chinese were far in advance of the rest of the world in matters of administrative organisation."

No one listening, except for Masataka (and perhaps the Dean), had ever heard a Westerner acknowledge a flow of wisdom from the East to the West. The inference always was that it could ever only flow the other way. Like gravity, things fell downwards, never upwards. What Masataka also knew was that most of this Eastern knowledge had come along the Silk Road with Arab traders and scholars, much of it in the Arabic language as well as in Chinese. As a girl, the stories Bella had heard of this great transfer inspired her interest in those two languages.

"It's interesting to note," she continued, "that this new knowledge of China reached Europe at a time when it couldn't fail to have an enormous impact. Great thinkers of the Enlightenment discovered to their astonishment that more than two thousand years before, in China, Confucius had thought the same thoughts in the same manner and fought the same battles. He became the patron saint of that 18th century movement. Even Voltaire went so far as to claim that the happiest period on earth, and the one most worthy of respect, was the time of Confucius."

The Dean's erudite nods gave Masataka great satisfaction. These continued unabated, as though his head and neck were locked into that pattern for all time.

"But eventually," Bella concluded, "the so-called Dream of China came to an end and adulation was replaced with denigration. The very fact that there had once been this great interest in China was forgotten, though Napoleon warned us some two hundred years ago that it would definitely return."

"And it has," the Dean observed. The PhD students were all nodding now.

"Bella," the Dean asked, "do tell us where you think Japan fits into all of this? Many people would say it has lost its way."

Bella pondered the question for some time, which in Japan was no mere deference to knowledge and learning. It was also an indication that you didn't think you knew everything.

"Professor, in my humble opinion," she responded, "I think Japan will in time decide to return to its roots. And I don't think that process will require it in any way to diminish its established links with the world beyond Asia. Maybe when Japan does that, and ultimately draws closer to China and South Korea, we might find ourselves truly living in what's called an Asian Century. The global contribution these three countries can make cooperatively could outstrip anything we've seen to date. I hope it's something I might see in my lifetime."

Masataka was quietly chuffed. This point, as well as the way in which Bella presented it, was something he could put to great use in the near future, and in a variety of ways. He would raise it with her as soon as they were outside in the fresh air.

His parliamentary driver was waiting for them at Akamon, the university's famed Red Gate, an ancient temple-like structure. As they drove off towards the city centre Masataka squeezed Bella's hand.

"I can't thank you enough for this morning," he said. "You were a hit with the students and most importantly with the Dean. But be careful. Don't assume because you can win him over you might be able to do the same with Hasegawa. No way. He's a very different kettle of fish. Rather than wasting your efforts on him I'd love to see you win over the few people around him he clearly trusts. That would be a real achievement."

"Well, I'll do my best," Bella replied.

A gentle autumn breeze dislodged a sprinkling of yellow leaves from the avenue of camphor trees nearby.

Chapter 3

Prime Minister's Former Official Residence
Nagatachō, Tokyo,
Monday, 1420 hours

Twenty-two people sat around a large rectangular table in the 1929 building designed in the style of American architect Frank Lloyd Wright. The room was musty, which fitted the eerie feeling of the place. That was one reason the Prime Minister had refused to live here. He was happier ensconced in the new, modern-style official residence that had been completed a decade before and was adjacent to the Diet, as the Japanese Parliament was known. That was his principal office as well as that of Ozawa Takahiro, the Chief Cabinet Secretary. It was where government meetings were held and where certain foreign leaders were welcomed.

The eight member MI6 team had arrived at the old residence early, along with the Tokyo Head of Station and a senior Japanese-speaking diplomat from the British Embassy. The team leader had been forewarned of the nature of the old building and on seeing it, regarded the location as a slight to the visitors and the goodwill mission that had brought them here. But that was not something he was going to complain about. After all, the British government wanted as much as it could get from this deal with the Japanese. There could be years of expensive training courses in it, as well as purchases of specialised gadgetry and technology, and a myriad other things beyond the realm of intelligence cooperation. The greatest prize of all would be the remarkable access MI6 would have to key Japanese personnel staffing the new spy service, especially if it were to be involved in the selection process. Prime targets for cultivation and recruitment could be readily identified at such a time. It was a golden window of opportunity and one that needed to be handled with exquisite care and finesse.

Ozawa now declared the meeting open and formally introduced the Japanese side. He was close to seventy years of age and had agreed with the Prime Minister that it was appropriate for him to attend the afternoon meeting and make a welcoming statement – or scene-setter, as he liked to call it. He would only depart when confident that the MI6 team appreciated that Western models didn't always fit snugly into an Eastern environment.

The PM had also instructed that Sakamoto Masataka not attend the meeting. The government's star politician had his finger in enough pies as it was. A call from Police Chief Hasegawa (who had helped the Japanese leader extricate himself from many a sticky situation) had convinced the PM that sidelining the Wonder Boy of Japanese politics would be wise in this instance.

The powerful axis between Sakamoto Masataka and his gaijin handmaiden, the Butter Bitch, as Hasegawa and his cohorts referred to Bella, should be nipped in the bud. They were simply too risky to have around together when key matters that could impact Hasegawa's plans for China were being discussed.

Speaking from prepared notes in English, Ozawa talked of the new world that everyone had lived in since the 9/11 catastrophes in New York, Washington and Pennsylvania.

"Nowadays," he said, "we find ourselves collaborating like never before. We're exchanging secret intelligence with governments and regimes that, twenty years ago, we'd never have imagined we'd want anything to do with."

Silent agreement surged from one end of the table to the other. This was not only in response to what Ozawa had said, but also in acknowledgement of the fact that he was a consummate politician and minister. He was a dab hand at painting on a broad canvas. Bella picked that up quickly and hoped he wouldn't waste too much time spinning his artistic web.

"Now, to grapple with all of this effectively," he continued, "we must ensure that we have the appropriate machinery of government in place. And moreover, that suitable mechanisms exist for sharing vital intelligence and know-how between our relevant agencies. I vividly recall something I was told by our American friends when I led a Japanese delegation to Washington after the 9/11 tragedies. And that was the dangerous role that intelligence silos had played in the American system, where hugely important pieces of information were simply not shared. Hence, the overall picture that top government decision-makers in Washington were presented with at crucial junctures was too often far from complete."

Another spate of agreement passed down the table.

"On behalf of the Japanese government," Ozawa said, "we are deeply grateful to our parliamentary colleagues in London for sending us a team of uniquely experienced officers from the illustrious British Secret Intelligence Service to help reorganise our ungainly apparatus. Britain and Japan have long been allies and the high degree of trust that we share allows this kind of assistance to be rendered. We sincerely hope that in the days and weeks to follow a concrete plan for the changes we most need to make will emerge from the dialogue between our two sides."

The veteran MI6 man leading the British team smiled as he caught Bella's eye in subtle recognition of these platitudes. The Japanese and British were unrivalled in their mastery of such empty language. Bella was wondering whether the Chief Cabinet Secretary might bow out at this stage, but he turned to a new page in his notes. What more could he possibly say without intruding upon the meaty structural issues that the meeting would itself soon have to address? She knew her team leader was thinking the same thing.

"My mind flashes back," Ozawa declared with some gusto, "to a lecture I attended many years ago as a student at the University of Tokyo. It was a talk by the head of the legal division of the Gaimusho, our Foreign Ministry, who enlightened us on the interrelationship between law and diplomacy. He spoke warmly, indeed passionately, about the great scholar diplomats that Britain, and almost Britain alone, had produced in the late 19th and early 20th centuries. These outstanding men were vital go-betweens as cultures interacted like never before. It was a time when the very building blocks of today's global community were being carefully put in place."

Bella could see where this was going. In a shared moment of eye contact with the Embassy diplomat accompanying the MI6 team, she knew he did too.

"What the Gaimusho gentleman emphasised in his lecture," Ozawa said, "were the extraordinary achievements of that great Englishman, Sir Ernest Satow, who wasn't just a scholar and diplomat but also an expert on Japan. He even married a Japanese woman. Satow was a brilliant linguist, an enthusiastic traveller, a writer of guidebooks, a dictionary compiler, an avid botanist, a mountain climber and a notable collector of Japanese books and manuscripts on all kinds of topics."

At this point, the MI6 team understood that the message in all this would come very soon, delivered – as the British themselves liked to say – with brutal subtlety.

"Satow was also a master of calligraphy," Ozawa went on, "which, as you all know, goes to the very essence of culture here in the Far East."

His addition of the archaic word far was obviously an historical dig he found too tempting to resist. Who could blame him? Bella was thinking.

After all, that was Eurocentric myopia at its peak.

Ozawa paused and opened a folder he had under his notes.

"I have here for you all copies of a classical piece in the great man's own calligraphy, in his own hand. It's a famous poem by the noted Tang Dynasty poet, Wang Bo."

Ozawa handed them to the Embassy diplomat to distribute to the MI6 guests. The copies were a high quality reproduction of Satow's work. Bella and the diplomat expressed their astonishment in Japanese to their hosts. Foreigners rarely excelled at this ancient form of writing, which was as much an art form of great beauty as it was a means of communication.

The Cabinet Secretary was delighted, which left Bella with a sense of cultural entrapment. But it would have been rude for her and the diplomat, fluent in written and spoken Japanese, not to have reacted in this way. Ozawa then went in for the kill.

"So, we trust," he said, "that in the spirit of Satow in the coming days, all of you gathered here will be able to construct a model that draws on Britain's rich intelligence heritage to take root here in the soil of Japan."

He paused to ensure that his message had registered, which it had. Bella recalled Masataka's warning: there'll be no outright copying of an MI6 template. Rather, it will be a game of compromise and negotiation at every turn. A game of cat and mouse. My God, Bella mused to herself, this could be tortuous as well as totally unproductive.

Police Chief Hasegawa had had enough history for his liking, though Bella could tell he was impressed with the masterful way in which Ozawa had delivered his message.

Of course, Hasegawa was thinking, some minion would have written his speech for him. All well and good for this exercise, but the possibility of a Pakistani jihadist strike right here in Tokyo is what we should be focusing on right now. His abject fear of an attack was emblazoned across the front of his mind and the Cabinet Secretary's waffle only highlighted the fact to those watching.

His mind drifted as Ozawa began his concluding remarks. At least I've stepped up surveillance, he thought, both physical and electronic, on suspects who might be linked to the terror cell, no matter how tenuous those links are. I have more police concentrating on this than anything I've done in recent years.

Hasegawa had set his phone on vibrate and was prepared to excuse himself at any moment to go to the bathroom if he felt the slightest pulsation in his pocket. Enough time had been wasted on this mindless tact and diplomacy.

Ozawa left without further ado, handing the meeting over to Hasegawa, who promptly called on Sir Crispin Grenville, the dignified middle-aged MI6 team leader, to outline the basic structure of Britain's secret intelligence service. Even in this simple task, Hasegawa was hesitant in English, needing to consult a large notebook he had in front of him. In Japanese, he invited Bella to interpret Sir Crispin's presentation, then settled back and lit up a cigarette.

Those who worked with Hasegawa knew his smoking habits well. At a meeting like this, especially with foreigners present, lighting up one meant he'd probably smoke his way through the whole pack. The air in the room was stale enough as it was.

Bella interpreted Hasegawa's indulgence as a display of supreme confidence, even cockiness. She did not feel it augured well. Grenville, ever the smooth British mandarin, provided a succinct rundown of MI6 in less than three minutes.

Hasegawa thanked him and then called upon a senior officer in his National Police Agency to provide an overview of Japan's recent intelligence history. This was expertly delivered in impeccable English, which drew high praise from Sir Crispin.

The NPA officer, Kuroda Takeshi, was in his mid-forties, had chiselled features and a pleasing and confident manner. He described the nature of Japan's fragmented intelligence system as it currently existed. The community had about 4,400 personnel split into units under different ministries. This had proved to be a major design fault, he said. He meant that communication and sharing between officers in any one part of the system were hampered by a reluctance to share secrets across bureaucratic divides. He made a passing reference to the silos that the Americans had discovered when examining the intelligence failures that had led to 9/11, especially those that existed between the CIA and the FBI.

Hasegawa nodded as each point was made, reflecting on how much better off he'd be if he too could make such presentations in English. Measuring himself against the other Japanese present, he concluded that he would be the worst performer in the room in that regard. That riled him no end. In his own obsessive way, he'd come to consider the quality of any Japanese person's English as an intellectual high jump. The norm appeared to be that everyone else could get over the bar, while he was the lone figure standing off to one side without plaster or crutches, attesting to why he wasn't competing.

Bella had already sensed this, as she had the esteem in which Hasegawa held his colleague making the presentation. Kuroda then ran through the various Japanese agencies involved. The main actors, he said, were his own organisation, as well as the Defence Ministry's Defence Intelligence Headquarters. Then there was the Foreign Ministry, the Cabinet Intelligence Research Office, whose staff came primarily from other ministries. There was also another body – the Justice Ministry's Public Security Intelligence Agency.

There was a fleeting pause, almost a hesitation, when he mentioned the PSIA. Bella noticed that Hasegawa looked down at the table.

The MI6 team was very much aware of why this was. Only the Deputy Chief of the PSIA was present, along with a colleague who was listed as Assistant to the Chief. The British Embassy diplomat, as well as Bella and her fellow team members, knew that the Chief himself was under a cloud. The latest MI6 reporting had suggested he was under suspicion of receiving payments from unspecified 'foreign organisations', which they knew meant he'd possibly betrayed his country's interests. It seemed that China was the culprit. This was a matter that had not yet attracted the attention of journalists in Tokyo's gaggle of exclusive media groups. Each belonged to a specific ministry and reported only what was fed to them. Hasegawa intended to keep it that way, at least until he was ready to strike.

Bella guessed what Hasegawa might be planning. He was closely aligned with the Prime Minister and a number of nationalist politicians in the government camp, who appeared to be receptive to his idea of folding the NPA and the PSIA into an American FBI-style body. It would be Japan's premier security organisation. Naturally, he saw himself as its founding head but he didn't want the new Japanese foreign spy agency to rank equally alongside it.

Hasegawa, Bella knew, was determined to be seen as someone who could not only handle change, but instigate it — massively upgrading Japan's intelligence capability in the process. But to do this he needed to have an in of his own into Beijing. And Bella was only too aware of how he might be eying her to fill that role.

I hold the ace card, Hasegawa was musing now as Kuroda continued speaking to the group. The PSIA knows nothing yet of the Filipino-Pakistani jihadist cell operating right under our noses here in Tokyo. That's hot new intelligence and I have no intention of sharing it with anyone at this stage. I'll use it to highlight the PSIA's chronic shortcomings. Right under their noses! will be the catch-cry when the truth is eventually out. Nothing cuts deeper than ridicule.

For Hasegawa to be called upon to establish a Japanese version of the FBI that incorporated an overseas spy agency, and to lead it through to the 2020 Tokyo Summer Olympic Games and thereafter, would be the pinnacle of his career. He was determined to maintain his strong position with the government as the custodian – indeed, even the driver and mid-wife – of this concept. He would be Japan's security and intelligence tsar.

He was pleased with how matters were progressing in today's meeting and impressed with Kuroda's presentation skills. It confirmed why he had selected the younger man for this task and to handle other delicate matters as well.

"There is reluctance," Kuroda continued, "for various parts of our system to work together cohesively and effectively. A combination of factors have given rise to this predicament and we all recognise these must be addressed. Help from our MI6 friends in this regard will be deeply appreciated. Put plainly, we lack cohesion and unity, as well as rules and guidelines for setting common standards across all of our agencies. We need to define fundamental issues like what secret material actually is, how it should be handled, and what to do to prevent leaks. We've recently introduced a state secrets law in Japan, but without mutually agreed standards inside our intelligence system it's proving difficult to enforce that legislation."

Hasegawa could not have been happier with

the points that Kuroda had made. One reason he liked him was that he never said too much.

"You can see why we need your advice," Hasegawa ventured in English, addressing himself to Grenville. "I think we have a big problem here with what I believe you call turf battles. Without common standards, the grass grows taller and taller to the extent that we lose ourselves in it."

Grenville had a horsey laugh and unleashed it in response to this observation. Hasegawa felt a warm glow inside. His offsider's briefing beforehand on useful – and safe – points to make in English had served him well.

Kuroda continued: "We have a great need in Japan for coordinated human intelligence collection to complement our existing signals and technical intelligence capabilities. As you would know, our most pressing intelligence priorities are China and North Korea, as well as the global terrorist threat. Many times, for example, our American friends have urged us to exploit more forthrightly Japan's under utilised assets in our business enterprises overseas."

Hasegawa again observed in English, "We hear that MI6 is better at this than anyone else, certainly far better than the Germans or the French."

Grenville smiled deferentially.

"With the ISIS killing of two Japanese hostages in the Middle East," Kuroda went on, "our system was disgraced. We simply had no real presence there and had to rely on countries like Jordan and Turkey for help. So Japanese public sentiment has now become slightly more receptive to the idea of beefing up our intelligence gathering and analytical capabilities so that we can do the job properly. Put simply, we must have boots on the ground, our own clandestine operatives abroad who can develop the contacts and secret networks we need."

There was nothing to disagree with in that, as Hasegawa readily perceived from the MI6 team's reaction to what Kuroda had said.

"We must never, never," Hasegawa ventured in cautious English, "see a repeat of our disaster some years back when the former North Korean leader, Kim Jong-Il, was ailing. Our best insights then came not from secret sources but from Kim's former Japanese sushi chef who published a memoir!"

Hasegawa laughed heartily.

Ever the diplomat, Sir Crispin opined, "Well, Hasegawa San, we've all suffered embarrassments like that, rest assured."

The NPA Chief was more than satisfied with the air of camaraderie that had developed in this first meeting with the British. Now, he mused to himself, let's see what we can get out of this bunch that's in any way relevant to what I want to do here.

So far, with Kuroda's help, it's a job well done. But any spy agency we eventually establish will be under my wing and nobody else's. And I'm sure the PM and those with influence around him will back me. After all, they're only too aware of what could fall off the back of a truck if they don't. But the greatest threat to me right now is this cursed jihadist cell in Tokyo. If it gets to launch an attack before I have a chance to crush it, then everything is lost.

Office of the Chief,
National Police Agency Headquarters, Tokyo
Monday, 1651 hours

It was the last thing that Hasegawa had wanted to happen, but there was no way he could buck a Prime Ministerial directive on such a pressing matter of national security.

He had briefed the PM on the intelligence the Chinese had shared on the Filipino-Pakistani jihadist cell operating in Tokyo, and the urgent need to find out whether Beijing knew more than it was letting on. The PM could hardly have been expected to act any differently. After all, Sakamoto Masataka was the go-to man for tasks like this with China. His success rate, admittedly, was good. Hasegawa had hoped to make the trip himself but had been over-ruled.

On reflection, he realised that if he were a Mandarin-speaker like Wonder Boy, he might have stood a chance. The most galling thing was the PM had instructed him to personally brief Masataka on what the Chinese had provided, what they might be holding back, and what favours they might ask in return for additional material. It riled Hasegawa that he was being outstripped by a politician, and one without a skerrick of experience in policing, security or intelligence gathering.

The saving grace for him in Masataka's trip was the possibility that he might return with something substantial that would help expose and destroy the jihadist cell. That would be a coup of the first order and one that Hasegawa would ruthlessly exploit.

Only time would tell.

Yet another irritant gnawed at his guts: the prospect of Masataka seeking the Butter Bitch's counsel on his upcoming Beijing trip. To have a gaijin involved in matters of high state was exasperating.

Bella's network in China was said to be impressive and if Masataka managed to tap into that there would be no way of knowing who he'd spoken to, when and where. Matters would be way out of Hasegawa's control. He still hadn't devised a means of worming his way into Bella's confidence. That called for serious thought before the next meeting with the MI6 team the following day. Extolling her virtues to her face might make him look like a fool.

I'll have to find other ways of ingratiating myself with her, he thought. Perhaps a word in Sir Crispin's ear might be the way to go?

Hasegawa briefly considered running a tech op – under the guise of a training exercise – to target Bella's and Masataka's mobile phones. But as tantalising as that option was, it was simply too risky to bug such a high profile and popular politician. The last time he'd set his eavesdroppers loose on a parliamentarian the operation had come horribly close to blowing up in his face.

For now, he would simply have to rely on his charm.

Chapter 4

Home of Sakamoto Masataka, Tokyo
Monday, 1935 hours

"At least this time the Gaimusho hounds won't be baying for your blood!" Bella said, which made Masataka and his wife, Midori, laugh. Japan's Foreign Ministry was never happy about a politician treading on its turf overseas, especially in a major capital like Beijing. They rightly believed that the Japanese ambassador and his staff there should be included in all government-to-government dialogue, no matter how sensitive. But on this occasion they would be unaware of Masataka's movements and the fact that he was on a secret mission for the Prime Minister.

Bella felt her conscience pricked in a way that was most unusual. How odd, she thought to herself, that I know where Masa's going, and why, yet the Gaimusho here doesn't. If I were running that ministry I'd be apoplectic. But then, intelligence work often throws up ironies like this, if not much greater.

The three were sitting in soft leather armchairs in the lounge room of the Sakamoto's home. It was in an up-market compound of town houses with large trees, which broke up the symmetry of Tokyo's endlessly angular architecture. They spoke in Japanese, with frequent bursts of English. Midori had done most of her schooling as well as university studies in Britain, where her father had served for more than a decade as the representative of a major Japanese bank.

They were sharing a quiet drink before dinner. The children had already eaten and gone to bed, with Aunty Bella having read them a story from a children's book she'd brought for them. Now, bringing the food to the table, Bella asked Masataka who he was scheduled to see in Beijing.

"A member of the State Council," he replied. "I've met him briefly before, but only for a personal chat. Not to raise anything like this. He oversees the Ministry of State Security, where I think you have an old friend if I'm not mistaken."

"I certainly do," Bella replied. "We were at Peking University together. If you have time, and want to, you should catch up with him. Li Weiming is a real wag. His sense of humour is way out there, like yours. Wacky but brilliant. If you do get to meet him, you'll know what I mean straightaway. He's one of the richest human beings I've ever met, and that has nothing to do with money. He's a walking encyclopaedia and has diverse interests to match, plus a few faults like the rest of us."

Masataka was keen to make Li's acquaintance. He'd heard Bella talk enthusiastically of him many times. Now and then, Masataka had asked her how they managed to maintain such a close friendship while working for their respective spy services. It presented no problem, she'd explained: they automatically blocked out no-go areas where they never asked questions, let alone gave answers.

They were able to compartmentalise various

areas of their professional lives so that conflicts of interest didn't arise. As they'd joked more than once, what were called 'Chinese walls' in English were what they'd created between them in real life. While some of Li's bosses would have preferred that no such relationship existed, they accepted it, hoping that one day it might be turned to China's distinct advantage. In the meantime, he was afforded a high degree of trust by the Ministry's hierarchy. But, as Bella explained to Masataka, there were a lot of global developments that were unaffected by their self-imposed restriction. Such matters were always up for discussion, and usefully so.

"I'll give you Weiming's personal number before I leave tonight," Bella said. "But when you see the State Councillor, it might be polite to mention to him that I know Weiming well and would like you to meet him, if that's okay. Most likely, the Councillor won't have any objections."

This was something Masataka looked forward to. Bella's friends were always interesting.

"Of course," she added, "Weiming may not know what you'll be raising with the Councillor, and even if he does, he probably wouldn't mention it. But in general terms he might be willing to chat about context and atmospherics."

Masataka nodded. No doubt he and Li would have a multitude of other topics to discuss.

He was also aware that a few short years after Bella's relationship with her Danish diplomat friend had ended abruptly, Li's family life was torn asunder. His wife and two children had been visiting her parents in southern China when a typhoon caused massive flooding in the area. The family home was close to a river and had been washed away. Li had lost his wife and children, as well as her parents and grandparents in one cruel act of nature.

Bella had been close to Li's wife and children in the same way she was to Masataka's family. She had taken leave to visit him in Beijing to help him keep his life, and his work, together. The pair had been even closer since then and Masataka knew that they had contemplated marriage.

He and Midori and a handful of others understood how this constantly tested Bella's emotional stability as her biological clock ticked down towards forty. And Li knew that only too well. Their dilemma was that if they were to marry, both would have to give up their intelligence work. If only one did so, the other would never be sufficiently trusted as a spouse.

Beijing International Airport
Tuesday, 1200 hours

Masataka's sleek government jet arrived in Beijing right on time. As the aircraft was descending the pilot had suggested to his sole parliamentary passenger that he look out of the window to relish a rare glimpse of sunshine that the heavens had bestowed upon the capital. Somehow the smog had gone missing.

He was met at a designated spot away from the international terminal by a middle-aged woman from the State Council secretariat. She advised him that the Councillor would see him at three that afternoon, unless, of course, he wished to rest. He'd been booked into a new hotel in the heart of the city and could check in there first. If he wished, he could later walk the short distance to the Ministry, though someone could meet him in the hotel lobby and escort him to where their talks would be held. Whichever he preferred.

Masataka found his own way there and was waiting in room eight – an auspicious and hopeful number for both Japanese and Chinese – by a quarter to three. His escort inside the Ministry had left him alone and arranged for tea, but moments later two men only slightly older than himself strolled in and closed the door. Masataka had met neither of them before and they refrained from exchanging name cards. He saw nothing unusual in this.

Standing, they made small talk for a few minutes, mainly about the exceptional weather and the absence of smog that generally blanketed Beijing. The air in the room was fresh, untainted by the stale odour of tobacco smoke. And there were no ashtrays in sight, which was unusual in China.

The men were friendly in an uncontrived way. They had heard about their visitor's fluency in Mandarin and were about to question him on where he'd acquired it when Councillor Yang strode in.

He was a proud and imposing man, in his late-sixties and balding, but with white wispy hair at the temples. To refresh his memory, Masataka had taken a look at his photo prior to leaving Tokyo, but in the flesh the man was much more impressive than he recalled. Yang had a commanding presence that no photograph could convey.

In the instant they made eye contact Masataka was reminded that Councillor Yang was renowned for his powerful intellect. It projected onto his personality and gave him a vibrancy that was immediately engaging. His eyes conveyed as much as his words. Extending his hand, he greeted Masataka courteously, but without undue formality. He gestured towards the seats at one end of the room's long wooden table.

"Welcome to Beijing, Sakamoto Laoshi!" he said with a smile, using a very respectful Chinese form of address. Hearing the two characters of his family name pronounced in native Mandarin always made Masataka feel accepted and a little proud of the effort he had put into learning this complex language.

The Councillor introduced his two subordinates, though only by name rather than position.

"I've heard a lot about you from my colleagues," Yang said, "so it's good to have some time together today. I think when we met a few years back it was only for a few minutes. But I've never forgotten the quality of your Mandarin."

Masataka nodded in response. This was praise indeed.

"With all the water that's gone under the bridge between China and Japan," the Councillor said, "I'd like to personally thank you for the role you've so often played. We appreciate the fact that you've bothered to learn our language, which is still quite unusual in your political world, and that you can grapple with China as it exists, rather than as something people tell us we should be."

Masataka acknowledged the remark with a slight bow of his head.

"Before we begin," Yang said, "do please tell me, how did you actually learn to speak Mandarin like you do?"

"With the greatest of difficulty and agonisingly strenuous effort," Masataka replied. This drew a loud cackle from all three Chinese, with one of the younger men observing that he had rarely met a Chinese-speaking foreigner who had mastered the language's notorious four tones.

Masataka waved his hand dismissively, suggesting he was embarrassed and it might be time to move on.

"Right, let's get down to business," Yang said. "You realise, of course, that you can be as candid as necessary. Our chat is completely off the record, as ever, and I hope you're prepared to believe that. Now, how can I help you?"

"Well, it has to do with reports on Uzbeks, Filipinos and a terror cell right under my government's nose in Tokyo," Masataka responded. "And with Pakistani jihadists who seem keen to carry out a major attack. We're deeply grateful that you chose to pass these reports onto us."

"Yes," Yang responded. "We thought this would be what's brought you to Beijing. The cryptic message we received from your Prime Minister's office about your quick visit didn't tell us very much."

"As you would understand," Masataka continued, "whether an attack is planned before or during the 2020 Summer Olympics, we want to track down the cell members and interrogate them as soon as we possibly can. Our security system has been on full alert since your reports came to hand and we have saturation surveillance on all likely suspects. But nothing has yet come to light. We're largely flying blind."

"We can well imagine the predicament you find yourselves in," Yang replied. "This is one of the worst challenges any government can face, especially when the attackers are already inside your castle."

The Councillor then fell silent. Masataka appreciated that it was for him, as the visitor, to state his case first. What, exactly, did the Japanese government want from China? As with previous missions to Beijing, Masataka knew he had to get straight to the point. A State Councillor hardly had time to dither.

"There are two things we'd like to raise with you," Masataka said. "One is the question of whether those reports were exhaustive. Might there perhaps be additional information ... marginal details ... that you believed might not be of interest to us?"

Yang looked him in the eye, though not menacingly. He was quietly savouring Masataka's ability to tactfully pose a question in Mandarin yet weave into it the subtlety and nuance that the

Japanese were so attached to. It was a skill he wished he had in English, and maybe he would have had if he were as young as this capable guest.

"Let me respond directly," the Councillor said. "I'm told there's nothing more that's of any great moment, at least not that we think would be meaningful to your intelligence and security people. There are, however, minor operational points and bodies of data that we can provide on the off-chance they might be relevant at some later date. My staffers here will discuss this with you after you and I have finished."

Masataka found the Councillor's demeanour receptive. It was a rare line of communication open into the heart of government in China.

"Pray, indulge me, my friend," Yang said with a wry smile, "and let me try to take the words right out of your mouth. As a man of senior years, I do sometimes forget things unless I articulate them straightaway. Oh, to be your age again! But I mustn't digress. Yes, we are seeking further information from the sources that provided the original reports. And yes, we're doing this expeditiously. We have as much interest in this kind of intelligence as you do, and, yes, we do expect more product to come from those Central Asian sources. Now, tell me, is that what you were thinking?"

His grin was avuncular.

"I'm pleased to inform you," Masataka said, "that you were one-hundred percent correct. You have emptied my mind." The Councillor chortled, as the other two men clapped.

"Not totally emptied, I'd hope," he said. "You said there was a second issue you wished to raise with me. Am I correct?"

Masataka felt honoured that a man of Yang's stature would coddle him in this way. It reminded him of his maternal grandfather who, in his dotage, lived in the Japanese Alps and spent most of his time reading books he'd missed out on as a young man.

"Absolutely," he said. "Though it's a matter of ... what should I say ... some delicacy."

"Please don't hold back," Yang replied. "I suspect it's something that we'll all enjoy pondering, something more profound and thought-provoking than the procedural nature of your first question."

"Well, some of my wiser colleagues," Masataka ventured, "have the impression that you might be reaching out to us in some way, that the reports are a reflection of what one could perhaps call a deeper intent."

He watched the Councillor's expression closely. There was a considered pause before his response was forthcoming.

"That's precisely what we're doing," Yang said. "Which is not to say we wouldn't have shared that reporting with you unless we'd had an ulterior motive. Rather, we considered this to be a good opportunity to send your government a message that there could be other areas where we might exchange things of value – by which I don't just mean secret intelligence...."

The Councillor left his sentence hanging, all the while maintaining eye contact. It seemed like a game that both were playing.

"Now, my friend," he said jokingly, "it's as though you're trying to empty my mind. At least, you're wondering if you can pre-empt what I'm going to say. Am I correct?"

"Definitely," Masataka replied.

Yang smiled.

"I would imagine," Masataka ventured, "that the relaying of these reports is not just an example of a more open exchange on the counter-terrorism front, but a prompt for us to consider having a closer and more diverse dialogue than we presently do."

"Yes," Yang said with gusto. "That is indeed what we're thinking! We recently held private talks here with a number of South Korean government politicians of your age, and with wits equally as sharp. We found a refreshing open-mindedness and receptiveness to our notion of some sort of agreement between our three countries, what one might call a 'Northeast Asian umbrella agreement', but ..."

"But?" Masataka queried.

"But unless Japan displays a similar open-mindedness," Yang said, "we're not going to make much progress. In effect, it's all in or none, if you see what I mean."

Masataka remained silent.

"Let me suggest to you," the Councillor continued, "that we now move onto something that we all know is dear to your heart, though you're more often than not berated, even condemned, when you have the audacity to raise it in public in Japan."

Masataka knew what he meant. "Japan returning to its roots, at least to some extent?" he said.

"Precisely," Yang responded. "As anathema as that might be to certain political quarters in your government."

Masataka wagged his head to indicate how soul-destroying it was to be called a traitor by one's fellow parliamentarians, even if the number involved was comparatively small.

"As you will appreciate," the Councillor said, "the South Koreans firmly believe that a gesture must come from Japan first before they'd consider any sort of tripartite agreement. In many ways it's a moral question, and an historical one, before one gets into the politics of such an agreement."

Masataka was silent again. He'd had this conversation on trips to Beijing before, but maybe this time – with Councillor Yang's seniority – there was a different purpose to it. He hoped that would be the case.

Yang leaned back in his chair and said, "I once heard a French academic proffer that the only hatred anywhere in the world stronger than that of the Japanese for the Koreans was that of the Koreans for the Japanese. If you follow that logic the Koreans are the world's best haters. But, of course, when Westerners make declarations like that, they rarely know anything of the background. They're oblivious to the ambition and the presumptuousness of your shogun, Toyotomi Hideyoshi, who twice in a decade tried to invade Big Brother China. That was in the late 1500s and it was the Koreans, with significant help from us, who repelled them. The vindictiveness and cruelty that Toyotomi's military visited upon the Korean people because of this repeated loss of face is legendary to us. Then Japan chose to make it inordinately worse by colonising the Korean Peninsula early in the 20th century. The Korean War of the early 1950s hardly made things better."

Masataka was unlikely to refute any of that. What's behind this recitation of historical fact? he wondered.

"The point I'm making," Yang explained, "is that these are the facts as one of the young Korean politicians presented them. As you well know, this bald portrayal of reality incenses Koreans, but what they articulated to us later was a different and more modern, more pragmatic, line of thought, one that's very much in keeping with you and other young people of influence in Japan, people who want to move on and put the past to rest. Not by burying it, but at least relegating it to the margins of our bilateral and trilateral relationship. Now, I do believe this is within the realms of possibility."

Masataka nodded in agreement. This time, the Councillor wasn't playing games. His expression said as much. What was coming was carefully considered and deadly serious.

"There's been a great deal of concerted discussion here, my friend, since we learned that you were going to pay us another visit. All of your other missions here, I am told, have been meaningful and productive. We like, indeed admire, the way you think and what you stand for. So this time, we wish to take things one step further."

The eye contact between both men said it all:

the Councillor was telling Masataka that as someone older and more experienced than him, and in a position of authority in the day-to-day governance of China, action needed to be taken. Things could not be allowed to drift any longer, with Japan regularly shying away from reality.

"We want to put you in contact with those young Koreans," Yang continued, "but with a specific purpose. You may already know some of them."

Masataka said nothing, though he nodded to indicate he understood.

"This time, my friend, we have a plan. It's hardly complete at this stage, but it's a start, and we hope you'll play a substantial role in bringing it to fruition."

"I look forward to it," Masataka responded, though he barely needed to say even that.

"You're a very different generation to me," Yang said, "and therefore, I wish you to discuss this in detail with those in our system who are your counterparts. Like you, they're up-and-coming. Later, hopefully, you'll do the same with people in Japan who share your foresight."

Masataka smiled.

"There's someone here," Yang continued, "who I want you to meet, who's virtually a carbon copy of you. He's in this Ministry and he's one of the most outstanding young minds we have, not just in looking ahead, but in finding ways to bring the future to us, rather than blithely waiting for it to arrive. He's keen to meet you and he'll introduce you to others of a similar age who share his thoughts and his approach."

Masataka thought he had a fair idea who it

might be but it was Councillor Yang's privilege to reveal the person's identity.

Office of the State Council, Beijing, Room 8
Tuesday, 1624 hours

"Sakamoto Masataka!" a bright young man the same age exclaimed, beaming.

"Li Weiming!" Masataka replied, with equal delight, recognising him from Bella's photos. He was immediately struck by Li's features and disposition, which were exactly as Bella had described. He was open-faced, had a cheerful demeanour and unusually round brown eyes. His short scraggly dark hair suggested he'd just got out of bed. There was something about him that reminded Masataka of Councillor Yang. When Masataka met the older man earlier in the day, his flashing eyes had said so much. In the first instant they'd made eye contact, Masataka had sensed his powerful intellect.

In this regard, the Councillor and Li could easily be father and son. But while the former had a scholarly manner about him, Li looked like an athletic, outdoors type who didn't care much about his appearance. He might have just stepped out of a kayak after a journey down the Yangtze.

They weren't talking for long before Masataka sensed a dimension to Li's character that Bella had spoken of. His problem, if it could be called that, was his tendency to get stuck on transmit. Bella told a wonderful story about their time together at Peking University, when, in answering a question, he'd gone on and on endlessly. Their professor, out of sheer frustration, had finally warned him that if he uttered one more word before the end of the term he'd be thrown out of the class.

"It's taken a while for us to get together, eh?" Masataka said.

"Absolutely!" Li replied. "Councillor Yang has great expectations of what our dialogue might produce. And as you'd appreciate, it's best not to disappoint State Councillors. What I need to do now is take you to another part of our office where I have things to show you that might be extremely helpful."

Masataka wondered what they could be.

Chapter 5

Office of the Chief, NPA Headquarters, Tokyo
Tuesday, 1814 hours

"Yes, please bring it to me straightaway!" Hasegawa exclaimed, smiling to himself as he put the phone down.

Maybe my prayers have been answered, he mused as he waited. He had quickly dismissed a number of section heads who'd been briefing him on administrative and personnel matters and pulled out a fresh packet of cigarettes. He felt tense, perhaps more so than ever before, and smoking always helped, at least to an extent. Minutes later, there was a knock on the door. He desperately hoped he might receive good news.

"Come in," he said, enthusiastically, recognising the distinctive rap used by the leader of his crack electronic surveillance team. But this time, it was repeated, which was the pair's code language for, 'You won't want anyone else present for this.' That was usually, but not always, an indicator of something positive.

Hasegawa hadn't felt like this since the Chinese shared those troubling terror reports. And now there was more! At least Wonder Boy's Beijing trip so far hadn't proved fruitless.

The surveillance leader, Saito Makoto, was a brawny man in his early fifties, with broad shoulders and a bearing that matched his endless skills in martial arts. But there was also a cerebral side to him; he was far from just muscle. He was one of Hasegawa's most trusted confidantes.

Early on, the National Police Agency had identified Saito's bent for this type of highly specialised electronic work. It required the patience of Job, a meticulous focus on detail, and unique powers of deduction. Saito had all three, and many more, which was why the Agency had paid for his degree course in electrical engineering and further study in the United States. The FBI frequently boasted that he was the star product of their high-tech eavesdropping course, for which trainees from allied agencies were occasionally selected on the basis of extensive psychological testing. This was pleasing to Hasegawa because it gave him more powerful boasting rights when advocating an FBI-type organisation for Japan.

"Why should we be sending people like him overseas for training?" he commonly asked. "We should do our own training, and to a level of excellence that would see foreigners coming to us!"

"So, what do we have?" Hasegawa said, as his visitor took a seat in front of his desk.

"A few worthy leads," Saito replied. "Not a great deal in one sense, but by their very nature they may take us where we want to go."

"Oh, really?" Hasegawa said, picking up on Saito's typical understatement of anything even mildly encouraging. It was generally accompanied by a pokerfaced look, which it was now.

"Yes, we've just had an urgent message come in from our wandering emissary to the Kingdom of Cathay, Sakamoto Masataka. And it's come via a secure link. At last our attempt to educate your favourite parliamentarian is paying off!"

Hasegawa knew what this meant. It clearly wasn't bad news. Things were looking good; enough perhaps to change his opinion of Wonder Boy. It was extraordinary that he'd been able to dispatch material electronically from Beijing on his NPA-modified and ciphered iPad so fast. Perhaps politicians did have brains after all.

They moved across to a table the Chief used for meetings, so that the NPA's eavesdropping genius could brief him on what the leads entailed. He ignored the cigarette he'd left resting on the edge of a cut-crystal ashtray back on his desk. He hardly needed a smoke when something this exciting was in the air.

Saito arranged on the table a variety of charts and technical spreadsheets that he'd printed out, explaining carefully the significance of each and how they were interrelated. They sat alongside each other, which was something that Hasegawa always enjoyed.

Hasegawa was an only child and had never found it easy to get on with other people, especially those who were outgoing and had no such problem. He wasn't the best of fathers himself and regularly clashed with his two children. Once they'd started university his children had drifted even further away.

But with Saito he could always relax, particularly when they were engrossed in crucial and challenging operational matters like this. Saito had his own demons but he was tough and resilient, though actually quite shy. When the pair sat together as they did now they felt like brothers conspiring to prove to their father how clever they were.

Hasegawa preferred to be briefed off hardcopies wherever possible, but had no problem with Saito also using his laptop to guide his Chief further into the thought processes behind his specific conclusions.

Saito underlined with a red marker the most salient pieces of information, or what he referred to as 'the leads'. What they led to he would circle in blue. Hasegawa was immediately struck by the techniques Saito used to extrapolate an identifiable trend or direction from seemingly meaningless bodies of data. He'd witnessed this previously but rarely on something as pressing as this.

Saito also had a gift for articulating in plain language why he'd elected to follow certain clues in a particular manner, which Hasegawa appreciated. Not all of his specialist teams, of which there were many in the NPA, were able to brief him like this. On this occasion he found no need to ask questions. What was in Saito's mind was effectively communicated to his boss.

He had another talent, too, which was shared between them and no one else – inside or outside the Agency. To others, it would have sounded trivial and simplistic for men in their responsible positions. Whenever Saito arrived at a point of inference, assumption or conclusion, he would commonly rate it on the Richter Scale for earthquakes. The higher the number, the better the news. The pair never laughed at this; it was a useful mechanism for Hasegawa when he was called upon to brief government ministers and occasionally the Prime Minister or Cabinet in a crisis. Saito's Scale, and the colours he used for each rating, helped his boss lodge things firmly in his mind so that during high-level briefings he could avoid having to speak from prepared notes.

"What the Chinese have given us," Saito said, in his customary deadpan way, "is a huge volume of data, only a fraction of which they've had time to analyse themselves. They saw no need to progress any further on it at this stage, but Masataka's smart contact in Beijing apparently worked out which bodies of data might hold something of interest to us. This wizard has somehow been able to place himself inside our minds and exercise his strategic judgement from there."

"What an extraordinary ability!" Hasegawa quipped, smiling sardonically.

"Well, it doesn't stop there," Saito replied. "He's even been able to throw up a range of priority targets for me and my team to concentrate on immediately. What he's done is to minimise, if not eradicate, any wasted time and effort on our part. He's pointed to where the bull's-eyes are most likely to be. Needless to say, this has proved extremely helpful."

Saito's emphasis lifted Hasegawa's hopes even higher.

"You see," Saito continued, "the Chinese have pulled in a wealth of electronic data from comms between the three-man Islamic State team from Uzbekistan while they've been in the southern Philippines. The team clearly and foolishly operates on the assumption that their specially modified equipment is totally secure, which it normally would be for corporate types or the military. But the Chinese have managed to crack it, with no difficulty I gather. They not only have great technological prowess but a formidable team of linguists and psychologists to support them. In one report back to IS in Uzbekistan and further afield, the visitors mentioned that the Filipino cell coordinator in Mindanao regularly enters Japan under the guise of a Christian preacher. The Chinese thought that was hilarious."

"Sounds like a classical weakness on their part," Hasegawa observed. "I mean, we hardly have thousands of Christian missionaries flocking to our shores every year! But one characteristic of humour for most people is that it's irresistible. If there's room for it, then most have to do something with it. Which is just what we want. Humour often spotlights something like nothing else can."

"Exactly," Saito said. "But, praise be to their Allah, they succumbed. What Masataka's contact has also highlighted is another slip-up that he feels might warrant follow-up on our part. In the report to IS, there was brief mention of the fact that the Preacher has a sister who lives in California. She runs a fishing business that covers a fair swathe of the west coast of the United States. The Uzbeks seemed to think she might be useful in picking up deliveries of weapons and explosives at sea."

Hasegawa now knew things were looking good, and his sense of relief showed on his face.

"What the Uzbeks recommended to IS," Saito continued, "was that a local Californian resident and clandestine IS supporter, whose codename is HADRIAN, checks her out. They provided the supporter with her address and her business's landline, plus her smart phone number."

Hasegawa remained silent like a studious child. He never interrupted Saito when the man was on a deductive roll.

"When we returned to the raw data," Saito went on, "we found just one call, one solitary call lasting just over a minute, from the Preacher in Mindanao to his sister. They spoke in English. All he said was that a Californian friend might drop by to see her. His name was Hadrian, and it would be worth her while to be obliging. She said she'd welcome new business, as things were very flat. That seemed to be a pre-arranged code phrase the pair used."

Hasegawa was all ears.

"Now this is a real nugget of gold," Saito said, smiling for the first time in his presentation. "The Chinese have carried out saturation coverage on all of the Preacher's comms and that's where this vital call to his sister was buried. It also threw up his smart phone number. Working with the other data the Chinese have passed on, we've been able to check for calls coming into Japan from that phone in Mindanao. There were just two, both from that same number and both coming into the Greater Tokyo area. In the second call, which was chatty and lasted about three minutes, similar to the first one, the Preacher said he'd recently watched a DVD on Mogul architecture and he'd noticed that the Great Mosque in Old Delhi was the same as the one in Lahore."

"Which is in Pakistan," Hasegawa noted.

"Exactly," Saito replied. "So, on the assumption that this almost certainly referred to Pakistani jihadists, we followed it up. And that's what has led us to two Tokyo addresses, one in Ikebukuro and the other on the city's outskirts in Saitama Prefecture."

Hasegawa punched the air in excitement. A lead only had value when it went somewhere and this one was taking them places.

"I have squads carrying out surveillance on both of them as we speak," Saito said, "and by that I mean physical, visual, electronic, plus a few other tricks I have up my sleeve!"

"Sounds formidable," Hasegawa said, his wry smile indicating not only exhilaration but also pride and professional satisfaction. Saito shared his sentiment. There was as much hanging on this for him as there was for his Chief.

After Saito left, Hasegawa returned to his desk and sat back in his swivel chair, swinging around to gaze out through the window. The view over the moat of the Imperial Palace and the reflections on the water were restful to the eye and the soul. It wasn't the lush green vista of summertime but its pallid autumn tones now conveyed a sense of tranquility. That was something Hasegawa had only ever had a modicum of through his life. Oh, what a relief, he kept repeating to himself.

Saito's mention of a DVD on Mogul architecture reminded Hasegawa of a late night TV documentary he'd seen the week before. It had examined the role of the Bletchley Park code-breakers in Britain and how their genius had shortened World War II by a matter of years. The program quoted Alan Turing, a brilliant mathematician who'd worked there and was considered by many to be the founder of modern computing. Turing's observation had stuck in Hasegawa's mind: Mathematical reasoning may be regarded schematically, as the exercise of a combination of two facilities, which we may call intuition and ingenuity. That summed up Saito to a tee.

Lakeview Hotel, Peking University Campus, Beijing
Tuesday, 1957 hours

Li Weiming had booked a table for three for dinner at the hotel ensconced within the University campus. A five-star, modern, six-storey building, it is set in gardens around an ancient and masterfully restored Chinese temple. They had arrived before daylight faded to take a stroll around the grounds and through that intriguing structure.

Visiting the University campus brought back vivid memories for Masataka, most of them warm. Others, however, relating to the rigours of studying international law in Mandarin, still made him shudder. Nevertheless, he mused, I wouldn't have the joy now of chatting away in Chinese if it hadn't been for all that mental exertion. Some endeavours pay off handsomely.

Now, in a small private dining room above the mezzanine floor of the hotel overlooking the garden, they took their seats at an elegantly set table. Only one of Li's colleagues, Wu Dapeng, with whom Masataka had spent time during the afternoon, was joining them. He had also known Bella during her years as a student in Beijing and, together with Li, had worked closely with her in recent months in the Chinese capital. All three, and a number of others, were focused on turning a vague concept of a secret Sino-British intelligence operation into reality. They had succeeded, but it had been a high-pressure venture where sleep had been at a constant premium.

A pleasant spinoff was that it had fused all three together as friends in a way they could not have imagined. They'd encountered no problems in crossing cultural and institutional divides that many had suggested would see the project fail before it was born. Bella had revelled in the challenge, as had the others.

Though the same age, Wu was a very different person to Li. He had a pallid complexion and was tall and gaunt, almost prematurely aged. A more retiring type than Li, there was nevertheless something engaging about him. He was patently a man of fewer words than Li and Masataka, but when he spoke his husky voice gave whatever he said a gravitas all its own. The other two, like Bella, tended to verbalise a lot of what they were thinking. Wu was the opposite. Earlier, in the Ministry car on the way from central Beijing to the campus, Masataka had been taken by a number of comments Wu had made on complex international issues – succinctly and concisely.

Masataka had thought to himself, Wu can say in thirty words what takes me at least three hundred. How does he do it?

Once Li had ordered the food, which he claimed was some of the finest Chinese cuisine he'd ever tasted, they reverted to a topic they'd been discussing earlier. All three readily agreed to abstain from alcohol in light of the weighty matters they had to discuss.

"What many of us in China and Japan need to focus on," Wu said, "is the collapse of the Islamic State concept of a caliphate and the thousands of foreign fighters who flocked to Iraq and Syria. Many are now returning home, including to China. Most are well equipped with military skills and a devastating network of contacts virtually right across the globe. And they've learnt how to feed their blood lust. They'll add enormously to the ranks of home-grown terrorists and psychopaths who missed out on the Syrian experience and still crave to kill. Key cities and infrastructure in both our countries are juicy targets, and it's not just places where large numbers of people gather. Water reticulation systems, transport networks, communications, major hospital facilities, the list goes on."

"Which is why we're so grateful for your tip-off on those Pakistanis in Tokyo. I hate to think what damage they might do if they're not tracked down quickly," Masataka responded

"Our pleasure," Li said. "But do let us know when you get back to Tokyo what your police and security people have extracted from all that data. Somehow, I think there are valuable clues in there."

"No doubt," Masataka replied.

"Which reminds me," Li added, "Wu and I must flesh out tonight the idea that Councillor Yang put to you. That's of prime importance, but before we launch into it I just want to mention something relevant to what Wu was saying about terrorism."

A waiter arrived with a pot of green tea and Li waited until it was poured.

"The other day, I read a liaison report from Canadian Intelligence which was a real eye-opener. Horrifying actually, though luckily here and in Japan we haven't let things go this far. You see, Muslim parents in Toronto have been protesting against their daughters having to take music lessons at school, which is compulsory for all students. They claim that Islam forbids listening to music and playing musical instruments, as well as singing the Canadian national anthem. It's plainly sinful, they say. Can you believe it? How can the West allow itself to be pushed around like this?"

"Ridiculous!" Wu growled in his gravelly way.

"If a host society," Li observed, magisterially, "can't protect itself by impressing upon newcomers their duties and obligations – rather than their self-perceived rights and entitlements – it only has itself to blame for the breakdown in the communal beliefs and mechanisms that bind its society together. Once that glue has gone, centrifugal force simply pulls the nation apart."

Once the dishes were brought to the table

and the three men were left alone, Li returned to Councillor Yang's idea. He gestured to Masataka to partake of the food from which faint spirals of steam snaked above the table, bearing the distinctive aroma of sesame oil.

"He's put Wu and I in charge of this," Li said, "and he wants us to explore the possibility of getting some sort of tripartite agreement off the ground between China, Japan and South Korea. As I gather he told you, the concept has already been quietly broached with the South Korean President, who was receptive and arranged for private talks with a group of younger politicians. The outcome was encouraging enough for Councillor Yang to then charge us with the task of further examining its feasibility. We're thinking of scientific and technological research first up. In the broadest sense, the first stage would be to establish a 'Northeast Asian Umbrella Agreement' under which all sorts of things could eventually be placed. It wouldn't in any way be a challenge to the United Nations and its subsidiary agencies like the Food and Agriculture Organisation, which do a lot of good work. In time though, it might well supplement what bodies like that do."

Masataka listened with interest, even intrigue, made obvious by his demeanour.

"In essence," Wu cut in, "we think it's about time the so-called Far East, as our part of the world is so quaintly described by Westerners, rallied its forces to make a grander and more coordinated contribution to the global community. One that draws on our rich heritage, our wisdom and our brain power."

Masataka thought to himself, that's it in a nutshell.

"As Councillor Yang's idea sits at the moment," Li continued, "the agreement would be largely free of politics. Probably, it would start with three-way research projects in nanotechnology, machine learning, blockchain technologies, data science, medical science and artificial intelligence ... areas like that."

Li reached across with his chopsticks to a dish of kingfish, which was one of his favourites. He took care not to drop anything on the starched white tablecloth, so immaculate that it warned any Chinese diner to tread warily. Masataka noticed this and it reminded him of how much messier the Chinese were as eaters compared to his own people.

Li then picked up where he'd left off. "Before anything can happen, Japan needs to establish a new link with South Korea. That's absolutely necessary. The Koreans aren't expecting your Emperor or Prime Minister to go to Seoul and prostrate themselves before Parliament. It's not just another gesture of atonement or apology that they're looking for. Let's face it, what Japan did on the Korean Peninsula for half a century is still too raw to be erased by words of contrition alone. All that's been done already, time and again, though a certain percentage of older Koreans still understandably demand more. We Chinese have long memories as well."

Masataka was nodding, fascinated by the direction in which this train of thought was heading.

"Rather than something that dwells negatively on the past," Wu added, "it has to be positive and from the present, something that helps build a better future. I know that sounds like the rhetoric politicians use, but there's no other way of putting it."

For the first time, Masataka noticed a change in Wu's expression — a cheeky, playful grin that he hadn't seen before.

Li continued: "That's the first thing we'd ask you to look at when you're back in Tokyo. What sort of gesture would Japan be comfortable with that would also assuage the Koreans? If you want Wu and I to come over to talk privately with like-minded people that can easily be arranged. And all off the record, as with the Koreans."

"Yes," Masataka responded. "I can certainly do that. I look forward to it very much."

"It hardly needs to be said," Li added, "that if Japan can come up with a gesture that the Koreans accept, it won't fail to be noticed here in China. Indirectly, it could constitute a gesture to us, too."

Masataka agreed. That was a point he hadn't thought of.

"Another dimension," Li added, "is that none of this requires Japan to give up its current alliances with, say, the Americans. Rather, it requires you to be more independent in outlook, and maybe sometimes to be an effective go-between when Washington finds it difficult ... even galling, dare I say ... to accommodate the change now taking place in the global balance of power."

"After all," Wu cut in, "we Chinese, the Koreans, and you Japanese as well, know what gall tastes like, don't we?"

Masataka nodded. There was nothing he could add to that.

"To Councillor Yang's way of thinking," Wu said, "if Japan can't come to the party and move on, China will just go its own way. If you have no wish to 'return to your roots', that's your loss, not ours. But we sense that your generation in Japan does want to move on, which is why we're talking to you now."

Wu had done it again, articulating things concisely.

"The Councillor has a wonderful story," Li cut in, "which is a historical parallel that resonates with us. You see, he came to know Bella's father quite well when he was here in Beijing as British Ambassador. Once, when they were discussing the gradual shift taking place between East and West, Bella's dad produced this particularly apposite analogy."

"As he is wont to do," Masataka observed, which brought a smile to both Li's and Wu's faces.

Masataka knew that Bella could live on analogies, allegories and puns, for breakfast, lunch and dinner. Her father had taught her well.

"It was a family story," Li continued, "and you may have heard it. I hadn't. Apparently, her father's forebears worked with the East India Company for a century or more. Some of them were pilots on the Thames when the huge Company merchant vessels came back loaded to the gunwales. When the British built up Kolkata as a major trading and administrative base in India, eventually making it their capital, the whole family moved out and lived there for over a hundred years."

Masataka had not heard this part of Bella's family history, though he knew her father almost as well as she did. And he liked him, especially for his love of history and how he could bring it alive. Wu seemed to be in the same boat.

"As Councillor Yang relates it," Li went on, "with generations of the family living in India, they saw wave after wave of change. They had a continuous strand of unbroken historical memory, unlike most of the British who served one term in that country then returned to Britain or were posted elsewhere. What Bella's dad said, which the Councillor has never forgotten, was that the family could see over many decades the gradual breakdown that led to what the British call The Great Mutiny of 1857. Naturally, the Indians see it very differently. For them, it was their First War of Independence."

Both Masataka and Wu saw the irony in that. Masataka now sensed where this was going and he wished he'd heard the story years ago when he'd often spent more time with Bella's family than his own.

Li continued, "Bella's father explained to Councillor Yang how the mutiny took the British completely by surprise, almost kicking them out of India. That's exactly where he believes the West is vis-à-vis the rise of the 'Far East' now."

Wu was greatly animated by this, clapping his hands to congratulate his colleague.

"Well said, my friend! What a fine story-teller you are. I had no idea. Are you sure that's Bella's father's story and not your own?"

They all shared a laugh but none of them failed to understand the validity of the point. It had certainly lodged itself in Councillor Yang's mind.

"When the Councillor passed this story on to Wu and I," Li continued, picking up the thread again, "he said it reminded him of an old Malay proverb, befitting the scenario of the West's widespread ignorance and criticism of the East at a key transitional point in history. *He can see a louse as far away as China but is unaware of the elephant on his nose.* What a gem!"

Masataka hadn't heard of this saying, neither in Mandarin nor any other language.

There was a brief silence before Li continued again. "What the Councillor is considering," Li said, "is an updated, 21st century version of the Vienna Convention on diplomacy, a framework that's served the global community well, regardless of which culture it originated from. There's the Geneva Convention on war, which has fared less well in recent times. Whatever, these were international agreements put in place to establish common standards, not always adhered to, but certainly better in their existence than their absence. We need something equally as grand at this point in history. Something that covers international standards for scientific research, technological exchange, genetic engineering, quantum physics and today's brave new world of cyberspace."

To Masataka, this fitted perfectly with the discussion he'd had with the Councillor earlier in the day. It was apparent now as it was then that the Councillor is a great intellect thinking great thoughts.

"This is why," Li went on, "Councillor Yang also wants us to look at the feasibility of proposing an international treaty on these important issues, a concept that might first emerge from our tripartite union here in the Far East, and later perhaps, move into the UN architecture."

Masataka was still pondering the significance of this statement when Li reminded him that there was a time in the late 19th century and early 20th century when many Chinese not only admired Japan for its rapid industrialisation and modernisation, but went to study Japanese ways. Zhou Enlai, Mao's deputy, was one of them. Unfortunately, that's something almost totally overlooked in today's Japan, he thought to himself. How different a path Chinese history might have followed if Mao had accompanied his future comrade in arms to Japan to study.

Chapter 6

Operations Room, National Police Agency HQ Tokyo
Wednesday, 0248 hours

"I'd prefer to listen to them in chronological order," Bella said, speaking in Japanese. "I find the sequence in tapes like these to be crucial to finding clues."

"No problem," Saito said. He smiled angelically at her, which she found unusually charming for a man so broad-shouldered and masculine. But she knew that the connection between them was very much on an intellectual plane. Their minds seemed to be working as one, something both found energising.

They were sitting in the underground operations bunker in the basement of the National Police Agency's headquarters. Saito and Bella had already struck up an instant and refreshing rapport, with their intellects engaging on the same wavelength. This was in evidence when they'd met at the early hour of two-thirty that morning.

Saito had picked her up outside the British Embassy where she was staying, and they'd driven straight to the Agency nearby. Hasegawa had no hesitation in calling her in to assist with this urgent task, especially after the unexpectedly pleasant encounters he and Saito had had at the last few meetings with Sir Crispin Grenville and his visiting MI6 team. Saito had been included by Hasegawa because of his technical expertise in the electronic dimensions of modern security and intelligence operations. Both had come to see Bella in a different light and had been impressed with the deferential form of the Japanese language she used when chatting with them. She was clearly a young woman who knew what she was about and her knowledge of Arabic and its variations in Central Asian languages, along with Urdu in Pakistan, was outstanding.

At first, Hasegawa had considered calling her directly himself, but on reflection had decided to get Saito to do it. If anything, he was closer to her in rank. Bella had immediately agreed and was waiting outside the Embassy within minutes, wearing her sky blue track-suit and matching Adidas running shoes.

Saito and his Chief, together with a handful of their close colleagues, had been in the NPA bunker for more than two hours when they'd reached a stalemate. The group now watched Bella and Saito seated together at a broad, raised control panel set above the square wooden table around which they were all gathered.

The panel, edged by a shiny black frame, was state-of-the-art. On the tabletop, were rows of switches, buttons and lights that reminded Bella of a recording studio. Both Bella and Saito were wearing puffy headphones covered in soft green leather. His offsider, an eager technician, switched off the various flashing box-like sections of the screen that were streaming data in an array of bright colours. The screen went black and Saito gestured his thanks to the technician. Visual distractions annoyed most people when they were focussed on sound.

What had stumped Saito's deductive mind was the potentially deeper significance of a statement the Filipino Preacher had made in his call to one of the Pakistani jihadists in Tokyo. It was the reference the Preacher had made to the Great Mosque in Old Delhi being the same as the one in Lahore. Saito had earlier thought it merely denoted Pakistan or Pakistanis. And indeed it had, but somehow that reference had stuck in his mind, buzzing around like a bee in a bottle. Instinct told him there had to be more to it than that.

Bella had listened to the full dialogue a number of times and had homed in, as Saito had done, on the greater import of that phrase. They agreed that it wasn't simply a pointer to Pakistan.

As they removed their headphones Bella turned to face Saito. "What a pity," she said, "that we don't have images of these people. A photo can tell you so much."

"Yes, I was just thinking the same thing," he replied. It was a matter-of-fact statement that highlighted how their minds worked in tandem.

Hasegawa and the others noticed this and exchanged hopeful smiles. One of Saito's colleagues said he'd check whether the Chinese had provided any images in some of the low-priority files that were only now being fully examined. It was the first time that any of those watching had broken their silence.

Bella had already concluded that the dialogue was a code that both parties to the conversation clearly understood. The Preacher used an accented form of English with the Pakistani, liberally sprinkled with Arabic and Urdu words.

The mix itself was revealing. I know he's using a contrived English accent, Bella thought. It's like the way people commonly speak English on the Sub-Continent. A bit like Peter Sellers taking them off. His natural accent is more American I'd say, possibly educated in the States. He no doubt feels his contrived accent will help the Pakistani understand him better, which it probably does – marginally.

Following on from the Preacher's Great Mosque observation was yet another statement which Saito thought was part of the same code. Bella now listened to that again through the headphones, with Saito replaying the tape whenever she signalled him. Occasionally, she scribbled English numbers and letters on a pad, as well as odd lines and circles that resembled doodling. Saito knew it was much more than that.

Sometimes Bella jotted down a few Chinese characters, kanji, which both the Japanese and Chinese used. Saito would glance at them and tick them when he agreed. No one in the bunker had ever seen a gaijin and a Japanese work together like this.

Hasegawa silently pointed this out to the others, inferring that they were all lucky to have two outstanding thinkers working with them like this Seemingly, the Butter Bitch had earned his respect. None of Hasegawa's subordinates had ever experienced anything like this with their Chief. Physical closeness to him in a room such as this was equally unique.

'Hardly a light-bulb moment!' the Preacher had

said in recognising that the two mosques were the same. 'No great flash of genius there!'

Bella listened to it over and over again, then signalled Saito to stop. They removed their headphones and sat in silence for some time. No one uttered a word. The only sound in the room was the low hum of the air-conditioning duct in the ceiling.

Hasegawa watched intently, somewhat in awe. It's as if their two brains are joined as one, he mused to himself. With luck, the power of two will lift their capacity to five, six or even seven. Pray that's what's happening now!

Bella turned to Saito and looked him in the eye, saying nothing apart from one raised eyebrow. Saito raised both in a response of sorts. To the others, they seemed to be communicating telepathically, which in an odd way they were. They were acknowledging to each other that the mosques and the light-bulb were definitely part of one coded message.

"Tsunagari dake ja nakute," Bella said to him: It's not just the linkage.

Saito half-smiled, which the others had already noticed was part of their pattern of communication. They were concentrating as intensely on the pair as the pair was on what they were doing.

"Furashu no kyōchō. Are wa, ichiban igi no aru ten," Bella added. "It's the emphasis on the word flash that's the critical point."

This was an English word occasionally used in Japanese and pronounced in the Japanese way.

"And it was deliberate," she continued, "because of both the bad line and the Pakistani's dubious ability in English comprehension. They're using a code language, one they mutually understand, allowing them to communicate in this way. There are obviously key words that have particular significance, especially when they are emphasised."

Saito nodded. He winked at Hasegawa, who smiled like a cat with a bowl of cream.

"I'm thinking of two things that are the same, but also different in some unique way," Bella added.

That sent Saito's mind into a whirl of analysis.

"Furashu!" they both said at the very same moment, facing each other: "The word flash!"

"Hiroshima and Nagasaki!" they added in perfect unison, shaking hands as they spoke.

The English word 'flash' was often used in Japanese to describe the moment when the atomic bombs exploded. But this realisation seemed to have much greater import to Saito, which Bella sensed must be related to the other matter he had mentioned briefly in the patrol car on the way to the Agency.

Just over an hour prior to Bella receiving the call at the Embassy, Saito's electronic eavesdroppers had intercepted a call to the other Pakistani living in Ikebukuro in inner Tokyo. It was a telephone conversation of less than half a minute, in what sounded like Arabic, taken on his smart phone and traced to a radio telephone on a vessel close to the major South Korean port of Busan.

The message was simple: All proceeding smoothly with holiday plans. See you there. All tourists like gurubbar, and if they don't, the fan island is always a winner.

As Saito briefed Bella on technical aspects of that communication, she knew instinctively that he'd already put two and two together. He was waiting to see what she'd make of it.

Bella put her headphones on again and listened to the tape in Arabic, while Saito, his Chief and the others waited expectantly. They all leaned across the table, focusing intently on her expression. There was only one other female in the room. Bella guessed her to be about 35 years old and of Korean-Japanese extraction. She'd greeted Bella warmly on entering the bunker though they'd not spoken at any length. From her demeanour there was little doubt she was a police officer.

Bella signalled to Saito to replay the tape, but halfway through the second run she removed her headphones and smiled at him.

"The caller," she said, "is almost certainly Central Asian, judging by his Arabic inflection. He obviously doesn't speak Urdu because if he did, that's what he'd be using with a Pakistani. He certainly wouldn't be speaking English. Now this is just an extrapolation on my part, but while I was listening to the caller's voice I thought he might perhaps be one of the three-man Uzbek team that visited Mindanao."

Saito and Bella leaned closer to each other and reverted to the type of exchange they'd already had a number of times. Their two minds were back in unitary mode. No one dared interrupt the high-speed deductive process under way.

"I can't swear to it," Bella said to Saito, "but it's more than just a long shot."

Saito was now displaying more expectancy than the others.

"Yes, I'd say he is one of the Uzbeks," she continued, "and I think he's on a vessel that's going to call into Nagasaki, or somewhere near that port, with instructions, weapons, explosives ... whatever. That's what I think is happening."

Saito put his hand up quickly and they high-fived.

"Chōdo onaji! Chōdo onaji!" he said. "That's exactly the conclusion I've come to!"

He was more excited than Hasegawa and the others had ever seen him but they all stayed quiet.

"And what about the references to gurubbar and a fan island?" he asked. He knew this would have been easy for her.

"Oh, that has to be Thomas Glover's house up on the hill overlooking the harbour in Nagasaki," she said. "And the fan island can't be anything other than Dejima Island, the enclave that the Dutch merchants were confined to for years. It's still there and still fan-shaped as it's always been."

Not all of Nagasaki was destroyed by the atomic bomb in 1945. Its valleys and gullies protected some areas from the blast, whereas Hiroshima, which was a flat basin, suffered maximum damage and loss of life. Saito was delighted with Bella's observations.

"Exactly!" he responded, beaming.

"But there's no mention of timings," Bella added, slightly puzzled.

"True," Saito said, "but we're not unduly concerned about that at present. We'll have both parties, and the vessel, under saturation surveillance, 24/7."

Bella nodded.

"Now for the rest of the story," Saito said, again in a one-on-one dialogue with her. For a moment, she was surprised there could be more.

"You see," Saito went on, "when the Pakistani received that call in Ikebukuro he immediately phoned his jihadist collaborator in Saitama on the outskirts of Tokyo. He used the same smart phone, but called the other man's landline. All he said, in Urdu, was the holiday's on. He was quite excited, despite his obvious effort to contain this. We ran a sound modulation check on his voice and the pattern confirms it."

Now Bella was the fixated listener.

Saito continued, "The Saitama collaborator's reply was, 'OK, I'll leave straightaway'. The Ikebukuro man said nothing and promptly hung up. But there's something very strange here. Saitama man didn't leave. He didn't go anywhere. Our surveillance teams were fully expecting him to, but he stayed put."

Bella was itching to ask what happened next, but held her tongue. Saito grinned at her anticipation.

"The one who did leave was the Ikebukuro man! He left his apartment with a swollen backpack about fifteen minutes later and headed towards the station nearby. He was still carrying his smart phone - a fatal slip in what seems to be a reasonably finely-tuned plan. We've tracked him into the train system and it looks as though he's heading down towards Nagasaki. In fact, as we speak, he's well on the way, but ... and this is interesting ... he's staying off bullet train lines."

"That is interesting," Bella said, still crunching the numbers in her head. Before Hasegawa dared speak, Bella conveyed something else to her new-found deductive soul mate.

"So, that's where we're heading, is it?"

"You took the words right out of my mouth!" Saito responded enthusiastically.

Hasegawa was about to suggest they all break for coffee when the technician nudged Saito who nodded in agreement. The technician keyed something into his laptop, which was linked to the main screen. A number of boxes came to life with grainy coloured images of two people. Some showed them walking, while telephoto images homed in on their heads and shoulders.

In that instant, coffee was off the agenda. A whole new dimension had opened up in front of them, a human one that told them a great deal.

PART 2

Chapter 7

Haneda Airport, Tokyo
Wednesday, 0642 hours

Dawn was breaking as they left the police helicopter and boarded an NPA executive jet parked away from the terminal complex at the airport, close to the centre of Tokyo. No one said a word about the fact that they'd worked right through the night without sleep.

If I can grab an hour on the plane, Bella thought to herself as the door of the jet was closed and secured, I'll get by somehow. I've done it for days before so there's no reason I can't on this operation, though I know Nagasaki is going to be full on.

Hasegawa would have dearly liked to have joined Saito, Bella and Kim, the smart young Korean-Japanese policewoman whom Kuroda had urged him to send with them. But he'd decided against it.

In Nagasaki, his profile as Chief might attract unwanted attention, even from inside his own Agency. Some months before, his presence in Hakodate, a port city on the south coast of Hokkaido Island, had been revealed by a junior administrative staffer who'd tipped off the media. That came close to threatening a major international drug haul, Japan's biggest ever, which he'd gone there to oversee.

After the jet took off and reached cruising altitude, Bella and Kim settled back for a chat, though

not a long one. They'd already agreed that sleep –
even just an hour – was the only thing that could
recharge one's mental batteries in situations like this.

"You know," Bella said to Kim, "what we did in
the bunker was exhausting! I know only too well that
at times like this, sleep is the first thing that goes by
the wayside."

"That's for sure!" Kim responded. In her early-
thirties, she was a friendly woman and Bella had felt
an immediate affinity towards her in the bunker. She
was a calm person to be around, a huge bonus when
constant mental focus was called for. Tempers often
frayed and people who were normally mild mannered
could unexpectedly crack under pressure. So far
nothing like that had happened.

The flight to Nagasaki would take just under an
hour and a half and once they were picked up at the
airport by a police helicopter events would develop
rapidly. Saito was already catching up on sleep and
the two women would soon follow suit, just as soon
as they'd addressed something important.

Kim, a quick-witted woman, wore her long dark
hair drawn up tight in a French roll, highlighting her
classical oriental features. There was a vibe about
her that said, 'I'm fully engaged with life. How about
you?'

Bella liked that and felt it probably came with
a sharp mind and good intellect as well. Despite
this, the pair maintained an element of reserve,
especially Kim. For a woman of mixed heritage to rise
in a male bastion like the NPA was an extraordinary
achievement, and Bella told her so. But Kim was

uncertain about the sudden appearance of this Englishwoman and whether or not it would impact her professional world. For the moment, she was not unduly concerned, while remaining somewhat wary.

What Kim wanted to discuss was something that had happened while they were still in the bunker.

She had been brought in to monitor all of the Busan Port Authority's communications with the vessel from which the call to Tokyo had been made. The boat had turned out to be a private ferry that could be hired for tourist excursions around islands in the Tsushima Straits between South Korea and Northern Kyushu. The captain and two crewmen were Korean, and had done something highly unusual by not reporting their destination. It was customary to do so with authorities on both sides of the Straits.

Hasegawa had no hesitation in instructing Saito and his team to eavesdrop on all South Korean communications, not just inside that country's territorial waters but also within Busan Harbour. The Chief told Saito that under the circumstances he could skip any formalities if he wished.

Soon after Bella arrived in the bunker and Saito had told her about the call from the vessel, she'd asked whether the South Korean authorities had been contacted, either for routine information or for specific assistance. It was merely a procedural question on her part and had been couched in polite terms in a bid not to sound intrusive. As someone who customarily operated across cultural borders and major geo-political fault lines, Bella was always careful to avoid treading on others' toes.

Saito had replied in the negative. Had Hasegawa expressly instructed him not to make contact with the South Koreans? No, he hadn't.

While Hasegawa was out of the bunker and in an adjacent room, Bella had asked Saito what his professional inclination was on a matter like this – just as a matter of interest.

"Oh, I'd let the South Korean Police HQ in Busan know that we're tracking a particular vessel and ask for any data they may have on it."

"Would there be anything wrong in doing that now?" Bella had enquired.

"No, certainly not. Why do you ask?" Saito had said.

"Well, it's not the sort of thing that I should be involved in, obviously, as a foreigner and all. But in this particular case, I suspect it might be better to be do it, rather than not."

Saito had readily agreed. He had no problem with that and was only too aware of Bella's sensitivity to delicate Japan-South Korean relations. Saito had then asked Kim to go ahead and discreetly contact her counterparts in South Korea.

Five minutes later, they'd received a swag of routine information on the vessel concerned. But what Saito and Bella found significant was the fact that the vessel had not yet provided a destination to the Busan Port Authority. Despite two reminders, it had still failed to do so.

"So," Kim now asked Bella, "whether this is women's intuition or just run-of-the-mill police instinct, I'm sure you had a professional reason for triggering that process. I overheard what you said to Saito." They exchanged a knowing smile, which put Kim at ease.

"Yes, I did indeed have a reason for suggesting it," Bella replied. "It's a long story, and if all goes well in Nagasaki we might be able to discuss it. Where I'm coming from as a complete outsider is simply this: if I see anything that might help Japan get on better with its neighbour I'll support it. I mean, it can't do any harm, can it? It's not that I'm trying to interfere."

"Absolutely not," Kim replied, confirming that she understood that as small a gesture as it was, it had indeed been worthwhile.

"It could prove to be pivotal," Bella observed. "I've seen it in a number of operations where a simple thing like this is the key to success."

Bella spent a few moments looking out of the window of the jet. They'd already flown past Mt. Fuji, which sported an early dusting of snow, and were tracking down the Pacific coast of Honshu, Japan's main island. She was thinking about how different it was to fly in a small executive jet rather than one of the huge A380s she'd travelled on numerous times.

"Just between us," Kim said, bringing Bella back to the discussion at hand, "I followed your lead and added a bit of spin that I thought might be helpful."

"Hontō? Nan deshō ka? Oh, really? What was that?" Kim laughed at what Bella had said in Japanese. "You speak like a local." Bella nodded her thanks.

"What I did," Kim continued, "was to use certain

honorifics that I normally wouldn't, plus other little things like referring specifically to the 'Korea Strait', rather than the Tsushima Strait, the term preferred by the Japanese."

Bella, with her interest in languages and awareness of how subtle messages could be conveyed in one while remaining absent in another, smiled broadly at Kim.

"In standard Japanese these days," Kim added, "Korea is referred to as Kankoku, rather than Chōsen, the name commonly used during the Japanese occupation of my homeland. These days, Koreans find that insulting, though every now and again some nationalistic Japanese will blurt it out."

"Back on Busan," she continued, "I also suggested, ever so delicately of course, that we might need to call on the Koreans for assistance, pending how things unfold with this suspicious vessel."

"Great." Bella replied. "Between us, I think you should do as much of that sort of thing as you can. Greasing the wheels, we might say."

"That sums it up beautifully," Kim said.

In that brief moment, Bella realised something quite significant. Kim, as a Korean-Japanese, wasn't just proud of her heritage. There was much more to it than that and Bella wondered what role it would play operationally in Nagasaki. Might Kim over-extend herself and put everything at risk? How could she be pulled back if this were to happen? How and when would they know?

It's going to have to be watched closely, Bella thought, from every possible angle.

Chapter 8

Nagasaki Airport
Wednesday, 0830 hours

"Approach from the south, then taxi to apron adjacent to Cargo Terminal," Nagasaki airport control instructed the pilot of the NPA jet. "There's a police helicopter waiting there for you now."

"Read you, thanks."

It was a bright sunny morning and the sea around the airport sparkled. Built on a long rectangular piece of reclaimed land in Ōmura Bay, it was connected by a long narrow causeway. This tenuous strip, similar to Osaka's Kansai International Airport, appeared to float on the sea.

"Hope your mission's successful," the controller added.

"Thank you. That's much appreciated," the pilot replied.

It was not uncommon in Japan and in other countries for air traffic controllers to identify instinctively with police, security and military pilots in this way. Dawn take-offs usually meant something important was under way.

Saito, who woke with a jolt as the jet's wheels touched the tarmac, was galvanised into action. He nudged the two women across the aisle, who were both still in a deep slumber.

"My wife sometimes snores," he quipped, "but

nowhere near as badly as you two! You both had such satisfied looks on your faces I didn't have the heart to complain."

"Glad you didn't!" Bella replied with a laugh. "Kim has a first dan black belt in karate and I topped self-defence on my training course. If we'd been woken in fright we could've made mince-meat out of you before we realised what we were doing!"

Saito grinned. He liked gutsy women.

As they waited for the aircraft's steps to be lowered, Bella mused on what an interesting threesome they made: a Japanese police mastermind, a Korean-Japanese policewoman with tact and sensitivity, and a well-intentioned female MI6 operative trying not to intrude upon other people's affairs. She got a real zing out of that. It's why Bella had gotten into the spy trade in the first place. It doesn't get any better than this, she thought.

Minutes later, they were in the helicopter and on their way to the NPA building in Nagasaki City, an eighteen kilometre flight. They were met on the rooftop helipad by the local police chief, a sprightly man in his forties with a bit of a paunch, who ushered them downstairs to the Operations Room.

"Not another bunker!" Bella whispered to Kim.

There'd been a number of intriguing developments on the vessel's movements while they'd been in the air. The Busan Port Authority had attempted to contact Kim at Tokyo HQ, but were told she'd soon be in Nagasaki and could learn of them then.

Refreshments were on hand in the Operations Room, with Bella picking up the welcome aroma of miso soup and grilled fish as they entered.

It was a slightly larger room than its Tokyo counterpart, with a greater array of separate screens covering one wall entirely. The technology was clearly more dated than in Tokyo, though the large plasma screen, right in the middle, appeared to be state-of-the-art. All sorts of lights were flashing and each screen, except for the main one in the middle, seemed to change images regularly. Those that monitored the shipping channels in the Straits stood out more than the others. Apart from a number of seats on a flat floor facing the wall screens and a control panel, the seating behind was tiered like an amphitheatre.

The twenty-odd staff, busily engaged in various tasks, immediately stood as their visitors entered the room and got their bearings.

Matsumoto Seiji, the local Police Chief, welcomed them and introduced the three newcomers to each of his officers. There were a few females, all young except one, a short, expressionless woman in her late fifties. Matsumoto, oddly, mumbled the woman's family name – Yamamoto – then pointed out that she was always addressed as Yumi Chama.

While Yumi was a standard female name, the addition of chama intrigued Bella. It was an affectionate honorific customarily used with kindly grandmothers. However, Yumi looked anything but. More like a prison guard, Bella mused, noting that there'd been no mention of her rank in the system.

Matsumoto explained that Yumi was his indispensible assistant, with emphasis placed on those words inferring she was more of a gatekeeper. Whatever role she played, Bella had the impression Yumi might be seriously challenged by the arrival two other professional women.

Most of Matsumoto's staff had met Kim previously, though not Saito, to whom they displayed great deference. He obviously has legendary status, Bella thought. Kim, though, is warmly received – more like a real person than an institutional apparatchik being parachuted in from the top of the Tokyo police hierarchy.

Matsumoto deferred to Saito when it came to introducing Bella.

"I take great pride," he said, "in presenting to you a top MI6 spy, all the way from Britain. As you will have been informed, she's in Japan as part of a team that's helping us set up a proper, modern Japanese overseas spy service – which I can tell you couldn't come a day sooner."

Those watching clapped. Bella knew this was a marked sign of respect, not just for her and her Service but for the close traditional relationship between Britain and Japan since the 19th century until militarism had overtaken everything in the 1930s.

Out of the corner of her eye Bella noticed that Yumi had not joined in the applause – due warning that there might be trouble lurking. By contrast, the younger women seemed eager to chat to their British visitor.

"Hasegawa San has asked that you all guard Bella's identity carefully while she's here," Saito pointed out. "But feel free to call on her experience whenever you wish. She's fluent in written and spoken Japanese, as well as Mandarin Chinese, Arabic and all sorts of other strange tongues. She's a great colleague to work with, as you'll see, and she asks for only one thing. That is, whenever there's a lull in operations that you remind her, me and Kim to get some much needed sleep."

The operations staff were aware of that, and already a number of portable beds had been set up away from the entrance.

"These two women snore like you can't imagine," Saito added, to another round of clapping. "But as any police officer knows, we deal with much worse than that! I think we're in for some heavy and trying work over the next few days, so let's all keep our spirits up and get to it."

Matsumoto stepped forward to deal with a few housekeeping matters that he knew would affect the visitors.

"We have a range of appropriately sized clothing of various descriptions," he announced, "which you should feel free to use. I know that Saito San and Bella San want to have a quick shower, while Kim's going to get straight onto the radio to strike up contact with Busan. She's going to respond first to the Port Authority's earlier call, then contact Busan Police HQ to ascertain which of the two will be overseeing surveillance of the target vessel in Korean waters. Kim will also get up to speed with any recent developments and once she has the lie of the land, she'll brief us when we reassemble."

Kim went straight to work and within a matter of minutes reported that the Busan Police would act as coordinator.

This was not the first operation Kim had been part of in Nagasaki and she was already a master of the room's dazzling array of digital screen maps. They could home in on any specific spot in the Straits, as well as on the broader northern part of Kyushu Island, Nagasaki City and its suburbs. The capacity to zoom in on buildings, vehicles and individuals with pinpoint accuracy had been welcomed by Bella before she'd gone off for a shower. It augured well for a successful operation.

Once the group had reassembled, Saito, Bella and some ten local police officers took their seats at the control panel. Kim stood alongside Matsumoto as she began her briefing. Yumi remained off to one side and had nothing to say, like an exam supervisor with the eyes of a hawk. Saito had a plate of grilled fish and pickles on the desk in front of him while Bella had opted for three bowls of miso soup to start with. The air in the small NPA jet had dried her out much more than a normal wide-bodied aircraft cabin.

She managed a quick word to Kim while the others were taking their places.

"What's with the battleaxe?" she whispered, which made Kim smirk.

"Oh, she's a strange one," Kim replied with a sigh. "She's the longest-serving policewoman in all of Kyushu. Divorced, no children, married to the

NPA. Hasegawa's kept her on well beyond her use-by date, though none of us know why. She handles surveillance right across the island and has stacked her squads with retired detectives – cronies who in most cases don't have much to offer. She also has a bad habit of interfering at the worst possible moment. Saito can't stand her. He'd bury her under twenty metres of concrete if he had half the chance. She can actually be quite helpful though, but you have to let her get to know you in her own odd way. I think she's going to be rather challenged when you and I start doing our thing."

Kim's wry smile said it all.

As the group started questioning her on the briefing she'd received from Busan, Matsumoto and his colleagues were shaking their heads at Bella's comfortable fluency in their language. He and the others – which included three women – found it extraordinary. They'd seen a fair few gaijin tourists around Nagasaki and others like her on TV, but never in the flesh. And she was a spy to boot, which made her more glamorous than she actually wanted to be. But as they all slipped back into their seats and functioned as a team, her distinctiveness rapidly dissolved. This pleased Bella, who knew as well as the others that highlighted differences never aided close professional teamwork.

"First up," Kim said, "I've been in contact with both the Busan Port Authority and the Busan Police HQ. It's the latter that we'll be liaising with for as long as this operation lasts. The police in Busan have already come on stream with some tantalising data."

She signalled to Jiro, the young policeman controlling the panel's displays, to bring up the entire Straits waterway. The main shipping routes in the area appeared instantly, displaying the dense traffic on the water at that moment. A flashing red light to the west of Busan Port denoted the ferry under surveillance.

"Before we switch to a less complex overview," Kim said, "please note that any vessel of any size or shape wishing to cross these busy sea lanes must – repeat, must – seek permission from the Port Authority. Our target vessel has not yet sought clearance to do so. It's not just a matter of their failure to report a destination."

Saito and Bella exchanged a quick glance. There was obviously something of relevance in this that had their two minds functioning as one again.

Kim continued, "Our police colleagues in Busan regard this as highly suspicious. Why? Because the vessel, a comparatively small ferry, has run along the coastline a number of times, always doubling back towards the port's entrance. It's obviously waiting for something."

Saito and Bella were at it again, which elicited an approving smile from Kim. A smooth working relationship had evolved between the three, which she was relishing. The major factor in this was Saito's ability to be atypically Japanese. He displayed no inclination to look down on women (with the exception of one) and in this respect, he was vastly different to Chief Hasegawa, his boss in Tokyo.

"Now, the Busan Police," Kim went on, "have

provided us with zoom images of the ferry master, its two crewmen and one other male person aboard. There are no apparent passengers. The shots you're seeing now on the screen were taken from CCTV footage in the dock area where the ferry departed from. The police confirm that the master and crewmen are South Korean citizens. They're residents of a small fishing town close to the western entrance of the port. The other male is unknown to them and due to his general appearance, they're concerned."

Kim could see that this had already registered with Saito and Bella.

"He looks awfully like a Central Asian," Bella suggested. Saito nodded in agreement.

"Do you think he might be an Uzbek?" Kim asked.

"Yes, indeed," Bella replied. "Saito San and I both think so. It's too early for the Pakistani from Tokyo to have arrived in this part of Japan, let alone to have made his way over to Busan. So it can't be him."

"Agreed," Kim responded.

Her clipped tone implied there was more to come. She liked the way Saito and Bella ran with the flow, avoiding any digressions. This really is a professional exercise, Kim thought to herself, like a well-oiled Rolls Royce engine humming away. But there's almost always a fly in the ointment, if not more than one.

Bella whispered something to Saito, who nodded in agreement. She then signalled to Jiro to bring up on the main screen grainy images that Saito and his colleagues had retrieved from one of the files passed on by the Chinese.

Five telephoto shots of The Preacher, taken from various angles in Mindanao, appeared one after the other in a looped sequence. He was of average height and build and after watching a number of rotations they now had a firm image of his facial features in their minds.

"One thing I'd point out," Bella said, "is his bearing - the way he carries himself. Instinct tells me he hasn't spent all his years in the Philippines. More likely than not he's been in the US or some place like that. He has a certain swagger about him that a Filipino would only have if he were a big time wheeler-dealer."

The others understood and agreed.

"Now, the next shot," she said, "is of one of his cohorts. They were photographed at the same place in Mindanao over a period of three or four days. We're pretty sure this chap's an Uzbek and member of the Islamic State team that's been training Abu Sayef rebels there. We don't know where he is now, but it's reasonable to assume he's directly involved in the IS plan we're trying to thwart."

Judging by the nods of agreement of those assembled, there was clear consensus on this assumption too.

"Kim's sent both shots across to our police friends in Busan," Bella added, gesturing to Kim to pick up where she'd left off.

"The Korean police are doing a computer scan

of all CCTV footage across the entire Busan precinct to see if they can find when and how that unidentified male entered the Port district," said Kim. "He wasn't at the dock inside the harbour when the ferry moored there late last night. The master and crewmen locked up and went off to a nearby bar. They returned about ninety minutes later, slept below-deck until around seven this morning when a throng of tourists started turning up for cruises. Somehow, he must have blended in, then jumped on board when one of the groups sauntered past our target vessel. The crowd milling around there at the time obscured the view, so we have no footage of him actually boarding, though we do have footage of him onboard."

"Do the police there see that as odd?" Saito asked.

"Generally, they wouldn't," Kim replied, "but in this case, the ferry's odd movements since leaving port make the sudden appearance of that male on board decidedly suspicious."

Saito and Bella nodded in unison.

Kim continued: "We might get something more on Uzbek 1, as the Korean police call him, later on. For now, let's go back to the ferry itself. The police are clear on the fact that the master is waiting for one of two things – to find a safe gap in the heavy bulk carrier and container traffic in the area to dart through and head out to sea, or he's staying close to the Korean coastline for some other reason, like a pre-arranged rendezvous perhaps."

The room was silent.

"Let me hand over now to Matsumoto San,"

Kim said, "who'll give us a round-up on how things are progressing here."

The local Police Chief seemed nervous as he stood with a file of papers in one hand and a clipboard that Yumi had just passed to him in the other. Bella had noticed that while he was relaxed with her, the policeman was twitchy when talking one-on-one with Saito.

Maybe he has an inferiority complex, Bella thought, or it might be a professional issue I'm unaware of. Yet, when she'd mentioned this to Kim, she was adamant it had nothing to do with rank or hierarchy. Saito wasn't that sort of person.

Matsumoto focused on the multifaceted surveillance being carried out on the Pakistani who was on his way down to Kyushu from Tokyo.

"What my HQ in the capital has told us," he said, "is that Pakistani No 1, or P1 as we should all refer to him from now on, is tracking towards Fukuoka by train. For some reason, he's staying off the main lines running down the Inland Sea via Hiroshima. It's a strange and tedious route he's chosen, but Tokyo has little doubt he's travelling to our part of Japan to link up in some way with what our Busan colleagues have observed. These two scenarios are almost certainly going to merge at some stage."

Yumi suddenly appeared alongside Bella and placed two more bowls of miso soup down on the bench in front of her.

"Let me know if you want any more," she said quietly.

Bella noticed a faint smile as she glanced up

to thank Yumi, quickly returning her attention to the evolving operation.

"P1's smart phone is magic for us," Matsumoto continued. "But in case he jettisons it along the way, we have saturation CCTV coverage of his movements at every station where he changes trains and even inside the trains themselves."

Saito liked that, nudging Bella to remind her that the NPA left no stone unturned, before asking, "Has P1 made any smart phone or public telephone calls to his associate back in Tokyo?"

"No, no communication with our second Pakistani friend, P2, at all," the chief replied, "though we're watching him like a hawk. To move on, we already have surveillance squads covering Glover House up on the hill and Dejima Island, both of which are usually crowded with Japanese and foreign tourists at this time of year. In the call P1 received from the radio phone on our target ferry both of these places were mentioned as possible rendezvous points — so we're already covering those sites. This is on the off-chance that UZ1, our possible Uzbek target on board the ferry, arrives here prior to his Tokyo associate and does a reconnaissance. As you can see, we're pulling all stops out for this operation, but maintaining a very low profile in the process, even inside our own establishment. Chief Hasegawa has been adamant on that point."

Saito glanced at Bella and smiled, his expression saying, 'This is how we do things professionally in Japan.'

"So, while we're waiting for P1's arrival,"

Matsumoto continued, "if it eventuates, all eyes remain focused on the target ferry and UZ1. How that puzzle unravels is anyone's guess, but at least we can be totally confident that our police colleagues in Busan have this under control. They're always good to deal with and very efficient but in this instance, there's a real sense of camaraderie I don't think any of us have felt before."

Kim didn't blink an eye at this comment but secretly she was very pleased and relieved.

"Now, that said ... " But the police chief was interrupted by Jiro, the panel controller, who'd been glued to the screen on his laptop, instead of the screen display on the wall, waving for them to stop. Something was happening in or around Busan that the police there wished to discuss with Kim.

Jiro quickly handed her a headset and mic and with a nod from Matsumoto brought the Busan Chief's image up on the main screen. Most of the police officers in the room had seen his stern features before and were well acquainted with his clipped manner. The Koreans were brittle at the best of times when interfacing with Japanese.

As Kim spoke to the Busan Chief her expression confirmed there'd been a significant development. The dialogue continued for some minutes while the others watched in silence.

Suddenly Kim said, "Gamsahamnida! Gamsahamnida!" followed by, "Thank you! Thank you!"

"I read you loud and clear," he said to Kim, "and look forward to hearing more."

After handing the headset and mic back to Jiro, Kim paused for a moment to gather her thoughts.

"Now, this really is interesting," she reported, reverting to Japanese and addressing the group as a whole. "A fishing trawler, larger than our target ferry, and from Kyushu, is approaching the main shipping lane and waiting for a break in the traffic so they can cross into Korean waters. Busan says it's noteworthy that this vessel is heading in a direct line towards our target ferry over there!"

Kim raised her hand to halt the chatter that had started up in the room.

"And that's not all," she said. "They've picked up direct communication between the two boats via smart phones."

Excited chatter sparked up again. Matsumoto ran his finger round the inside of his collar and asked Yumi to find someone to turn the air-conditioning up.

"There's been banter," Kim continued, "between UZ1 on the Busan side and an unknown Japanese – in broken English – who's on the fishing trawler approaching our target ferry. It's apparently a practised script, very touristy, even tedious, and instantly suspicious. Busan is convinced it's a coded dialogue about a shipment of goods at sea on the Korean side of the Strait. It seems that the Japanese fishing trawler will try to find its way through the traffic in the shipping channel, perhaps through a larger gap between those super-tankers and container ships heading north at the moment. Smaller craft always steer clear of them, so it's the Japanese trawler that will make a dash for it."

Kim pointed to the largest of the digital displays on the wall panel. The position of both target vessels appeared in the Straits in different colours, as did the larger ships they were trying to dodge.

Jiro zoomed in on the immediate area where the trawler, in green, could be seen on the Japanese side and the target ferry, in red, in Korean waters.

This is brilliant! Bella thought. The colour coding makes it very easy to follow. If Masataka were here, he'd be like a kid in a toyshop!

Kim explained, "This is real-time, and you'll notice that Busan and us are now using the same target codes. The ferry sticking close to the Korean coast is KF, Korean ferry. JFT is our Japanese fishing trawler heading towards Korea from the Japanese side. When we're operating across linguistic borders, as we are with Busan, it's crucial that early on we agree on a common coding system. It's the only way to avoid misunderstandings."

Suddenly, Jiro held his hand up again, signalling a high priority call coming through. "It's Chief Hasegawa in Tokyo and he wants it on speaker-phone," he said, flicking a switch which put the Chief's image and voice up on the main screen.

"Greetings to all of you," Hasegawa said, with his usual gravelly tone.

Saito and Bella realised straightaway that there must have been a positive development of great importance. It was written all over Hasegawa's face.

"Beijing," he revealed, "has just provided us with a load of extra material that can only be described as intelligence gold. We're pulling the vital data out in Tokyo and will send it down to you within ten minutes. This kind of cooperation from the Chinese is unprecedented."

For Hasegawa to acknowledge any Chinese contribution in this way meant that the operation they were currently involved in was broader, deeper and possibly far more dangerous than anyone had envisaged going in.

Bella studied his face, realising she had witnessed similar things at MI6 Headquarters in London, and more than once while embedded with British and allied military forces.

"I'll give it to you in a nutshell," Hasegawa said. "Chinese operatives in Central Asia have identified all three Uzbeks in the team that visited Mindanao. Two are still in the Philippines, with their exact positions now clear to us compliments of our Beijing colleagues."

Saito and Bella exchanged a quick smile. Beijing colleagues was a description neither had expected to hear from Hasegawa. That was a fascinating development in its own right.

"The pair in Mindanao are planning to slip into Japan sometime in the next two weeks, making their way to Tokyo to meet up with P1 and P2," Hasegawa confirmed. "By the way, we're all locked into your English-language coding now, which nicely crosses all three borders: Japanese, Chinese and Korean. We now know the Mindanao pair will be doing the groundwork for a major terror attack in Tokyo, the scale of which is mind-boggling."

Hasegawa had wasted no time presenting the facts concisely. Bella was impressed; Saito was stunned. He'd never seen his boss in a hands-on situation quite like this, especially a cross-cultural one.

"Now, let's concentrate on your bailiwick down there," Hasegawa said. "A load of high explosives, extremely powerful but not bulky, has somehow been delivered earlier by sea to the target ferry master of KF in Korea. He's had them stored in an onion shed of all places just outside the town where he lives not far from Busan. Those explosives will be transferred from KF to JFT tonight in exchange for a large cash payment."

Suddenly, everyone in the room realised the Nagasaki operation was just the tip of an iceberg.

"UZ1 is a nasty piece of work," he continued. "He's been an organiser of suicide squads for Islamic State in Syria and Northern Iraq. Now he's branching out into new and grander operational domains. Tokyo is the first cab off the rank. He apparently considers it the softest of all targets. China's operatives in Central Asia have reported that he's known to boast that he wants to outdo 9/11, this time on Japanese soil. With the explosives he now has at his disposal, and placement at the Tokyo sites he's pinpointed, he could well achieve that goal. He and his fellow jihadists have apparently studied the engineering of the various sites and major buildings involved in minute detail. In that sense, it certainly rates alongside Mohammed Atta, the pilot who flew the first aircraft into the World Trade Centre towers in New York. Atta had been doing a doctorate in town planning in Hamburg and had gotten hold of the plans. He knew every square centimetre of those buildings."

"We all have a lot of preparation to do," Hasegawa said. "So I won't keep you any longer. The transfer is due to take place around 0300 hours tomorrow morning. I've just been talking to my counterpart in Seoul and he has his government's approval to allow it to go ahead. After that, the Koreans and we will stay on this case until every jihadist involved in this horrible affair is exposed."

Hasegawa had clearly been busy. "It's been agreed with the Prime Minister here," he said, "that we'll allow our trawler, JFT, to deliver its load as planned to an inlet some distance from Nagasaki. P1, the Pakistani jihadist on his way to Nagasaki, via a circuitous train route now, apparently chose this location weeks ago.

Jiro threw a visual of this coastal site up on one of the wall displays as Hasegawa continued.

"P1 will go directly to the inlet when he arrives in your area. There, he'll meet up with UZ1. They'll lie low there for a few days and then drive a van with the explosives up to Tokyo via back roads."

Saito, Kim and Bella were all wondering how such a complex plan had been devised right under the noses of Korean and Japanese authorities? That was worrying. Hopefully, in Nagasaki at least, it wasn't due to any shortcomings on the part of Yumi and her much-vaunted surveillance network.

"We'll get all this information down to you shortly. I'm very tempted to come down myself, but when the PM asked me whether I thought that option was wise, I told him no. But I'll be available to you all 24/7 until this is over. Many of us will be bedding down in the bunker here in Tokyo whenever we have the chance, so feel free to call us at any time."

He hesitated briefly, searching for words. Saito and Bella could see that his thoughts were racing. Bella gathered that Hasegawa was only now becoming aware of just how many officers, specialists and experts were doing their best to bring this complex operation to a satisfactory conclusion. No doubt he understands how he is dependent on a large number of people with greater and much more diverse skills than his own.

Winning high office through influence and cunning was one thing, Saito thought to himself. Strategically, collaboration like this was a far better option, albeit far more difficult to manipulate. Nevertheless, Saito considered that his boss was acquitting himself well.

Hasegawa's voice trembled as he continued. "We all have so much to thank our Chinese colleagues for," he said before lapsing into silence again.

Most in the room thought this marked the end of Hasegawa's briefing when he suddenly added, "Before I go, I want to mention something to our MI6 colleague and friend. Can you read me, Bella?"

"Yes, Chōkan," she replied, using Hasegawa's formal title of Chief in Japanese.

"It's your friend, Li Weiming, in Beijing who's been coordinating all this, you know. He said to say that he's been granted permission to come to Nagasaki if we think it would help. Let me know offline and I'll attend to it without delay. As you, Saito and I well know, getting Li here would be no straightforward thing. There'd be many implications and political hurdles. However, I don't believe the PM would have any objection."

On that note, Hasegawa signed off – for the time being at least.

Bella glanced at both Saito and Kim. "Do you think we should bring him across?" she said.

"Why not?" they both replied at the same time.

"What's your view?" Saito asked Matsumoto. "You're in charge of the operation here."

Bella was touched by this deference on Saito's part. He could easily make this decision himself but the gesture was clearly appreciated by the local Police chief. Bella was slightly taken aback when Matsumoto turned to Yumi, who nodded her agreement after a pause. This riled Saito, something Bella also noticed. Neither of them had any wish to have the local chief's sidekick included in high-level decisions like this.

"If you three are all for it," Matsumoto said, "we are too. Let's get word to the Chief in Tokyo ASAP!"

Bella mused about how fascinating it would be to see how all this panned out. So far, we have Japanese, Koreans and me involved, she thought, and now a Chinese spy is about to jump into the mix!

There was also another factor in the back of both her and Saito's minds, that could scuttle the whole mission if it reared its ugly head. Something that none of the others had yet picked up on.

Chapter 9

Operations Room, Nagasaki
Wednesday, 2127 hours

"JFT trawler crossed shipping channel at 2055 hours and is standing just outside Korean territorial waters three nautical miles from KF ferry," the Busan Police Chief reported to Kim on their secure link.

Speaking in Korean, his voice sounded strong and in control, while his image on the main screen showed a man more at ease with what he was handling. His cooperative spirit was very much in evidence and his harsh features far less intimidating, a relief to everyone.

This is Kim's doing, Bella thought. That stone-faced look that Korean officials feel obliged to adopt when dealing with the Japanese has more or less gone. Working quietly from the sidelines Kim has brought this about. Brilliantly subtle and very effective!

Alongside the main screen, another display showed precisely where the Korean ferry, marked by a flashing red dot, and the Japanese fishing trawler were and the courses they had taken up to that point. A green dot marked the trawler.

Kim waited until the end of the contact with the Busan Chief to brief the room on what he'd said.

"JFT is not anchored and it's drifting due to a south-westerly wind and choppy seas. Deck line of both vessels differs slightly, so we assume they will wait for the wind to drop before attempting cargo transfer. Overcast sky. No ambient light from the moon."

With this meteorological observation as a prompt, Jiro brought up images of the night sky from different angles on three of the smaller screens. Two of these were from Korean islands in the Straits, a link-up that Kim had quietly arranged with her counterparts in Busan. They had contacted Jiro in Nagasaki and fully integrated their network with his. Bella and Saito exchanged a knowing glance at this significant achievement.

"Under cover of darkness, our patrol boats are passing nearby on a regular basis using scanning technology to pick up conversations onboard," the Busan Chief said. "Presently, the master and three crewmen are sitting together in the stern section of the JFT trawler. All are Japanese. There have been two brief smart phone communications between KF and JFT, both instigated by UZ1 using broken English. We believe he's using coded phrases from a written English-language list with which the trawler master is conversant. But his thick accent is obviously making it hardgoing."

Through all this Kim didn't take notes. Bella and Saito had earlier become aware of her exceptional memory for anything from visual imagery to the spoken word. Bella had undertaken training in MI6 to achieve just that. She and Kim had already discussed what an advantage this afforded to their respective professions.

"Will revert when situation changes," the Busan Chief reported.

Kim signed off with her routine friendly banter, then turned to brief her colleagues. The night sky visions on the displays had now been replaced by detailed information on tides, currents, winds, the drift of the target vessels, territorial boundaries and weather forecasts, all being constantly updated in real time in English, Korean and Japanese. Night-time movements of all other shipping, both in and out of the main channel, were also featured.

Saito revelled in this use of state-of-the-art technology, pointing out to Bella various ways in which the data could be cross-referenced with other relevant factors. He and Jiro seemed determined to show her what their technology could do.

"Men and their toys!" she quipped. This brought a smile from both of them, as well as from Yumi, who'd overheard the comment as she glided around mothering the younger members of the staff. This clearly annoyed Jiro, though he refrained from articulating his thoughts. That didn't last long however. While Bella and Kim were otherwise engaged, Saito sidled up to him.

"Sonny, you're doing a great job here," he whispered, pointing to something on his laptop screen to cover their dialogue, "and I'll make sure you're rewarded for it when this is all over. The person who's most likely to fuck this operation up for us all is that cursed woman, roaming the control room like the dinosaur she is!"

"I totally agree we have to take care," Jiro

responded, smartly pointing to something else on Saito's screen.

"This is a truly complex operation," Saito said, "with dimensions most of us have never had to deal with before. I don't want anything to go wrong, so I'm taking precautions, if you understand my meaning."

Jiro nodded, his eyes fixed on Saito's laptop as if comprehending some technological innovation.

"What I'd like you to do," Saito continued, "is to monitor everything she does. Of course, this is strictly between us, but you have my permission to listen in to her communications with her surveillance squads, who'll be crucial to this operation before very long. If you come across anything you think I need to know, give me a signal. If you can't tell me here at the panel, send me an instant message that I can open at the bottom of my screen. No one else will be able to access that."

Jiro nodded gravely.

"I know you have a lot to handle already," Saito added. "Are you okay to take on this extra task?"

"Absolutely," Jiro replied, quietly but intently. "I'm honoured, Saito San, that you'd place so much trust in me. I won't let you down."

"I know you won't. You've already earned my trust. And there may be additional tasks I'd like you to take care of for me."

Jiro smiled and Saito knew he was chuffed.

Bella was starting to feel very tired, though Saito and Kim were still in fine form. There was a good deal of associated communications traffic for them to sink their teeth into. Other displays around the room were monitoring police surveillance units in and around Nagasaki, including the designated inlet where the explosives and their carrier, UZ1, would disembark.

She was about to excuse herself and head towards one of the portable beds when caterers arrived with large trays of sashimi, sushi, miso soup, sandwiches, coffee and even kimchi for which Bella and Kim shared a liking. Sleep would have to wait for a while.

"Don't worry," Yumi said to Bella, pre-empting any concerns she assumed the gaijin spy might have about caterers in the control room. "They're all on our police payroll."

Bella thanked her. It was the first time she had felt that Yumi accepted her presence, though something about the woman didn't sit well with her. She might be unwinding a bit, Bella thought, but there's something off about it. It's much like what I sensed in Hasegawa's display of emotion over the Chinese inputs to this operation.

The atmosphere in the room was buoyant and not unduly tense. Everyone was ready to jump to as soon as an alarm sounded. With this sort of operation anything could happen at any moment. To soothe those with frayed nerves two or three of the smaller screens, when not in use, featured beach scenes with waves, morning mist clearing in mountain valleys, and birds flitting around in trees in a forest.

When Bella had asked Jiro whose idea this was he'd proudly stated that it was his own. "We Japanese love nature," he'd told her, "and to bring it into an ops room like this has a calming effect on those who feel stress more than others. They can select those channels any time they want and bring up the sound on their headphones."

So Japanese, Bella thought. It reminded her of an eight-hour brain operation on a fellow-MI6 officer that she'd had to witness in Jordan for legal reasons. Standing alongside the surgeon throughout, she'd been fascinated by his explanations of how he was repairing the damage that her colleague and friend had incurred in a major traffic accident. Soft classical music had been playing in the background and when she'd questioned the surgeon on this he'd replied: "How else do you expect us to handle the stress?"

Suddenly, a sharp ringing sound from Jiro's desk sent him scurrying back to his seat. This silenced everyone in the room, as though they'd been placed in suspended animation.

"The Chief's coming through again from Tokyo," he announced.

The air of expectancy could be cut with a knife. Bella was left holding her miso bowl halfway to her mouth.

"Good evening everyone," Hasegawa said, as soon as his image appeared on the main screen. "This thing just keeps getting bigger."

His stark expression left no doubt that he wasn't jesting.

"Our Filipino Preacher is back in the game!" he said.

That facilitator – some even saw him as the mastermind – had long ago drifted to the periphery of the operational focus.

"When our Chinese friends sent us a number of images of him, procured from Mindanao, we had Saito San's experts here at HQ do some correlation with our bio-databases."

"The result of this analysis," Hasegawa went on, "is that we've discovered a totally different ID for our preacher man. And on this latest trip he's used this new ID to enter Japan via Fukuoka International Airport on a flight from Manila."

Looks of surprise fanned out in the room as they realised that anyone with one extra identity was likely to have other IDs as well. That could have all sorts of consequences.

"He's in Nagasaki as we speak, this time entering the country as Dr. Roberto Cruz, born in Luzon in 1968 and American-educated. He's posing as an academic, an anthropologist. His US passport as well as his Japanese visa application and the rest of his documentation are in meticulous order. This is clearly a case of high-level, sophisticated falsification, most likely with the connivance of one or more of the bureaucratic systems involved, including Japan, I regret to say. The implications are alarming and we've now deployed an expert surveillance team to monitor him 24/7. As we all know, when someone has multiple identities it's not always easy to work out which is the original."

The room was silent, processing this alarming development.

"It seems that it's Preacher Cruz who's done all the reconnaissance in Nagasaki over the past ten days," Hasegawa said. "This almost certainly included the fishing village outside Nagasaki Harbour. He's staying at a small, up-market tourist hotel, a new one, in the old quarter near Dejima Island, not so far from Glover's House up on the hill behind it. At this stage, we have no idea how those historical sites fit into the scheme of things."

The silence in the room was unbroken by questions.

"He's booked two twin rooms alongside his own, which is puzzling," Hasegawa added. "We can imagine one of the rooms being used by P1 when he arrives from Tokyo, and possibly UZ1. But why another twin room? We're working on the assumption there are other people involved in this whole thing that we have yet to learn about."

Saito and Bella's eyes met. The scenario they were working on was expanding at a worrying pace. It no longer had boundaries, even approximate ones, within which the police could realistically extrapolate what they might not know. It was the dreaded blight of the unknown unknowns.

"Chief, might I cut in here briefly?" Saito said.

"Please do," Hasegawa replied. "I was about to ask you what you make of all this."

"You've no doubt realised," Saito responded, "that we're heading into a blizzard of information, variables, assumptions, analyses, and exponentially expanding parameters. It's what we don't know that could be our undoing."

There was absolute quiet for a moment, before Hasegawa broke the silence.

"My thoughts exactly," he said. "That's why I want to appoint you as the key coordinator of the whole operation in Nagasaki. You have Matsumoto and his team and their wealth of local knowledge. You also have Yumi as a free-ranging troubleshooter who can pick up on anything you might have missed in the barrage of information."

Saito shuddered at this.

"And you have Kim, Bella ... Oh, that reminds me ... I concur with Bella's proposal to have her Chinese friend, Li Weiming, come over from Beijing. The way things are going, I suspect we'll need to call upon his talents and knowledge."

Bella nodded. Li's help could be a game-changer, she mused.

"He'll fly into Nagasaki in an unmarked Chinese government jet," Hasegawa announced, "at around 2315 hours your time. You'll need to liaise with air traffic control there. I suggest you allocate one of our special NPA designations to the aircraft. His presence must be kept absolutely secret, something both governments are insisting on. Any questions?"

Nagasaki Operations Room
Wednesday, 2205 hours

"Busan Police Chief on the line for you Kim!" Jiro called out.

Small teams were busy monitoring visuals and data streaming on numerous display screens, but as soon as Jiro's voice was heard above the buzz, the entire operations room fell silent.

Matsumoto had brought in more police with specific expertise and a number of these were working in groups spread throughout the room, liaising directly with undercover colleagues around the city and its environs. Yumi was in charge of coordinating these activities.

No sooner had Kim taken up the mic the Police Chief stated baldly, "Cargo transfer now complete! A sudden drop in the wind and a change in the current are responsible. The KF master used his radio to contact the master of JFT and urged him to take advantage of this positive window in the weather before it changed again. It only took a few minutes for the vessels to successfully lash themselves together. Once that was done the transfer was remarkably smooth. Crewmen on both vessels were so adept that we assume this has happened a few times. Either that or they'd trained for this particular scenario."

Those watching Kim's face could tell something significant had taken place.

"A total of eight boxes of explosives were transferred," the Busan Chief continued, "which is more than expected. Some must have already been aboard the ferry prior to our surveillance at the dock. The transfer included two other boxes, probably wooden but a different shape, which must have already been aboard as well. Our guess is that they may contain weapons. One Korean crew member transferred to JFT along with UZ1, for reasons unknown. Though we were able to monitor much of their dialogue on the ferry there'd been no mention of this arrangement."

Kim nodded as she digested these details.

"Unless you have any objection we propose to block all communications on KF from now and will apprehend the craft at sea. We think this will facilitate an unimpeded raid on the onion storage shed during which we hope to find evidence that may be vital to both you and us. JFT is now heading back towards Kyushu. We'll continue to track it until you signal your readiness to take over. "

"Will revert soonest on that," Kim responded before the Police Chief signed off.

Kim quickly briefed everyone on Busan's plan and there were no objections. Then she rejoined Bella who was prioritising data just received from NPA HQ in Tokyo. They sat together at a desk adjacent to Saito.

"You know it's extraordinary," Kim whispered to Bella, "just how efficient and professional women can be, isn't it?"

"I heard that," Saito said in a low voice, grinning but without turning away from his laptop. "Except for that old bat who hovers around like a disgruntled headmistress! She unnerves me, in more ways than one."

Bella and Kim chuckled, aware that they shared his misgivings.

Saito was studying a police map of Nagasaki showing the location of the many surveillance teams now operating across the city and their targets. He asked Jiro to put the city map up on one of the displays. He then suggested to Matsumoto that if he and Yumi agreed, she should direct her teams to consult regularly to stay abreast of how things are evolving. Such communications, Saito recommended, should be streamed on designated screens so that everyone in the operations room could tune into who was reporting what to whom. The surveillance squads could bring up the same information in their vehicles, while plainclothes patrols were equipped with wristwatch displays and unobtrusive earpieces.

Yumi visibly baulked at this suggestion, but before she managed to utter a word Saito asked in a polite but authoritative tone, "Do you have a problem with that? Your own experience and professionalism, and that of the teams under your command, are pivotal to what we're doing here. We can't risk any misunderstandings or gaps in our comms."

Jiro and the others were cheering on the inside but remained silent and solemn on the outside. Matsumoto was relieved that Saito had put Yumi in her place. He'd dreaded the thought of being directed to ensure she toed the line.

Only Saito and Jiro were aware that Saito had discreetly introduced his own, secret hi-tech innovations into the existing communications system. Those using the comms were unlikely to detect the various ways in which input was being directed and supplemented. Saito regarded the Nagasaki operation as an ideal opportunity to test these innovations – which he'd been working on for more than a year – before they were officially rolled out.

He immediately requested an update from Yumi on the squads assigned to tailing the Preacher who, in the early evening, had taken a forty minute taxi trip to the inlet where JFT was due to return. He'd asked the driver to wait and then had spent just twelve minutes inside a large timber shed built over a boat ramp on the shoreline.

The Preacher hadn't used his smart phone during that excursion, nor had the driver seen anyone else emerge from the boat shed to greet or farewell him. Discussion with the driver had revolved around Portuguese activity in Nagasaki in the late 1500s and early 1600s, and the driver's own family experience in the atomic bombing of August 1945. This all seemed conveniently innocent, which meant the conversation was contrived.

Yumi's delivery of this report was procedural and to the point, though she was still smarting from Saito's recent rank pulling. The taxi driver, she reported, was a part-time police surveillance operative and, at her direction, had hovered in the vicinity of the Preacher's hotel on the off-chance he might take a taxi-ride somewhere. The ploy had worked and was an encouraging development in what was, overall, a sophisticated and carefully integrated operation covering many square kilometres.

The driver's impression of the Preacher was that he was cocksure, patronising, and had worked hard to establish a tourist aura around himself.

Now back in his hotel room, the Preacher – or Dr. Roberto Cruz – Yumi continued, had not long had a meal delivered when he'd received a call on his smart phone from a public telephone on platform two at Shimonoseki Station. This station was located at the far-western tip of the main island of Honshu where a narrow waterway separated it from Kyushu. The call was from P1, who reported he would soon board a train and cross the straits to Kitakyushu where he would change again for Nagasaki. He would arrive at Central Station at 0822 hours the following morning and would make phone contact again before exiting the station.

Cruz-the-Preacher had no quibble with any of that. In keeping with his 'tourist' cover story, he'd asked only one question of P1: are you taking lots of photos along the way?

The response was, yes, quite a few.

While Saito was pleased with Yumi's presentation, he still didn't trust her. Bella sensed this and wondered what sorts of precautions he might be taking. Perhaps the father-and-son chat she'd spotted him having with Jiro was part of that? Bella too, had warmed to the young man and was impressed with how he went about his job marshalling numerous streams of information.

Operations Room
Wednesday, 2325 hours

While the Japanese trawler headed south towards the coast, Bella, Saito and Kim managed to get nearly an hour's sleep. Matsumoto had insisted that they not be disturbed unless absolutely necessary.

All three were now back at the panel and had been brought up to speed on a number of minor events. Bella was contemplating how the pace would soon quicken when Jiro called for silence again.

"Busan for you," he said, pointing at Kim. She quickly picked up the mic and watched as the Police Chief appeared on the main screen.

"We have significant developments to report," he said. "The master and remaining crew of KF have been apprehended and interrogated. Their involvement in the importation of explosives and weaponry into South Korea is far more extensive than we'd earlier assumed. The Korean master has spent many years living in Japan operating pachinko pinball parlours – becoming closely associated with the yakuza in the process. Initially, he helped with contraband trade in handguns and amphetamines, popular with long-distance truck drivers. The economic slump greatly reduced his income stream and he returned with his family to his home, a fishing town near Busan. There he turned to the ferry trade where he developed two revenue sources: passenger excursion trips, plus facilitating the importation and flow to Japan of goods prized by the yakuza. This ultimately led to his introduction to criminal elements within Japan's large community of Indian, Pakistani, Bangladeshi and other overseas workers, a significant percentage of whom are Muslims."

Kim could see the plot unfolding.

"We plan to send your NPA an extensive report on this later," the Chief continued, "but for now, let's focus on what we've learned that's of direct relevance to your immediate operation. The KF master from our side is a frequent visitor to the boat shed and fishing operation managed by the master of your JFT trawler. This is the designated point of JFT's landfall away from Nagasaki where the explosives will initially be stored. The KF master claims that two young Indian nationals, whom he refers to as fish labourers are employed there on short-term contracts drying bonito for katsuobushi, the shaved fish garnish. The town's inhabitants have been told they hail from the Coromandel Coast in south-eastern India, where a similar tradition of fish drying and shaving exists. I'm no expert on India, but that sounds spurious to me."

Saito and Bella studied the intense expression on Kim's face as she listened, instinct telling them that something noteworthy had emerged in this small detail. When Kim swung round towards them, and raised an optimistic eyebrow, they knew she was aware of it too.

Another front had just opened up in the operation.

The Chief continued: "Our KF master believes the two men to be Indians in name only. He's intermittently involved with genuine Indians through his importing of spices and other substances for Korean suppliers to the Chinese medicine trade. Some of them are Tamil-speakers from that same part of India, but the language he's heard the labourers speaking sounds nothing like that. To the limited extent he understands such things he thinks they use a mix of Arabic and other tongues. He's overheard occasional references to well-known places in Central Asia and the Middle East, but he's never ventured to question either your JFT master or the labourers on where they were born or their families' places of origin. They're also very close, he observed – like brothers."

Kim knew that Bella would feast on this new information. She interrupted the Busan Chief to emphasise how valuable the information was to the Japanese side of the operation and to thank him. He nodded to indicate his appreciation.

Saito quietly chuckled to himself. He had never expected the Koreans to be so forthcoming, but he knew that if anyone could soften them up it would be Kim. He'd told her to do anything she thought necessary to bring them on side. Clearly, she was masterful at it. When he and Kuroda had backed her for promotion they knew they were on a winner. It had not been easy to obtain Hasegawa's approval, however. In his biased view, the very idea of a capable female Korean-Japanese police officer was as much of an oxymoron as military intelligence!

"Our KF master," the Busan Chief continued, "opened up after he'd been further incentivised, telling us he thinks there's some relationship between UZ1 and the two labourers. While the cargo transfer was under way at sea he overheard UZ1 asking your JFT master if they were ready, and had they been maintaining a low profile. Our KF master had the impression that his Japanese counterpart couldn't wait to be rid of them. We'll continue pursuing this and will let you know if we turn up anything else."

"Gamsahamnida," Kim said: Many thanks.

"Now, there's one other thing," said the Chief, "which is worrying in the extreme. UZ1 spent a lot of time by himself in the onion shed. Our KF master told us that he seemed to be busy with some sort of clothing, padded jackets actually. Nothing else, just jackets. It appears he was doing some sewing. The master asked him what he was doing and whether or not his wife could help. UZ1, whom the KF master describes as unflappable, said he was sewing extra Kevlar panels into jackets he'd purchased in Hong Kong prior to coming to Korea."

"Does he have the jackets with him onboard JFT?" Kim enquired.

"Yes, he does. Two of them."

Kim and the Chief exchanged a knowing look. There was a brief pause while he checked for any updates.

"Yes, here we are," he said. "UZ1 has three wooden crates with him. Two of these would need at least two men to move them. The third crate's much lighter. Our ferry master tells us he got to see inside one of the heavier ones when it was left open in the onion shed. It's full of automatic weapons, like AK-47s, wrapped in thick grease-proof paper, and he told us there'd be at least three layers of the weapons in it. The paper had been torn open on the top layer and that's how he spotted them. He didn't dare touch them or take one out for a closer look."

Kim bit her lip nervously. Bella and Saito turned to look at Matsumoto who understood a fair bit of Korean. The intense look on his face indicated that the information Busan was providing was well beyond what they'd originally imagined.

"The second crate of the same size," the Chief

went on, "has different markings on it and it's not quite as heavy as the other one, but he's not too sure what's in it. All he knows is that when they were heading out to sea to meet up with JFT, UZ1 took a large revolver out of that crate and loaded it. While the lid was off the box, the ferry master noticed it was stacked with tightly wrapped packages a bit bigger than house bricks. At first he thought it might be cocaine or something like that, but the smell was more like industrial chemicals. Plastic explosives flashed through his mind because he'd recently seen a movie that featured some things like that where someone had commented on the distinctive smell."

Kim grimaced at the mention of that.

The Chief continued, "Our ferry master asked if he could handle the revolver and UZ1 agreed. It was quite a solid piece and UZ1 said it was the most powerful hand-gun on the market. From the little we know, it might be a ·38 calibre Super Edge, a pistol that really packs a punch! Now the third box, with green masking-tape across the top and down the sides, was never opened. The ferry master wouldn't hazard a guess about what's in that, but UZ1 was extremely careful with it. He actually lugged it onto the boat by himself."

Kim was about to thank him and wind up the report when the Chief mentioned one other small thing.

"By the way, we found in the master's wallet two black-and-white photos, like you use for visa applications. One, of an Asian, had a name like Roberto scribbled on the back in pencil, which may mean something to you. The other is of a younger man, unnamed, probably late thirties or early forties, who could be Iraqi or Afghani. It's hard to say. Looks like a pretty nondescript sort of person. The master claims the photos fell out of UZ1's pocket in the onion shed. We've run a check on the unnamed man but nothing's come up. We don't think he's in Korea whoever he is. He may well be over there. We'll send scanned copies of both photos over to you in a few minutes."

Kim thanked him again for the effort he and his colleagues had gone to in this operation, remarking that it could have positive consequences further down the track. Busan's Chief was clearly alert to the import of what she was saying, as was Matsumoto. He sensed there was something of significance in the exchange, though he was unaware of its nature.

Saito, Bella and the others were eager to be briefed on what had transpired. Saito asked for the room's full attention and then gestured to Kim to begin.

Operations Room
Thursday, 0036 hours

Li Weiming's arrival was welcomed by all in the room, with the exception of Yumi who for some reason had absented herself. Apart from Saito and Bella, no one had previously met a Chinese intelligence officer, nor had they considered how they might deal with such a person.

What they saw was a sprightly man in his late-thirties, with unusually round brown eyes and short scraggly hair. His smile – some would say grin – put everyone at ease.

Before Bella formerly introduced him, Saito reminded everybody of the strictly clandestine nature of his visit.

"He's not really here at all," Saito said, whimsically. "You've never seen him, but from what Bella's told me I think we're all going to enjoy his company and the operation will benefit from his formidable professional skills. Li speaks Japanese, though he modestly claims it should be much better than it is but even one solitary word is a plus over here!"

That sent a ripple of laughter around the room, lightening the mood a little. Only a few minutes were devoted to this welcome, added to by Matsumoto. Time was now of the essence, especially in light of the vital information that Kim had passed on from the Busan Police Chief.

As the others returned to their tasks, Saito, Bella and Kim huddled with Li to brief him on what was happening. Bella interpreted in Mandarin whatever Li indicated he had not fully understood from Saito's rundown in Japanese. Saito, laconic by nature, was highly proficient in the art of briefing. He moved skilfully from peak to peak in the mountain range, rather than losing his listeners in the foothills, which so often happened with people who didn't think like him.

As Bella had expected, the amiable Kim warmed to the new arrival. It was Saito's reaction that concerned her. Would he feel challenged by the younger man's intellect and remarkable deductive capacity?

She watched the pair closely, along with everyone else in the room. They'd never witnessed an interaction like this and were equally as intrigued by the role Bella played. Even Jiro glanced at them frequently while still managing to coordinate his various screen displays. On the face of it the two men seemed ready and willing to engage professionally, but under the surface they were like wary dogs sniffing each other out. As the room fell completely silent, Bella could sense the rapid assessments Li and Saito were making about each other on a host of different planes.

Anxious moments passed as Saito fiddled with his laptop without saying anything. Bella wondered if Li might be offended by this. Saito was frustrated because a file he wanted to show Li wouldn't open.

"Bakayaro!" he said, a common Japanese swearword carrying the same weight as fuck in English.

"That's not a term I've heard before," Li pronounced, with a grin.

"Actually, it's the first time I've used it myself," Saito chuckled in reply.

Once the file had opened, Saito invited Li to sit next to him to be shown a number of matrixes he'd drawn up to help everyone comprehend the multi-layered situation they were grappling with. Bella had already seen these and appreciated what her colleague was doing.

"Li," Saito said, his tone markedly trusting, "I'm an unashamed IT nerd. Please stop me if I go too fast, and especially if I go too slow."

"I sit at the feet of a master," Li responded, following Saito's overview intently before posing a number of rapid-fire questions. There was a fleeting moment of silence before they smiled at each other.

Bella heaved a sigh of relief. She watched in awe as the pair found a means of communicating in a mix of Japanese sprinkled with English words like algorithms, quotients and axes. Their fast-moving dialogue was already beyond Bella's and Kim's range of technical comprehension.

Together with Matsumoto and Jiro, the two women looked on in silence. Yumi suddenly appeared with a lidded mug of green tea – not a typical drinking vessel used by the Japanese – that she placed at Li's side. It was a small cultural gesture that pleased Li, and one that Bella had least expected from the nuggety schoolmistress.

"What puzzles you most at this stage?" Li asked Saito. "For me, it's those two Indian labourers. There has to be more to them than meets the eye. What are they really here for?"

"I agree," Saito said, with obvious enthusiasm.

Both men looked at each other in silence. Li sat back, rubbing his chin, before mumbling a drawn out 'Hai': Yes.

He looked Saito in the eye and said, "There's something in that wealth of material that my Beijing colleagues and I received from Central Asia and Mindanao that might hold a critical clue. It's in a load of secondary data we haven't sent across to you yet. It didn't seem relevant at the time, but I have it on one of the memory sticks I've brought with me."

He reached down for his backpack on the floor.

"This man," Saito declared convincingly to those watching, "speaks mathematics like me. Li is a man after my own heart and I'm so pleased he came over to join us. It's our privilege to have him here."

There wasn't a hint of smarminess in Saito's statement, unlike Hasegawa's earlier praise of the Chinese. Bella, Kim, and even Matsumoto were gobsmacked.

They'd never seen Saito this animated, nor had they expected the two men to connect in this way, and so quickly.

"Where does he get his talent from?" Saito asked Bella, while Li was rummaging around in his backpack.

"From far back in his family history," Bella said, "to a unique place in China called Wenzhou. He'll tell you all about it when all of this is over, I'm sure. And you'll probably be given a much more intricate and scientific rendition than I've ever been privy to. All I know is the broad historical outline of the place – that's remarkable enough even before you get to his family's role in it. In Wenzhou, they breed Einsteins like mushrooms."

Saito was greatly intrigued, which was exactly what Bella had intended.

Chapter 10

Operations Room, Nagasaki
Thursday, 0041 hours

"Kim!" Jiro called out. "Busan again."

"The wind's come up, and quite strongly," said the Police Chief, as everyone in the room stopped to watch him on the main screen. "So the master of JFT has opted to take shelter, probably until daybreak, in the lee of Tsushima Island. It's in Japanese waters, but if you agree, we'd like to get one of our Navy special boat squads here in Busan to try to place listening devices onboard while the master and crew take a nap. We know there are Japanese Self-Defence Force units stationed on the island, but we believe we could handle this effectively and we're ready to go now. What do you think?"

"Hang on and I'll check," Kim replied, well aware this was a politically explosive suggestion, but a job that needed to be done fast.

Bargaining between the South Korean Navy and the Japanese Maritime Self-Defence Force would waste valuable time. Kim understood that the Police Chief was pushing the envelope to see just how cooperative the Japanese could be.

She explained the situation to Saito and Matsumoto.

After a brief exchange Saito said, "Let's run with the Busan idea, but keep it to ourselves. Let the Chief know we're deeply appreciative and that we won't be consulting Tokyo on this. Technically speaking this isn't really happening."

"All clear to go," Kim reported to Busan with a smile. "And we'd be grateful if this can be kept strictly between you there and us over here."

The Police Chief chuckled openly, his demeanour changing markedly from a robotic cardboard cut-out dealing with formal procedure to someone with a warm personality. Bella gave Li a nudge, suggesting he observe this unusual discourse.

"Okay!" the Chief said. "Just give me a second."

Kim heard him instructing someone to pass on the message: Go ahead!

"This is brilliant," he said when he turned back to Kim. "Do you realise we've done all this in under a minute? Are you as amazed as I am?"

"Unquestionably!" Kim replied with a warm smile of her own.

"We'll confirm placement of the devices and will relay anything we receive directly to you ... just you in Nagasaki! A pleasure doing business with you, Officer Kim!" the Chief said as he signed off.

Kim chuckled as she handed the mic back to Jiro who, with the flick of a switch, replaced the Chief's smiling face with the multi-coloured map of shipping movements in the Straits.

Saito was delighted with the outcome of the discourse between the male Korean Police Chief and his female subordinate. Korean men had a similar reputation to Japanese males when dealing with women at work.

"So they're going ahead?" he asked.

"Yes, they're off and running already," Kim replied.

"It's good that Busan trusts us enough to suggest this course of action, isn't it?" Saito observed.

"Indeed it is."

It took Kim a moment to gather her thoughts. She'd never been afforded this degree of professional respect before. She'd never even 'dared' to think it could happen. But it just had.

Operations Room
Thursday, 0044 hours

"Here we are," Li said, a picture of concentration as he brought up a block of data on his laptop. "I'm pretty sure what we're after is in here somewhere."

Saito moved his chair closer to him as Bella and Kim looked on with keen interest.

"What I have here," Li said to Saito, "is a series of matrixes of my own. I started working on them after we received the initial reports on these jihadists from our operatives in Central Asia, and added to them when the intercepts from Mindanao turned up. They're not complete, but at least they're a start."

He moved his laptop around so Saito could get a better view.

"If you look at this first one," Li said, "then jump across to the next by clicking here, you'll see where I'm going."

Saito was engrossed and asked Li whether he'd mind having Jiro project the matrixes up on an electronic display so others in the room could follow his thinking.

"No problem," Li replied. "In fact, it'll be helpful to have more eyes on this."

When the matrix was up on the screen, Li moved to stand before them.

"Saito San has seen all of these," he began, "and he knows how my mind works. I believe we're on the same frequency."

The attention of the operations room was now fixed on him and the screen. Everyone seemed aware that something of great relevance to what they were doing was about to be revealed.

Li went through the matrixes first, his Japanese now gaining in confidence, thanks to his productive dialogue with Saito.

"Now, I'd like to give you all a summary of the conclusions I've drawn, or should I say, I'm inching towards with Saito San's help."

The room was totally silent. Li had everyone's undivided attention.

"It seems there's a powerful familial link between most of the characters in our scenario," he said, "and it's something that follows patterns we don't have here in our part of the world. For us, brothers and sisters are plainly brothers and sisters – full, half, adopted and so on. But in India, Pakistan, Afghanistan, and across Central Asia and the Middle East, they have a concept of cousin-brothers. I asked an Indian acquaintance once, how many brothers he had and without blinking an eye he said sixteen. These cultures have a much grander notion of what we call 'extended family'. Whether we're talking about blood relatives, or people who have somehow come to be included under that umbrella, the links remain powerful. They'll kill for each other, certainly to protect the broader family's honour."

Li paused for a moment to take a sip of green tea.

"I must be honest with you. I'm feeling a little tired and standing makes it worse. I hope you don't mind if I sit on the desk here. I promise I won't put my feet up on it like the Americans do. In China, your boss would clout you around the ears if you did that!"

A titter washed over the operations room and Bella and Kim exchanged a subtle glance: this man knows how to handle an audience.

"So, returning to our characters, based on what I know from the material my intelligence service has gleaned, P1– the Pakistani jihadist from Tokyo – is a cousin-brother of his associate there in Tokyo, P2. UZ1, I think, is also related to them in a similar way. Exactly where he fits into this extended family biologically is hard to say. He also has so many different identities that we've been unable to ascertain who the original UZ1 actually is. One thing I'm pretty sure of, and Saito San and Bella now agree, is that the two so-called Indian labourers working for the trawler master of the vessel now sheltering near Tsushima Island, are in fact twins. I think UZ1 wants to use them as suicide bombers, possibly here in Nagasaki, but definitely somewhere in Japan."

A frisson of reality ran through the room.

"It would seem that these twins are somehow

related, probably directly to P1 who'll be arriving in Nagasaki later this morning. Now, before we continue mapping out these complicated relationships, it might be useful to drive straight into the heart of the extended family we're wrestling with here. This family has a chequered history and a great deal of bad blood as well. Indeed, the hatreds are so intense most people would find them difficult to comprehend. The patriarch and matriarch of this family were originally living in Afghanistan. The old man worked closely with Osama bin Laden, while the woman lived in Herat, in the west. He died in the American bunker attack in the Tora Bora Mountains from which Osama managed to escape, as we know. But the old man is entombed there, along with many others. The matriarch was killed when the Americans accidentally bombed a bus on its way to Kabul which was unfortunately passing a targeted Al Qaeda convoy of trucks at the time."

When his voice became noticeably hoarse, Yumi took Li's mug away for a refill.

"Thank you," he said.

Wow, he's already become part of this family, Bella thought.

"Now, a son in that extended grouping of people," he continued, "was at one stage working in the south of India and was married to a Muslim woman there. The twins I mentioned earlier are the product of that marriage. The family spent very little time in Madras, or Chennai as it's called nowadays, moving to Pakistan for a few years when the father picked up a job in Peshawar, not too far from Kabul just across the border. It's there that the father of the twins became radicalised. He was loosely affiliated with Al Qaeda, but when they were driven out of Afghanistan this man moved on to Northern Iraq, eventually becoming a die-hard supporter of Islamic State. His family stayed back in Peshawar."

Li took another sip of tea.

"He was killed by an American, or more correctly, a Coalition bombing of an ammunitions dump near the Syrian border. We believe this man's brother may well be UZ1."

A picture was definitely emerging.

"Back to this man's twin sons for a moment, one of them is, strangely, hopeless at languages, while the other is outstanding. One speaks no Tamil, the language of his birth, and has only acquired 'marketplace' Urdu plus a smattering of Arabic and English from his family's time in Peshawar. His other half also has little Tamil, but is very good in Urdu, and particularly Arabic and English. He's even picked up some of the Pashtu languages from the tribal area on the border between Pakistan and Afghanistan, north of Peshawar. Between themselves, they seem to speak a mish-mash of all of those languages. One of my service's operatives has told us that it's mutually intelligible to them, but quite impenetrable to anyone else."

Li cleared his throat as he scanned the group. Clearly, they were all intrigued by the way this jigsaw puzzle was coming together. As Bella watched him she thought of the sheer might and scope of the Chinese spy apparatus that Li had at his disposal.

Saito was thinking the same thing, which was at once intriguing and frightening.

"Now," Li went on, careful to keep things as simple as possible, "the twins' mother went off to Iraq when she learnt of her husband's death, hoping to bring back at least some of his possessions. Despite having only a smattering of Arabic she somehow managed to meet up with the fighters who'd been with her husband when he was killed. It's one of those men that radicalised the mother. When she returned to Peshawar, she exhorted the boys to go to Syria to join up with Islamic State, which at the time appeared unstoppable. But the twins' uncle, UZ1, could see that the tide was turning and insisted they fight alongside him on a new front. UZ1 arranged, via the Preacher – Dr. Roberto Cruz – for them to work with the master of the Japanese trawler in his fishing business. UZ1 wanted them to get a feel for Japan until he was ready to use them in a suicide mission."

Saito, Kim, Bella and Matsumoto, sitting in front of Li, all shook their heads at once.

"So, that's what we're dealing with," Li said, "and I won't bore you with any more detail for now."

That raised a laugh from the room.

"The cast in this deadly play is grand enough as it is. Saito San and his colleagues have agreed that I should message my superiors in Beijing outlining everything I've just told you. It's possible someone in my set-up can expand on what we already know or even challenge the conclusions we've come to. What we particularly need to find out from my colleagues in Central Asia and the Middle East is how the other two Uzbeks in Mindanao fit into this matrix, if indeed they do. I think they do, but we must be sure before they leave the Philippines and head for Tokyo in the next few weeks, if not sooner. I'll stop there. Thank you for your attention."

The room burst into applause. Bella was pleased for Li's sake that he'd been able to carry it off so well, especially in Japanese. This surprised even her, and she thought how mentally exhausted he must be. Bella always was after dialogues like this in languages other than her native English.

She turned to Li and said, "When you send that message to Beijing, could you include one other thing please?"

"Certainly, what is it?" Li replied.

"Before you arrived, the Busan Police Chief sent us electronic copies of two black-and-white passport photos. UZ1 had dropped them in a shed where the explosives were stored before being loaded onto the Korean ferry. When the master was interrogated in Busan he was asked why the photos were found in his wallet. The master said he'd picked them up and kept them, despite knowing they belonged to UZ1."

Bella asked Jiro to bring the photos up on one of the screens.

"As you can see, one is obviously the Preacher, and the picture had Roberto scrawled on the back. The other, however, had no name. He looks like an Iraqi or an Afghani to us. Which raises the question of who he is and why UZ1 was carrying his photo. We know UZ1 is acquainted with the Preacher, so maybe he had his photo on the off-chance he needed to show it to someone so they could recognise him? That, we can understand. But who's the other man? He must be of some significance. Is he linked to the matrixes you've just shown us or is he someone in the mix who hasn't been identified yet?"

Li thought for a moment. "Bella, if you had to name just one reason why UZ1 had that photo what would first come to mind?"

She answered without hesitation. "I'd say he's somehow mixed up with the bunch we're dealing with here, but UZ1 hasn't met him and that's why he had the photo."

"When and where will they meet?" Saito said, joining this deductive process. "That's what we need to know."

"Maybe here in Nagasaki," Bella suggested. "If not, perhaps at the inlet where the trawler's going to dock. A worse scenario would be in Tokyo. In any case, it's definitely going to be somewhere in Japan."

"What makes you think that?" Li asked.

"Instinct," Bella said. "Any of us in police and intelligence work, and let's face it, we're basically the same animal, the outlier is the one we fear. That maverick who pops up at the worst possible time to play a key role we couldn't possibly have foreseen."

There was general agreement to the validity of this point. The unmarked photo had to be significant. It was highly unlikely UZ1 just happened to be carrying a picture of some old school friend.

"Instinct tells me it's sinister," Bella said.

"OK," Li said immediately. "I'll include the shot and see what Beijing's database throws up."

Once Li had dispatched his message, Saito called for a break.

He could see Li was urgently in need of rest.

"OK, Li/007," Saito declared. "The consensus is that you should catch up on a few hours sleep. We've made up a bed for you and we don't mind if you snore!"

Operations Room
Thursday, 0135 hours

While Li was tucked up in bed, Saito called Matsumoto, Yumi, Bella and Kim together to review the state of surveillance on each of the targets being monitored. They needed to put in place a protocol for apprehension when the time came.

Would this take place at different times, in separate stages, or would all the targets be taken into custody in one synchronised action? If not the latter, Saito explained, there would be a danger that one or more of the targets, using, say, a smart phone that the police were yet unaware of, could tip off the others, sending them deep underground. The careful coordination of these events was critical to the success of the operation.

Yumi spoke briefly on how the surveillance teams were deployed and the high degree of maneuverability they had. She appeared nervous at first, addressing such a mixed group of specialists, but a number of questions Kim tactfully put to her elicited sound responses that clearly boosted Yumi's confidence.

"One final thing to add," she said. "The inn where the Preacher's booked rooms uses an 'outside' servicing company to handle cleaning, changing bed sheets and that kind of thing. We have one of our own people in the company's management and he's had those rooms equipped with listening devices. So we have another way of monitoring any dialogue between the occupants."

She glanced at Bella and smiled, clearly suggesting that an MI6 operative would be well acquainted with this kind of surveillance. Bella's gracious nod confirmed it, establishing a professional link between the two women that Yumi seemed to appreciate.

Well, that's a start, Bella mused. I was beginning to think she was too hard a nut to crack. But she hasn't won me over yet, not by a long shot. There's something about her that's unsettling. I just can't put my finger on it, yet.

Yumi turned to Saito asking his permission to outline the nature of the surveillance technology. It would be no great revelation to Li, but Saito nodded his assent for the benefit of others in the group.

"Well," Yumi began, "we aim electronic beams onto the glass windows of the rooms involved, from which we pick up vibrations on the glass from human speech. That's how we can overhear what they're saying. That's matched with our line of sight into the room and, from there, we're able to create a 3D image of the interior – who's sitting where and who's addressing whom. If the curtains are closed, we can still build an image from voice lines, aided by the listening devices already planted in the room. This new technology is already in place across every site involved in this operation, and, of course, it's supplemented by night vision."

Saito thanked Yumi, then moved methodically through each of the targets, starting with the Preacher. He seemed to be central to the jihadist network that had already been dispersed across Japan. Whatever was to happen when P1, the Pakistani from Tokyo, arrived at Nagasaki Central Station at 0820 hours and met up with the Preacher, could be pivotal to any action taken against the other targets. The place of their meeting was still unknown, as was the point where either, or both, would rendezvous with UZ1.

Another factor that was likely to become critical was the arrival of the Japanese trawler at its small home base. What would UZ1 do first? Who would he make contact with? The multi-layered surveillance exercise now under way across all of these targets would, with any luck and a great deal of skill, be the net from which none could escape.

Over and above all of this, however, Saito and his team were sweating on something else.

Operations Room
Thursday, 0148 hours

"Kim, you're being called again!" Jiro shouted out with his now familiar verve. He brought the uncharacteristically chirpy Busan Police Chief up on the screen. Something else must have gone well, Kim thought.

"When you gave us the all-clear to send our Navy squad in," he said, "they had already put to sea. Strictly between us, they were in fact very close to the target vessel. That gave us a head start and it's paid off. We've managed to place three listening devices onboard your JFT trawler. They're small, virtually undetectable, but highly effective. They've been positioned around the cabin area and have already proven they can pick up speech clearly. The technology filters out extraneous sounds like water lapping the hull and the anchor chain when it's pulled tight. The trawler's sitting in a sheltered cove, which we gather the master has used before."

Kim was eager to hear about the yield, but had no intention of interrupting.

"Before they bunked down something unexpected happened. We're well aware that UZ1 is a volatile character but to put it mildly, he has a very short fuse. You might like to alert your colleagues and let them hear the recording for themselves. This says it better than the transcript."

Apart from Li, who was left undisturbed in his cot, everyone was ready to listen.

"Let it roll," Kim said.

"OK, this is UZ1 addressing the master," answered the Chief.

He pressed a button and the dialogue began. It was in broken English with the odd phrase or two interrupted by a Korean crewman from the ferry who was accompanying UZ1.

"Our agreement," UZ1 shouted, "was that you'd employ the twins until I needed them. That's all there is to it!"

"Kuso!" the master responded angrily with a much-used Japanese expletive: Shit! "That's completely wrong. The agreement I reached with your Filipino sidekick was that the longer I employed these two in fish-drying, the more you'd compensate me when you took them away. They're doing a real job here, remember, and that's given you the cover you wanted. I'm trying to run a fucking business here!"

"No, no!" UZ1 yelled back. "The lump sum I'm paying you covers all that, as well as the pay for your crewmen!"

"Bakayaro!" the master, responded, cursing him more than once: You bastard!

"Take it up with the Filipino," UZ1 screamed. "He handles the money side of things. Don't bother me with this trivia!"

The master seemed surprised that their relationship had suddenly turned bad. He had previously been unaware of this ugly side to UZ1's character, now fully on display.

"Don't mess with me!" the master shouted, the shrill pitch of his voice piercing as he must have been in close quarters to the listening devices.

Everyone in the operations room then heard the distinctive sound of a gun being cocked.

"Bakayaro! You're mad!" the master shouted. "You're crazy! You ..."

The master's voice was suddenly lost in a jumble of sounds. Metallic pots and pans were crashing to the floor and glass shattering.

There'd obviously been a struggle over the

gun. Presumably, the Super Edge revolver UZ1 had retrieved from one of the boxes had been pushed into the master's stomach or face and he'd fallen backwards into the galley. The Korean crewman pleaded in Japanese with the master not to pursue the matter.

"Firipino to hanshinasai. Kochi no yatsu wa abunai yo!" he screamed: Take it up with the Filipino. This man is dangerous. Don't push him too far!

UZ1 was relentless, cursing in Arabic and other languages that made Bella blush.

Then a shot was fired, almost deafening those in the operations room. The sound of buckled metal suggested a bullet had gone through the fishing boat's cabin structure near one of the listening devices.

"You no talk to me again about this!" UZ1 was heard shouting.

Then the dialogue suddenly stopped. UZ1 must have stormed off. Maybe he'd gone to the bow of the vessel to get away from the others. Shortly after, another device picked up an exchange between the master and the Korean crewman.

The recording was faint, possibly because they were standing in the uncovered working area at the stern of the vessel.

"Please understand, it's best left until we're onshore," the crewman said in deferential Japanese.

The Busan Police Chief stopped the tape there.

"That should give you some idea of what you'll have on your hands with UZ1," the Chief quipped in Korean. "The recordings are far more extensive than this and they'll be sent across to you shortly. I'd get ready for fireworks when the boat arrives. Come back to us if we can be of any further help."

Kim thanked him and then provided her colleagues with an interpretation of his closing remarks. There was silence for a moment as everyone considered the implications of what they'd heard.

"Right!" Saito said, snapping them back to reality. "Forewarned is forearmed as they say in English. And thanks to our Korean counterparts, we are. They've done an outstanding job. I'll call Hasegawa right now and let him know what's happened."

Matsumoto pointed to the time on the wall clock.

"I'll call him anyway," Saito abruptly reacted. "It's not as though we're playing mahjong down here."

Li was still asleep when Beijing's response to his message came in. It flashed up on his laptop screen, which he'd left switched on, but required a password to open.

The heading was in Chinese and Bella checked to see if it warranted waking him up. It related to the man in the unmarked photo that UZ1 had dropped in the onion shed. She decided to rouse him and it didn't take long for him to crawl out of bed and join them, oblivious to the fact that he was only wearing socks and underpants.

Once he'd opened the message he decided that everyone in the room should be aware of the information it contained. He asked Jiro to bring it up on the main screen and then went through it point by point in Japanese:

Subject is Afghan by birth. Spent formative years in Northern Iraq. Age: 38. Was early recruit to Islamic State. Moved into Syria with IS and played key command role in IS HQ in Raqqa. Was involved in initial beheadings and mass executions of hostages and prisoners. Uses numerous aliases but most commonly known by jihadist name of Abu Mukhtar. A fervent Islamist also renowned for cruelty. Is indisputably a rabid psychopath. Frequent intercepts of his colleagues' communications indicate they refer to him as King of the Killers. He disappeared inexplicably three months ago and is believed to be active in South East Asian region. We suspect he has linked up with the unidentified Uzbek fighters training Abu Sayef. Dangerous in the extreme. Will revert with additional photos of him when to hand. Do your best over there.

Zhang/Command Unit,
Central Data Division.

Bella and the others stared at the screen, everyone wondering the same thing: where is Abu Mukhtar right now?

Chapter 11

Kiyomizu Fishing Village near Nagasaki
Thursday, 0510 hours

Yumi's surveillance teams were the first to pick up movement by Dr. Roberto Cruz. Middle-aged and slender, the Preacher had graying hair around the temples and a dignified, even scholarly look about him that fitted neatly with his academic research cover. His benign looks served him equally well when he was spreading the Christian gospel.

It gives me a measure of the man, Bella mused as she watched the surveillance footage up on the big screen. Visuals can tell you so much. He's definitely a man of conviction, even if it is perverted. But it's what drives him that we need to know.

The Preacher had collected an unmarked delivery van from a local hire service the previous evening and left it in the car park at his hotel. There had been only one incoming call for him, on his smart phone, and that was from UZ1 saying that he expected to arrive in Kiyomizu around 0600 hours. The call was truncated by the Preacher in an odd way.

'Is ...?' UZ1 said, attempting to ask another question before the Preacher terminated the call.

'Yes, yes,' the Preacher had replied petulantly, cutting across him mid-sentence before hanging up.

The abrupt end to the call told those in the operations room that UZ1 had carelessly strayed into extremely sensitive territory. Clearly, he should have known better.

The Preacher had slept for a short while before getting into the van and heading out to the fishing village at one side of the inlet. It was an ancient settlement renowned for its clear water springs. For centuries, fishing vessels had called in there to replenish their water supplies, delivered directly onboard via an elaborate network of bamboo pipes.

He'd reached the boat shed and ramp belonging to the trawler master just before daybreak. After waking the master's Japanese employees who worked and lived there, including the Indian twins, they all shared breakfast together. The Preacher told the employees that he and the twins would soon be embarking upon a research trip around villages and towns in Japan that were fading away, many even closing down, due to the exodus of young people to the cities. In these places, the elderly were left to fend for themselves. Aid packages were coming from Korea on their master's fishing boat and would be distributed during this trip.

Over breakfast, the Preacher noticed that the master's three young local workers and the twins had developed quite an affinity. This worried him, not because they might reveal the terror plan they were part of, but because their current lifestyle and the friendships they'd formed might prompt second thoughts about their mission.

The plan for Japan, of which the Preacher appeared to be the prime architect, meant everything to him as a Muslim. Bella was about to brief everyone in the operations room on why that was so. Only minutes before, a short background report on the Preacher's motivation, provided by Chinese operatives in the southern Philippines, had been received by Li from his Beijing headquarters. Bella had no wish to waste time translating it into written Japanese and instead was verbally interpreting it directly from the message in Mandarin.

Bella stood facing the group before saying, "I won't soften the language in this, nor the content."

Only Li knew what that meant. Valuable time would be lost in trying to accommodate the sensitivities of any of their Japanese colleagues. Being polite in spoken Japanese was a complex process – flowery and longwinded – no matter how gifted the foreign interpreter.

Jiro sensed from Bella's warning what might be coming. On his own initiative he placed all of the wall's display screens on mute, dimming their colours and images. It was the first time he had done this in the course of the operation. Everyone in the room knew this to be an important moment.

"The Japanese military," Bella started, "decimated the Preacher's family in Mindanao during WWII, with most of the womenfolk raped and murdered. Babies had been bayoneted and tossed in the air. No war reparations have ever trickled down to the few family members who survived. Some decades after rebuilding their lives, the burgeoning Japanese economy paid high prices for soft woods used to decorate new homes or for billions of throwaway chopsticks. Japanese loggers were not only paying off politicians and bureaucrats in the capital but were themselves directly supervising the destruction of old-growth forests."

Saito was watching Bella's facial expression intently as she delivered these unpalatable words. He fully endorsed the way she'd chosen to present them. It left sentimentality out of the equation. Bella, he thought, never fails to surprise. To interpret directly from Chinese into Japanese like this is really impressive!

"It wasn't just a matter of clearing trees," she continued reading from the report. "Local criminal elements were recruited to the task of eradicating influential farmers, villagers and anyone else who voiced their objections. The Preacher's wife and three young daughters were, at this time, kidnapped, raped and killed, as though the Pacific War had never ended. Such crimes were generally attributed to rebel forces, even to Maoists. Not long after, much of the male Muslim population of Mindanao was classified as subversive and pushed off their traditional lands. Many of those caught up in this campaign were innocent. But with no effective recourse to law, throngs of young men joined up with Abu Sayef, the separatist movement. To them, it was the only way to fight back. Before long, they were seen as fully-fledged terrorist jihadists and treated accordingly."

Bella indicated this was the end of the report. In the space of ninety seconds everyone in the operations room came to understand what motivated a man like the Preacher to plan an act of great vengeance on the Japanese. Islamic State and its fanatical Uzbek adherents had furnished him with the opportunity he had long dreamt of.

Matsumoto now rose and stood alongside Bella.

"We are fairly sure," he said, "that the trawler master in Kiyomizu is blissfully unaware of this. To him, any business deal that supplements his regular income is welcome. The less he knows about the back story, the better, and that suits the Preacher and his associates just fine."

*****

When the Preacher arrived at Kiyomizu he reverse-parked close to the jetty where the trawler would moor, so the boxes could be loaded straight into the van. Despite his well-laid plans, he was oblivious to the fact that Yumi's teams had bugged both the van and the boat shed. Every word was being recorded and transmitted to monitors in the operations room, as were all of the various targets' movements.

Once the trawler left the cove on Tsushima Island, the Busan Police Chief had ensured that monitoring of the listening devices onboard the trawler was seamlessly transferred to the operations room in Nagasaki. The vessel had headed directly for the northern coast of Kyushu in mild weather with a sea breeze behind them.

Meanwhile, the master's employees in the boat shed set to work on repainting a wooden craft bright yellow on the slipway. The Preacher took the twins aside and gave them a pep talk. The dialogue, mainly in English, was directed largely toward the twin with the flare for languages, who occasionally interpreted for his brother.

Bella listened carefully for any subtle inflection that might reveal who knew what and why. She could brief the others later when an opportunity presented itself, though, as was her habit by now, she scribbled notes as she went for Saito, Li and Kim.

The Preacher said, "You should both feel honoured to be chosen for a mission like this. It will avenge the losses your family has suffered and soon you'll be reunited with them in a wonderfully peaceful place. Now, when you see Amin, greet him warmly and leave him in no doubt that your resolve is as strong as ever."

The name Amin had not previously been heard by the surveillance teams, though it somehow rang a bell with Li, who launched into another data search.

Saito was engaged in conversation with Hasegawa in Tokyo, briefing him on how the various strands of the operation were starting to converge. Hasegawa, in turn, was routinely briefing the Prime Minister.

The long hours of surveillance in its myriad forms was beginning to pay off. Li praised Matsumoto and Yumi for the diligent and agile manner in which they juggled so many diverse tasks. Though it was early days, these sorts of positive comments seemed to be influencing the attitude of both Matsumoto and Yumi towards Saito. As Li had noted to Bella, it's probably more a matter of Matsumoto lacking confidence in his own ability than fear of Saito's intellect, or his legendary status within the NPA. On Yumi, however, he wouldn't hazard a guess. She would now spend much of her time outside the room, monitoring her teams relaying information directly to Matsumoto.

Whatever the dynamics between the pair, the operation was coming to a decisive point. Yumi's skill managing the forces on the ground was now paramount. They had come too far and even a minor slip-up could ruin everything when they least expected it.

Kiyomizu Fishing Village
Thursday, 0620 hours

As soon as the trawler moored and UZ1 stepped onto the jetty, Yumi's surveillance team zoomed in on the Uzbek's features. The visuals taken from different angles came up on the screens in the operations room and were much clearer than those provided by the Busan Police.

UZ1 was in his late forties, dark-featured, with an unusually sinister look about him. Though the close-ups showed a kindly face, perhaps with a touch of innocence about it, the eyes were intense. Someone in the room, thinking aloud, observed that they were the eyes of the Devil.

On the jetty, UZ1 pulled the Preacher aside and asked him to settle the money issues with the Japanese trawler master. One of the listening devices on board the vessel picked up the first part of that exchange, but it faded slightly as the two men turned towards the boat shed.

"Don't bicker over money and get the master offside," the Preacher was heard to say. "He could wreck everything. Don't you understand that? Pay him double and don't quibble. After all, it's not our money, is it."

UZ1 gave a surly grunt in return but it seemed to satisfy the Preacher. Those listening closely in the operations room now had a fix on the Preacher's degree of authority. His word carried weight.

Their voices faded temporarily but came back when they entered the boat shed and were joined there by the master. The transaction took place quickly. The Preacher's sports bag contained a large amount of cash in ¥10,000 notes as well as high denomination US currency.

The master was more than happy with the sum he received and wandered off to attend to business matters, joined by the sole Korean crewman who'd accompanied them on the trip across the Strait.

"Let me know when you're leaving," the master said in a gruff tone to UZ1, "and we can say our final goodbyes."

The statement oozed sarcasm but drew no reaction from UZ1.

In the meantime, others in the room had focused their attention on the Indian twins. Without any assistance, the pair had transferred the three boxes, as well as UZ1's personal bags, into the van. They'd dutifully followed the Preacher's instructions and left the wooden box with the green masking-tape bands until last. That done, the double rear-doors of the van had been closed and locked.

"Do you think there's any significance in the masking tape?" Kim asked Bella.

"Well, I doubt it's to secure the box," she replied, "so it must denote something special. Perhaps it means the box needs to be handled with care? Green is also symbolic of Islam. All we really know at this stage is that we need to keep a close eye on it."

No one else in the room had any idea what the box contained, nor why it should be afforded special attention. No reference had been made to it in the interrogations of the Korean ferry master and his crewmen carried out by the Busan police. The only thing they'd gleaned was, when one of the crewmen sat on the box, UZ1 promptly told him to get off it. No reason had been provided.

Once the rear doors of the van were locked, the Preacher, UZ1 and the twins had huddled inside the shed, away from the master's office, an enclosed, windowed area in the inner-most part of the building.

UZ1 spoke in Arabic directly to the gifted twin, addressing him as Murad, a name the operations team hadn't previously heard. It was, however, on a list that Li had now retrieved. The name Murad was a significant lead for Saito and Li, whose combined matrixes were proving invaluable.

Bella was once again called upon to listen in on UZ1 and the twin Murad speaking Arabic for just a few moments. She started interpreting simultaneously what she was hearing to those in the room.

UZ1 was doing the talking and clearly saw no need to interpret for the Preacher. This suggested the latter was already acquainted with the topic of discussion.

Adopting an avuncular tone, UZ1 stressed, "You do our whole family proud in taking on this brave assignment. I am particularly proud of you both and it won't be long now before we're all reunited in Heaven."

Bella signalled to the others that UZ1's use of the word heaven was notable. His intonation displayed great and obviously intentional reverence. Murad relayed all of this to his twin brother with the same emphasis.

Both twins acknowledged UZ1's praise and expressed their gratitude as well as resolve. Reaffirming their conviction clearly put the Preacher at ease. Though he said nothing, UZ1 relayed how impressed Dr Cruz was with them.

"I've already rigged the two vests for you," he went on, "so once we've checked into the hotel in Nagasaki, we'll slot the explosives in and do the wiring. This can't be done on a bumpy road. Before we get there, though, I want to take you on a practice run around Dejima Island and Glover's House. Dr Cruz will join us on that excursion. He's already scouted the area and knows where the densest concentrations of tourists will be. Any questions?"

"No questions, Amin. We're ready to go, ready to do our duty," the twins replied in unison.

Saito and Li exchanged a glance. UZ1 had just been addressed as Amin – another positive identification.   Saito had something to ask when Bella had finished interpreting.

"Is there anything significant, like atmospherics, that you've drawn from this dialogue that we need to know?"

"Yes, most definitely," she replied. "The Preacher chose to say nothing, reinforcing my initial impression that he's the one ultimately in charge. UZ1 defers to him in that regard, but not in a subservient way. There's a mutual dependence."

UZ1 and the twins exited the boat shed and climbed into the front cabin of the van. The two young men moved back in the van's rear with the boxes and soon after the Preacher jumped into the driver's seat. Surveillance cameras showed the van traversing the driveway to the boat shed before turning onto the main road that would take them to Nagasaki.

For a moment, everyone in the room focused on the main screen where Jiro had projected footage of the van's departure. There was a brief silence as everyone realised that this operation was about to enter a new phase – a much more dangerous one.

"What are you thinking?" Li asked Bella in Japanese.

"That our level of concentration is about to get much more intense," she replied. Saito, Matsumoto and Kim all nodded.

Li turned to Bella and raised one eyebrow. This habit of his always presaged a shared moment between them. "What are you feeling right now?" he said in Mandarin.

"I'm feeling good," she replied, reflectively. "I

always do at a juncture like this when we're all about to flip into top gear."

Li grinned back at her. They'd never imagined a day would come when they'd be sitting alongside each other in the thick of a complex intelligence operation like this. Up until now, whatever operation either had been involved with while working for their respective services was simply not up for discussion. It was an unwritten law Bella and Li religiously followed. Now, they were duty-bound to put their heads together and share their thoughts openly. It was a strange but exhilarating feeling.

"How the worm turns!" Bella observed in Mandarin, and both of them laughed.

One young policewoman whispered to another beside her that she'd never seen a white woman and a Chinese man get on so well.

Chapter 12

Uemura Inn, Nagasaki City
Thursday, 1012 hours

During the drive to Nagasaki, UZ1 dozed off while the Preacher was at the wheel. The twins had remained in the rear of the van fixing large adhesive labels to the boxes, including the one with the green tape. The Preacher had had these printed in the Philippines prior to flying to Kyushu. On a white background, in both English and Japanese in red and blue lettering, the text matched Roberto Cruz's cover story: *Welfare for Japan's Elderly – A Project of the University of Virginia.*

A listening device in the rear of the van had picked up the duller of the twins asking his brother what was printed on the labels. The explanation was proffered in both English and the mish-mash of other languages the pair commonly used.

All four of the van's passengers checked into the Uemura Inn before P1 – the Pakistani who had travelled down from Tokyo by train – called the Preacher's smart phone from Nagasaki Station on arrival. He would join them at the Inn shortly after.

The Uemura was a new ten-story ferro-concrete structure painted in a soft ivory colour. Situated in a narrow street that sloped down towards the harbour, the area was a maze of small thoroughfares that followed the original layout of old Nagasaki. The car park alongside the Inn had spaces for around fifteen vehicles and was bordered by rows of slender pencil pines. From the outside, the building had clean modern lines, though the architecture and design were still in keeping with Japanese tradition.

The twins had been provided with false American documentation. They were supposed to be university students on a study tour of Nagasaki researching the impact of early Portuguese presence in that city. They shared one of the extra rooms that the Preacher had booked at the Inn. P1 and UZ1 would share the other. All were on the top floor, with good views from the rear of the building out over the central part of the Harbour. A massive shipbuilding yard sprawled along the opposite shoreline.

In the operations room, Bella, Li, Saito, Kim and Matsumoto were studying images of P1 from a number of CCTV cameras at Nagasaki Station.

He was the next person they needed to get a fix on. The Pakistani and the Uzbek bore quite a facial resemblance, though it stopped at the eyes: P1's seemed glazed, which suggested he might be on drugs. One of Matsumoto's colleagues named a combination of substances he thought P1 might be taking and Bella concurred. She'd seen the same thing in other Central Asian men – Afghanis and Pakistanis in the main. P1 was tall and gaunt, with a strange air of resignation and detachment about him that couldn't simply be ascribed to drugs.

It was as though he had only one foot in this world, the other in his grave or the heaven he thought was waiting for him.

Jiro brought up new images of P1 as he made his way to the Inn and when he'd arrived there. He lingered outside in the street and sent a text to the Preacher, who came down to the lobby to check him in. It was an effusive greeting, which struck those watching as more genuine than feigned.

This sent Saito and Li off on another electronic search to see whether there was any record of a previous relationship between the two. Li promptly sent a message to his colleagues in Beijing to check this out.

"It may be just a woman's intuition," Bella whispered, nudging Kim, "but it's almost as if it's a father-and-son closeness."

"I agree," Kim replied. "Somehow, I sense this relationship goes way back, too."

"OK folks," Jiro called out. "A new batch of visuals for you."

The police had hacked into the Inn's CCTV system and an image now appeared on the main screen of P1 and the Preacher exiting the lift on the top floor. Once the two men entered the Preacher's room, which was a larger suite, the discussion UZ1 and the twins had been having there stopped abruptly. That dialogue had been focused on arming and detonating the suicide vests, although these hadn't yet been brought up from the van.

The mechanics of the Preacher's introduction of the new arrival were revealing. UZ1 was clearly meeting P1 for the first time, while P1 appeared to already share some affinity with the twins.

Yes, there's certainly something between them, Bella thought as she glanced at Li. He seemed to read her mind and nodded, which she interpreted to mean he would check that out with Beijing as well.

The targets soon got down to business in the Preacher's room, with UZ1 taking the lead on the nuts and bolts of their plans for both Nagasaki and Tokyo.

Bella caught Saito's eye and they exchanged a quick smile. The rubber was about to hit the road, they could almost smell it here in the room! Anything could happen now, and it did.

P1 suddenly remembered something and reached into his travel bag. He pulled out a device the size of a hairdryer and held it up in front of the Preacher.

"I'm so glad you brought that," he said. "It's always best to be on the safe side."

Jiro adjusted the focus on the sight line they had through the large, floor-to-ceiling window into the Preacher's suite, zooming in on the device. As soon as it appeared clearly on the screen display Saito was sure he knew what it was.

"That's a scanner for bugs," he said, "a battery-operated one."

While the Preacher and the others remained quiet, P1 stood and switched the device on. But before he had done so, Jiro sent a pulse down the line that immobilised the bugs in the suite so they wouldn't register.

P1 scanned the walls and the furniture and even went into the bathroom, going about the task in an unusually casual way – almost ritualistically. No positive readings came up.

Those in the operations room watched on in silence but they were not unduly concerned. Even if P1 had bothered to get down on the floor and look up under the furniture, it was unlikely he would spot anything. The hi-tech bugs they were using were incredibly small and so carefully placed that they were virtually undetectable.

As soon as he switched the scanner off, Jiro re-activated the devices in the suite. It was such an expert procedure, Saito slapped Jiro on the back by way of congratulations.

"I feel better after that," P1 declared, and the others agreed. "By the way," he said, clearly addressing the Preacher, "I also brought that other stuff."

"Fine, but not now," was the response.

They were about to resume discussing their plan when there was a knock on the door. Those watching knew the Preacher had arranged for bowls of hot noodles to be delivered. Once the waiter left with his trolley their conversation returned to serious issues.

No matter how sophisticated bugs were, especially those placed under wooden or metal tables, the sound of cutlery on crockery always produced unwanted interference, jolting for those listening in. But with chopsticks – wooden, ivory or plastic – that didn't happen. When the Preacher had called room service earlier, they'd all hoped he wouldn't order something served on plates and eaten with metal knives and forks. In light of the ethnic and religious background of his collaborators it was feared he might, but he didn't. At that point Bella had declared, "Praise be to Allah!"

As the group's dialogue recommenced, it was immediately apparent to those listening that a mother-load of information was about to emerge. All of the key targets were now in one room, except for P1's accomplice still in Tokyo.

Bella was focused on the dialogue between UZ1 and P1, using her headphones to block out extraneous noise in the operations room. They spoke in a mix of Arabic and Urdu. P1 assured UZ1 that everything was ready to go in Tokyo. He foresaw no problems, though there were a few minor matters they could take up once the twins were prepared for their mission.

After a brief lull, the Preacher took over. He used English peppered with common Arabic phrases.

"Tomorrow morning," he explained to the twins, "Amin and I will take you for a walk around those historic sites. I have cameras for you both, so take lots of shots. After all, you're meant to be here on a study tour."

Amin was obviously the name UZ1 was best known by.

"This afternoon," the Preacher continued, "we'll put the vests in my carry bag and bring them up here. While we're out tomorrow, Yousef will prime them and rig the cords that you'll pull to trigger them. Apart from the vests, everything else is now ready to go. Once Amin, Yousef and I are satisfied that you have the optimal sites firmly lodged in your minds we'll take our leave and head off on our long drive up to Tokyo. Once we're there, and ready for action in the big city, we'll text you both. That'll be the final signal for you to do your duty."

"And without delay," Yousef – P1 – cut in. He'd already repeated in Urdu what the Preacher had said, clearly determined to ensure that the twins were left in no doubt. He spoke with a gravitas that almost placed him on an equal footing with the Preacher's authority.

"And let me emphasise, now, right from the start," Yousef said, "you two must remain together until you detonate your vests. If you do happen to get separated, and it's unlikely you'll get back together again, blow your vests then. Make sure you're surrounded by people. Is that clear?"

"Yes," both twins dutifully replied.

Bella held her hand up to signify that she had something to relay but would wait until that dialogue finished. After a brief pause, the conversation split into two, one between the Preacher and the twins and the other between P1 and UZ1. Matsumoto indicated that he and Yumi had a monitoring team in the operations room that would focus on what the Preacher was saying to the twins. Bella knew they would record that dialogue in case she wished to listen to it later.

Meanwhile, she focused on what P1 and UZ1 were saying to each other in Arabic. Jiro dulled the sound of the other conversation and highlighted the one she was following. By raising or lowering her hand she signalled whenever the sound line between the men changed, as it did when UZ1 dropped the tone of his voice. These were the exchanges that Bella was most interested in. Clearly P1 and UZ1 didn't want the twin with the language skills to pick up on what they were saying.

Li thought it looked like Bella was conducting an orchestra. She's on the scent of something important, that's for sure, he mused. She was indeed, and it wasn't long before she lifted her hand and held it steady to indicate that Jiro should hold the sound at that level.

Lowering his voice slightly, UZ1 said, "I'm so glad you brought them with you, not that the twins will need them. The way I've rigged their vests, we can blow them with a signal from Tokyo. We'll follow their movements on GPS, though they don't need to know any of that. But listen, don't pull them out of your bag now. Wait till we get to our room."

"Of course," P1 replied.

It soon became apparent that the group was about to break for a rest. UZ1 and P1 obviously wanted to wash and catch up on a few hours sleep, and discuss whatever it was that Bella had picked up on. The Preacher clearly had the same idea. The twins left the room with UZ1 and P1, but Bella knew that Jiro would record their separate conversations. She stayed focused on UZ1 and P1 and was rewarded when the pair reached their room and after P1 had done a quick scan.

Bella nodded slowly, indicating to those around her that whatever she'd heard hadn't come as a surprise.

A few minutes elapsed before P1 handed something to UZ1, which the latter put in his pocket. Then P1 headed for the bathroom. While Bella monitored their exchange, she also watched the visual feed coming up on one of Jiro's screens. Finally, she removed her headphones and swung around in her chair to face Saito and the others.

"Something we'd assumed would happen has happened," Bella said in Japanese. "The twins' suicide vests are equipped with smart phones that can be triggered off remotely by the Preacher or the others in Tokyo should the twins look like they're chickening out or straying too far from their target area. They'll be tracked by GPS the whole time and needless to say, they know nothing about it. I can't imagine that the more cerebral one wouldn't have worked it out for himself, but whatever."

Bella's expression warned that something else she'd gleaned from UZ1 and P1's chat was even worse that this.

"Those small metal tubes P1 brought with him from Tokyo – one of which we saw him hand to UZ1 - contain glass vials that hold a powerful nerve agent, much more effective than cyanide, according to P1. The way it works is one removes the vial from the tube and puts it in a pocket, preferably close to the heart. The glass vial can be easily snapped and it contents kills almost instantly on contact with the skin."

Bella paused for a moment looking grave, before continuing. "But there's another important attribute to this device. It spreads through clothing quickly and will kill anyone who comes near it. P1 says they have a large supply of the nerve agent in Tokyo and not just in individual vials. That sounds like a bulk quantity to me."

There was a moment of silence while the others digested the significance of this revelation. They were dealing with a nerve agent much more potent than Sarin.

"Yet another dimension for us to deal with," Kim said with a sigh.

Saito said, "Kim and Matsumoto, you should get ready to check whether we have any HAZMAT experts on Kyushu, especially if they're within helicopter range of Nagasaki. There are two I know of in Fukuoka. See if they can get here ASAP. If not, we'll need to check if there are any university people in that field who could get here fast. Of course, we don't want to cause any alarm so this will have to be done discreetly."

Kim nodded. As a multi-tasker, she could handle this easily. She also knew that Fukuoka being such a large population centre the chances of finding someone quickly were good. Matsumoto indicated that he already had someone in mind. Saito then reverted to what Bella had first told them.

"Before we move on, there's something I want to be clear about. Do you think there's any real chance that the twins could chicken out?" he asked. "Did it sound like P1 and UZ1 are actually worried about that possibility? Not that we'd ever allow the twins to 'do their duty', as the Preacher likes to put it."

Bella thought for a moment, then said her

impression was that the two men were only raising it as a contingency rather than a possibility.

She pointed out, "UZ1 stressed to P1 that the smart twin is absolutely determined and there's no way he'll let his brother pull out – no way at all. We need to bear in mind that blind determination. While not all Islamic State diehards back up their words with actions, when they're committed, it seems there's nothing that will stop them."

"Exactly," Li chimed in. "My colleagues in China who keep close tabs on IS attacks say the younger suicide bombers often pose the greater risk. They'll go even further, indulging in overkill by taking things into their own hands. But one thing they don't do is go weak at the knees."

"Which means we're going to have to grab the twins before they even don those activated vests, right?" Saito cut in quickly.

"Correct," Li responded. "The Preacher's plan is that the Nagasaki blasts are a precursor to something much grander in Tokyo. They'll draw attention away from the capital while he and the others go in for the big kill."

Li was right: the attack on Tokyo was the main event. That was what this operation had to pre-empt while nipping whatever was planned in Nagasaki in the bud.

As an aside to Bella, Li said in Mandarin, "What if we succeed here but the IS cell already in Tokyo has the wherewithal to go ahead anyway?"

"That's what we're all worried about," she replied.

Uemura Inn, Nagasaki City
Thursday, 1124 hours

"Late tomorrow afternoon," the Preacher said, "we'll get out of this place and head for Tokyo. I've gone over every minute detail of our trip and have it down to two nights and two days. We'll text Ramsi to let him know when we'll arrive at the spot he's designated on the outskirts of the city for the handover."

Another new name: Ramsi. It had to be P2 who had stayed back in Tokyo.

The twins were sleeping, but after a bath, P1 and UZ1 had returned to the Preacher's suite.

Bella and the others had managed an hour's rest when Jiro – who never seemed to sleep himself – alerted them.

Addressing UZ1, the Preacher stressed in his distinctive mix of English and Arabic, "We only need to hand one thing over to him – the contents of the smaller box you brought over with you. I doubt he'll see any need for weapons, but if he wants them he can have them. We have more than enough for our own mission."

Neither P1 nor UZ1 asked what was in the box with the green tape, confirming that they already knew what was inside.

It has to be high explosives, Bella thought, maybe a massive amount of C4? Would a crate that small contain something that powerful? Perhaps it's something else?

The Preacher went on, "When you've primed

it, Ramsi will load it into his delivery van and head straight for the Diet."

A shudder rippled through the operations room where enough people understood what the Preacher was saying. It sounded like some kind of massive bomb.

"The freight company Ramsi works for has a longstanding contract to supply the Diet complex's early-morning load of food, newspapers, stationery, dry-cleaning and so on. He's a sociable chap, as Yousef will tell you, and he's been on that run for quite a few years. He's so trusted that he's rarely, if ever, asked to show his security pass. He can get his van right down into the basement of the building. Can you believe it? The memory of 9/11 has faded faster in Japan than it ever could in the United States, and yet our plan is based precisely on the 1993 attempt to bring down the World Trade Centre Towers. The idea of bringing down two towers with a bomb in the car park of one of them could have worked but didn't. But they got it right the second time with aircraft."

UZ1 was impressed by this powerful parallel. "So, Ramsi will trigger the detonation as soon as he's underneath the building?" he asked, his tone deadly serious.

"More or less," the Preacher responded. "We've studied the plans of the Diet Building in detail and it hardly matters where he triggers the device once he's down there. I mean, the blast is going to pulverise the entire complex as well as most of the buildings within a kilometre radius. There'll be nothing left standing in the central part of the city and we estimate between a hundred and two-hundred thousand people will be killed instantly. The radiation will make greater Tokyo uninhabitable. It will have to be evacuated immediately. Just imagine more than forty million people suddenly on the move, desperate to escape? Where will they go?"

The Preacher paused for a moment. "It'll be mayhem!" he added gleefully. "And, of course, there'll be no way Tokyo would be able to host the Summer Olympic Games in 2020!"

A deadly quiet descended on the operations room as the unimaginable ramifications of a nuclear blast in Tokyo sank in.

But this was no ordinary bomb. Even if UZ1 and his IS associates in Uzbekistan had managed to acquire a supply of plutonium – a likely proposition – their best efforts at weaponising it would only give them a massive dirty bomb. There was no way a bomb like that could cause such radical damage in central Tokyo. Maybe they'd somehow gotten hold of a tactical nuclear weapon?

The very notion that Japan could be subjected to a third nuclear attack, with the seat of government in the capital as the target, was devastating. It was an irony too cruel to consider.

Li had never seen Bella so worried. She signalled again to Jiro to raise and sharpen the pitch of what she was hearing through her headphones. Targets that endlessly changed their sitting position were the scourge of eavesdroppers, no matter how sophisticated the technology.

The Preacher suddenly cut across their

thoughts. "Once Ramsi closes the doors of his delivery van and heads off for the Diet," he continued, "we'll go straight for the Sky Tree — Tokyo Tower Mark II. The Nips will think it's Godzilla all over again!"

The Preacher gagged on his own heinous joke and started coughing. His hatred of the Japanese couldn't have been clearer. The passage of time had not dulled it; quite the opposite in fact. It was now at full pitch.

UZ1 sniggered, then asked, "So, we'll sign off at the Sky Tree?"

"Yes," the Preacher replied. "Unless Ramsi gets in first. I thought we should have a back-up plan just in case something goes wrong."

His colleagues agreed. UZ1 decided to make some coffee, which truncated their dialogue. The Preacher and P1 chatted cursorily about how predictable the traffic was in Tokyo, even extolling the virtues of the organizational prowess of the Japanese.

This gave Bella a chance to brief the others. Jiro would alert her as soon as the targets returned to serious discussion.

Saito, Matsumoto and Kim launched into action. Yumi was directed to contact each of the surveillance teams deployed around Nagasaki City, calling on the Top Secret Alpha Blue code. All senior officers were familiar with that code, even though they'd only heard it used once before, after the Fukushima earthquake and resulting tsunami. The code placed them and their subordinates on the highest alert, indicating a major threat to the nation as a whole. They could request any support they required, be it manpower or equipment and technology.

Saito announced that he'd get onto Chief Hasegawa straightaway, suggesting he call on the Prime Minister immediately.

"The PM will then alert the chiefs of the Self-Defence Forces in case we need to bring them in too. I'll also ask Chief Hasegawa to rally our top experts on radiation," he said. "While he's doing that, we should undertake our own research to see if there's anyone in that category in this locality."

Saito turned and was about to say something to Bella when she held her hand up: the Preacher had more to say.

"We've been extraordinarily lucky bringing all of our gear into Japan without being detected," he said gravely. "That's a mighty achievement and I don't want to push our luck any further. We have to focus single-mindedly on our task here in Nagasaki and put Tokyo out of our minds for the time being."

Bella relayed this to Saito and the others. With Saito's agreement, Matsumoto immediately put the operations room on lock-down. There would be no more casual drifting in and out. Each staff movement would require justification. Jiro brought up the positions of each of the surveillance teams on his screens while Bella stayed focused on the continuing dialogue in the Preacher's suite. Missing a minor inflection on a seemingly innocent word could make or break the operation.

"Getting hold of a Russian nuclear suitcase

bomb was a major coup for us in the first place," the Preacher exclaimed, "let alone a late-model one!"

P1's silence suggested to Bella that he was already acquainted with this. It was UZ1's expression on the visual feed that explained why the Preacher provided more information.

"The old Soviet Union," he continued, "produced a number of models over time. All up, I believe over one hundred were made. The device we have is from the final batch, part of Osama bin Laden's arsenal of four and the only one not taken into the Tora Bora cave complex. The device was first smuggled into Uzbekistan and then all the way to Mindanao, where we managed to get it onto a small freighter to Korea."

Saito gestured to those with whom he wished to huddle as soon as the dialogue that Bella was monitoring had ended.

"So, my dear friends," the Preacher said, "our clever act of destruction and our own martyrdom will bless our extended families with a unique place in the history of Islam. We need to have clear heads for what we're about to undertake, so I suggest we get some sleep."

Then, P1 handed the Preacher one of the small steel tubes.

Chapter 13

Operations Room, Nagasaki
Thursday, 1202 hours

"Can you two check out the suitcase bomb?" Saito said to Bella and Li. "We need some idea of what we're dealing with here. Explosive power, fragility of the device, radiation yield, how it's armed, which it probably isn't right now ... you know what I mean."

With the Preacher having a bath and UZ1 and P1 back in their room watching TV, the operations room had some welcome breathing space.

Li was already at work on his laptop, seeking information from Beijing on such matters.

Matsumoto provided the room with a quick recap on where surveillance squads were deployed and their maneuverability.

Saito was relieved protocols were in place to adjust to sudden changes of events like this. What they were contending with now was in a category all its own and he knew holding his nerve would be fundamental to keeping the whole operation together.

"None of our surveillance teams are to be told about the nuclear device," Saito stated. "The last thing we need is to start a panic."

It was not unknown in operations like this, for officers to crack under pressure. They might attempt to warn their families or worse, to join them in fleeing. Mayhem would spread like wildfire if this were to happen. Saito knew they couldn't risk it.

Matsumoto went away to craft a carefully worded alert to distribute.

"When you have a moment," Saito whispered to Bella and Kim, "walk around a bit and keep an eye out for anyone you think might be feeling the pressure. I need to know if the team here is solid. We have enough to contend with outside, without having cracks opening up inside. You both command enormous respect here and even affection. Your calmness and clear-thinking are infectious. Matsumoto's pre-occupied with operational matters, so don't let him twig to what you're doing. I'm not so much concerned about him, but Yumi is a different proposition entirely. Chat to the staff, especially the young female officers. See if you can pick up anything on how they think she's handling the situation."

Kim had seen Saito in an operational environment like this once before and she knew he coped well with stress. On that occasion, there'd been a threat to blow up an oil refinery near the densely populated Kobe-Osaka area. Explosives had already been planted throughout the sprawling facility and Saito's deductive powers, critical thinking and his negotiating skills had saved the day. Oddly, his success had almost nothing to do with the hi-tech end of an operation that he customarily dealt with. He'd been drawn into the operation tangentially but ended up being put in charge of it. This was no doubt due to his outstanding networking skills and his ability to work in unison with a wide variety of specialists, like he was doing now.

Kim watched as Saito received an urgent message from Jiro that popped up in the corner of his laptop screen. He waved to Jiro to join him, and the younger man pulled Bella's vacant chair up alongside. He pointed at the laptop screen to give the impression they were discussing some sort of technical issue.

"It's Yumi," Jiro began in a low voice. "Some of her surveillance teams aren't up to scratch. A few of the older men have fallen asleep in their cars, and one went off to collect his stereo system that was being repaired. He spent more than thirty minutes in the shop chatting with the dealer."

Saito nodded. He sensed there was more and that Jiro had started with the good news first.

"Two more things of note," Jiro continued. "Yumi's been communicating with some of the older members of her teams using her own secure mobile. They've also been calling her on theirs."

Everybody involved in this operation, either in the field or in the control room, was supposed to be hooked up to one networked comms system. Yumi's departure from this strict protocol was both unprofessional and dangerous. Saito nodded grimly, his forehead creasing slightly.

"Worst of all," Jiro said, "she's monitoring and recording – over and above our formal comms network – all of the innovations you're testing here. I know because I've been tracking everything she records. Is there any reason why she'd be doing this?"

"No, none whatsoever," Saito replied, astonished and annoyed. "The only three people who know about this new technology are you, me and Chief Hasegawa. Let's keep this to ourselves for the time being. No need to tell Kim or Bella, and certainly not Li. I trust him, but we have to remember where he's from."

"I understand," Jiro said. "That's all I have to report."

"Thanks. I appreciate your efforts. Just keep doing what you're doing and let me know if you turn up anything more. I'll tell Matsumoto that I think poor Yumi's approaching saturation point; could he stay in touch with her constantly and help her out, until further notice? He can attribute it to my not wanting to see her stressed out. I'll even say she's too valuable an asset to lose with all her experience."

Jiro grinned. He knew he was watching a master at work.

"Also, please give me the names and car numbers of those older surveillance men," Saito continued. "I'll tell Matsumoto I want them back here in the ops room so I can draw on their experience. He'll know which younger officers Yumi will probably replace them with."

Pausing for a moment, Saito then asked, "Do you think I should pull Yumi back in here too, under the same guise? I'm tempted to do that right away, but I want to give Matsumoto a chance to get on top of it first."

Jiro nodded his agreement and Saito continued, "He mustn't know that you're monitoring this for me. I'm very worried about why Yumi's scrutinising the technical innovations, but the situation at hand is my highest priority. If you find it too demanding keeping an eye on her for me, just let me know. I can word Kim up to help share the load if you need."

"Will do," Jiro replied under his breath, simultaneously pointing one last time to something on the main screen.

All the while, Jiro had been wearing an earpiece in case anything occurred during his brief chat with Saito. Something came through as he returned to his seat only metres away. He called to Bella who quickly returned to her chair and put on her headphones.

UZ1 and P1 had decided to check on the Preacher. They seemed to draw solace from talking with him, particularly when the twins were otherwise engaged. Understandably, this was something the Preacher embraced: they were part of the Tokyo team and that was the main game. It was when they left their room that Jiro alerted Bella.

When the two men joined the Preacher in his room they chatted briefly about the air conditioning and how annoying it was to have to regularly adjust it. UZ1 then suggested they read passages from the Qu'ran together. Jiro had guessed this would happen. He'd seen them carrying a book each when they'd left their room.

All three read aloud which Bella found interesting. She scribbled the word Qu'ran in Japanese and nudged Saito, who immediately checked the visual feed from the Preacher's suite. It certainly looked devotional and in no way contrived.

This continued for almost fifteen minutes, during which time Kim returned to her place and reported to Saito that none of the staffers in the room seemed likely to crack under pressure. But there was one thing of great concern: every single one of the young female operations officers had privately expressed to both Kim and Bella their disquiet over Yumi. They each had the distinct impression that she wasn't fully focused on her operational duties and had seen her use her smart phone to carry on what appeared to be a separate dialogue with some of her team members. The police officers had been fearful of reporting their suspicions to Matsumoto, let alone to Saito, and were relieved when Kim assured them she would handle it.

Hot on the heels of this discussion, Li reported to Saito that Beijing might be able to help on the suitcase bomb. They both agreed that a briefing should be deferred until such time when the proper focus could be placed on the problem. Li returned to his data searches, the results of which had so far proved vital to the operation. He patted Bella affectionately on the shoulder as he passed by but could tell from her intense concentration that something was afoot.

The Preacher had just closed his Qu'ran and began broaching an entirely different matter with UZ1 and P1.

"I say, where do you think Abu Mukhtar is now?" he asked.

Bella recognised the jihadist's battle name straightaway and signalled to Jiro to lift the volume of the feed. Mukhtar was the person in the unmarked photo that UZ1 had dropped in the onion shed and that Li's colleagues in Beijing had identified.

"Neither of us has any idea," UZ1 replied.

"Well, I'm confident he knows how to handle things like this," the Preacher said. "He'll be moving around watching out for surveillance, and if there is, he'll let us know. But otherwise, he'll simply blend in with the landscape; that's something he's expert at, which is why I chose him for the task. Let's face it, there are foreign tourists galore in Nagasaki and in all shapes and sizes. If he doesn't spot any danger he'll meet up with us briefly tomorrow before we head for Tokyo. He'll suddenly appear out of nowhere and nudge us from behind as if to say, 'look who's here!' That's what he does, Amin. Of course, the twins don't know anything about him, which is why he'll be watching them later from a safe distance until they get the final signal from us in Tokyo to go ahead."

"You think of everything, don't you?" P1 observed.

"Well, I have to," the Preacher replied. "I've been working on this for a very long time and I've gone over the plan again and again. There's probably nothing I haven't thought of but it's the unexpected we have to watch out for. That's why Abu Mukhtar's role is so important. He's another set of eyes and ears."

The other men nodded, obviously assured.

"Does he have one of these?" UZ1 said, pulling the steel tube out of his shirt pocket.

"Of course!" the Preacher replied. "He's the one who supplied us with the vials and our bulk container in the first place."

UZ1 removed the glass vial from the tube and

examined it against the light from the window.

"Hey, be careful with that!" P1 exclaimed. "We don't want you killing us all before we even get to Tokyo!"

"Alright, I'm not stupid!" UZ1 snapped back. "It's just that I feel better with it close to me — ready to use. After all, we're in hostile territory and anything could happen."

"Come on, let's not argue over such things," the Preacher said, sounding like a father cajoling a wayward son.

UZ1 slipped the tube into his pocket. Jiro, the keen observer, noticed that he hadn't bothered to screw the top onto the tube properly. He pointed this out to Saito. After a moment of silence all three Jihadists went back to reciting in turn from their Qu'rans.

This gave Bella the opportunity she'd been waiting for.

"We have an outlier!" she whispered sharply to Saito and Kim while beckoning to Li and Matsumoto to join them.

"It's Abu Mukhtar," Bella explained. "The man in the onion shed photo dropped by UZ1. He's obviously the group's lookout who only links up when it's safe. We've discussed the possibility of something like this, and now we know for sure. The Preacher's as cunning as a fox but he's about to become unstuck!"

A crack military anti-terror squad was already on its way to the Uemura Inn by helicopter, dispatched from a nearby naval base. An armoured car had just joined the surveillance teams close to the hotel, tucked into a side street well out of sight. Swift action had to be taken.

Li brought up additional shots of Mukhtar received from his HQ when the jihadist was first identified. The selection of photos included full-body images, head and shoulder shots, as well as facial close-ups. There was also a link to a video clip so they could get a fix on his voice.

"Right!" Saito said, addressing Bella and Li. "Are you two willing to get out there quick smart and try to spot him? We can easily dress you up like tourists. You can wander around the streets near the hotel and see if you can get a fix on this killer. With the rest of his gang all up on the top floor it's possible he's not far away."

The pair had no objections to that, deciding in a split second of eye contact between them. Saito asked Kim to find them sets of inconspicuous earpieces and mics, along with tourist maps to match their disguise. Bella and Li could choose whatever clothing they wanted from racks at the back of the room. It wasn't long before they were kitted out and ready to go.

Saito was thankful the two were both Special Forces trained and able to take on this task without hesitation. Unlike the police, both Li and Bella were skilled in the arts of self-defence and offence. During an earlier quiet moment in the operations room, Saito had asked the pair to brief everyone present on what they sardonically referred to as the spy's five rules of survival. Bella had even demonstrated on Li just how easy it was to kill somebody instantly, without as much as a second's warning to the victim.

"By the way," Li said to Saito, "a brief round-up of the late-model suitcase devices should pop up on my laptop soon. It'll be in Chinese and English and should also give us more information on Mukhtar's background. When you see the pop up message just key in 14PNQX78 and you'll get direct access to the document."

Saito memorised the password effortlessly, as Li knew he would, and they exchanged the briefest of smiles. Saito had never expected to experience such a bond of trust with a foreign spy, least of all one from China.

Uemura Inn and surrounds
Thursday, 1227 hours

An unmarked patrol car dropped Bella and Li off and their first sweep was along the street where the hotel was situated. Li looked nondescript in a plain navy blue jacket, while Bella sported a beige Burberry raincoat and a pair of sneakers. They were both armed with Browning 9mm pistols from the Nagasaki Police HQ armoury.

Arm in arm, they strolled down the street, looking like a typical tourist couple despite their ethnic origins being so different. They communicated seamlessly with surveillance teams close by via connected earpieces. The communication between everyone on the network was tight and effective. The pair could even speak without visibly opening their mouths, as the earpieces were sensitive enough to pick up vibrations from their vocal chords and could also transmit them. This was hi-tech connectivity at its most advanced.

So far, they'd heard no aged voices, which suggested that Yumi and her cronies might have already been recalled to the operations room. If Abu Mukhtar was sighted, plain-clothes police teams would be mobilised very quickly. The photos sent from Beijing were invaluable.

Spotting the hotel up ahead, Bella and Li stopped to consult their map and undertake a little visual reconnaissance. Tourists in any country were always looking this way and that, as well as pointing at things, so their cover was ideal. With Abu Mukhtar's image firmly planted in their minds, they were confident that spotting him would be relatively easy. Visitors to Nagasaki with Middle Eastern or Central Asian features weren't all that common.

"OK," Bella said to Li in Japanese. "Are you in character?"

"Sure am," he replied. "We must look like a cute married couple but on second thoughts, it might be best to keep our arms free."

"Smart thinking," Bella responded, referring to one of the fundamentals of her undercover surveillance training: always be ready for action. Saito cut in from the operations room where he was watching them.

"We're using the city transport authority's CCTV system as well as our own surveillance to track you," he said. "There are cameras on some of the higher buildings nearby, so we'll warn you if we're able to see our target from a fair distance."

They decided to stroll past the hotel without paying it any attention, then casually turn into a side-street that led up a steep hill. Not too far up, they could see the top floors of the hotel when they looked back.

"This is the kind of vantage point Mukhtar might use to keep watch on the place," Li observed.

"Correct," Bella responded, just before she saw something about five hundred metres further up the slope.

"I'm sure that's him!" she said quietly but urgently.

Saito replied, "Hang on, Jiro's trying to get a good facial shot from the CCTV."

Jiro confirmed their suspicions. It was Abu Mukhtar and he was walking down the hill towards them. Bella and Li continued at their relaxed pace, giving nothing away as a plain-clothes team a few hundred metres off reported they were closing in on foot.

As Abu Mukhtar approached he looked straight at them with a slightly furtive demeanour that he couldn't disguise, certainly not from experienced spies. While there was no crazed look in his eyes like that of UZ1, he was definitely sizing them up.

Mukhtar headed towards the hotel but for what purpose it was impossible to tell. Was he planning to enter the building or was he simply scouting for signs of surveillance? Wearing a pale khaki jacket with several pockets, the type popular with war correspondents, his cream shirt was unbuttoned low enough to show a silver pendant inset with a gold coin hanging against the dark hair of his chest. His tan leather shoes were trendy and apart from a slight limp he looked muscular and fit.

As Mukhtar was about to pass Bella and Li, two security guards in police-like uniforms suddenly emerged from a small office building nearby and started walking in his direction. This clearly put Mukhtar on alert, though he did a good job of concealing it.

The tourist couple stopped to look in a souvenir shop window, using the reflections in the glass to see where he was going. Without looking back, he turned into the street where the hotel was situated some three hundred metres away. But something appeared to have alarmed him. As he approached the hotel, he veered off the road into the car park at the side entrance to the building. Though he wasn't walking briskly, there was more purpose to his step.

"Here we go!" Bella said, under her breath. Both she and Li knew from experience that for a target to approach a building where his associates were gathered – without attempting to enter – meant that something unexpected was likely to happen.

"Action stations!" Saito declared across the network. "He has a smart phone on him. One of our teams close by has picked up the number on their electronic scanner. In the event that we need to distract him, we can make the phone ring."

"We read you," Li replied. He and Bella had sauntered back down the hill and were now entering the hotel's street at a relaxed pace. In a few seconds they'd be at the mouth of the car park.

Mukhtar was standing still alongside the van rummaging for something in one of the chest pockets of his jacket. He pulled out a bunch of keys and quickly found the one he needed to open the rear doors of the van. The keys were left hanging in the lock. Bella and Li stopped where they were to check their map, hanging back from the entrance to the hotel, taking care to maintain their line of sight to the van.

Mukhtar gingerly dragged the wooden box with the green tape towards the open doors of the van. He deftly tipped the box on its side then produced a Swiss Army knife from another pocket in his jacket. Opening its main blade, he cut the green tape, all done so methodically that he'd probably practised it.

"Certainly knows what he's doing," Saito observed, "and he's clearly more than just the Preacher's eyes and ears."

Using the knife blade, he gently prized open the lid of the box then lifted out a shiny aluminium suitcase very slowly, blocks of bright green foam rubber packing falling away as he did so. The suitcase looked just as Bella and Li had expected, so ordinary it would not have been out of place on an airport carousel.

He carefully placed the suitcase upright on the ground then gathered up the pieces of foam rubber and stuffed them back into the box. Closing the doors of the van, Mukhtar locked them and placed the keys back in his pocket.

Now what would he do? Attempt to take the suitcase inside the hotel or remove it from the site?

"Whatever he has planned," Saito said, "one thing's certain: Mukhtar has to be separated from that suitcase without delay. Let's throw him off guard with a phone call."

In the next instant Mukhtar's phone rang in the lower pocket of his jacket. This clearly startled him but he made no attempt to answer it. He lifted the case without any effort, though it seemed quite heavy, and then turned to exit the car park. He looked as though he was headed towards the hotel entrance.

"Retrieve the suitcase immediately," Saito instructed, catapulting Bella and Li into action. As soon as they tackled Mukhtar, police squads would move in to support them. Li knew what Bella would do; they'd discussed it in advance.

"Excuse me," she said to Mukhtar in French, as Li held out his map.

Mukhtar was fazed. He looked past Bella to Li and his map first, perhaps thinking a male posed more of a threat than a woman. With his head side-on to her, Bella struck him with great force in the temple using her knuckled fist. She drove the joint of her middle finger as far into his head as possible. More a matter of power than penetration, this action would either render him immediately senseless or kill him instantly. Uppermost in both her's and Li's minds was the possibility that he might be carrying a nerve agent vial without its protective steel tube.

As Mukhtar went down, Li grabbed the case before it hit the ground. It was all over in a matter of seconds. Plain clothes and uniformed policemen were on the scene fast, along with a backup squad to guard the van and the front of the hotel. Mukhtar lay slumped on the ground. Bella bent to check his pulse – he was dead. Two police specialists wearing hazard suits moved in to check his body. They found nothing.

Soon after, the body was loaded into a paddy wagon while the suitcase was carefully placed in an armoured car, to be whisked off to a designated site far from Nagasaki city and suburbs. There it would be examined by the nuclear experts the Nagasaki operations team were currently trying to locate.

Back in the operations room a spontaneous round of applause went up, driven by admiration for a successful effort as well as an enormous sense of relief. But the moment of congratulation was short-lived as Saito refocused the networked team on the next, crucial part of the operation.

Bella and Li clung to each other where they stood in the car park, not quite believing they'd pulled off such a feat.

A tactical police squad had just entered the lobby of the Uemura Inn, ensuring there was no one on the reception desk or in the surrounding area who could sound the alarm to the hotel's occupants. There were no passers-by in the street as police wagons had blocked off both ends. Saito told the squads on the ground that if anyone asked what all the excitement was about it was to be referred to as a major drug bust.

Plain clothes police scanned the surrounding shops and buildings opposite the hotel to identify any witnesses, urging them to refrain from posting to social media or alerting the news media. As an extra precaution, Saito ordered the jamming of any private smart phones located in the vicinity.

"Stage one completed," Saito announced across the network, "now we have to round up the rest of them! Bella and Li, jump into one of the surveillance wagons and you'll be able watch on screen what's unfolding inside the hotel. We may need your expert help again."

Chapter 14

Operations Room
Thursday, 1244 hours

Two crack police anti-terror squads waited for the all-clear to go into the Uemura Inn and up to the top floor. They'd been forewarned that UZ1's vial might be loose in his shirt pocket and to be careful in restraining him. Electronic surveillance of the Preacher and his cohorts confirmed they were unaware of what had just transpired in the car park. UZ1, P1 and the Preacher were in his room, while the twins were still asleep in theirs.

Saito had hoped that the military squad would have arrived by now but he could wait no longer.

"In you go!" he commanded.

Any dialogue inside the operations room was no longer being transmitted across the comms network. Only Bella and Li were purposely left online as they waited outside the hotel. Saito needed them to cross-check the progress of the operation on the ground in case a vital step had been accidentally overlooked. The fog of war applied equally to police and intelligence operations as it did to military battles.

Without the now marginalised Yumi in tow, Matsumoto stood beside Saito, providing a quick rundown on the police personnel who were now closing in on the hotel's entrance. Twenty-eight additional officers were now in position, ready to provide back-up.

A visual feed from Jiro's monitoring of the target rooms was streaming to the small screen attached at eye level to the helmets of those heading to the top floor. The Preacher was poring over a map of Tokyo to identify alternate routes to the Sky Tree, briefing UZ1 and P1 on a number of contingencies he'd drawn up. He planned to wake the twins within an hour to take them out on a reconnaissance of their target area in Nagasaki.

The hotel's landline phones had been blocked, along with those in adjacent buildings and shops. All electronic devices, like smart phones, iPads and laptops – not just inside the hotel but in the immediate vicinity – had been similarly jammed.

Back in the operations room, Saito turned to Kim. "Please get on to Chief Hasegawa and ask him to stay glued to the display console in his office. He can monitor our streamed feed there in real-time. He'll need to brief the PM once this part of the exercise is over, but ask him not to mention the suitcase to anyone at this stage."

As he spoke he watched the images on Jiro's screens in front of him. One of the attack squads was using the elevator to get to the top floor, while the other group was vaulting up the stairway. The first to arrive would smash in the door of the Preacher's suite, securing any weapons then forcing all these men to lie on the floor on their backs in case any of them were carrying nerve agent vials in their shirt pockets.

Like a whirlwind unleashed the following squad

would enter the twins' room in the same manner. All had been briefed on the necessity of immediately separating each of the five targets once apprehended and keeping them individually guarded. If taken alive, the opportunity for any of them to communicate should be nil, even during their transfer to the interrogation cells at HQ.

Miniature camcorders mounted on the helmets of each squad member provided real-time coverage of events as they unfolded inside the building, supplementing the remote monitoring already being undertaken. Back in the operations room the younger officers eagerly watched the images Jiro was constantly putting up on the screens. For most, it was their first time on such a complex and multi-faceted operation. The blizzard of action mesmerised them, as did the sophistication of the NPA's surveillance technology.

But this was no guarantee of success. When operations went awry, it was almost always at this very juncture.

Uemura Inn
Thursday, 1247 hours

The squad members travelling up in the elevator took care not to knock their weapons and equipment against the metal walls. Their colleagues climbing the staircase were equally vigilant.

"Quiet!" UZ1 whispered urgently.

This surprised everyone in the operations room: the listening devices in the Preacher's suite had not picked up any external noise.

Somehow the wily Uzbek was instinctively aware of approaching danger. Neither of his cohorts queried him, straining to hear whatever it was that UZ1 had detected. All three were standing now and UZ1 moved closer to the door.

"Stay here," he said in a low voice. "I'm just going to check outside."

The first squad member stepped out of the elevator to see UZ1 outside the room, peering over the banister rail down into the stairwell.

The other squad members were halfway up that stairwell and while he hadn't yet spotted them he heard the sound of their rubber-soled boots on the concrete.

In two strides the squad member from the elevator confronted him, aiming his Styr rifle at his heart.

"Watch out!" UZ1 screamed in Arabic to the Preacher and P1, who was holding the door to the suite open. In the same instant, he leapt head-first over the rail. Two men from the elevator squad tried to block his fall by grabbing UZ1's boots but his laces were untied.

"Abunai, Sarin!", one squad member shouted to alert his colleagues on the stairs below: Danger, Sarin gas!

Two of the men climbing up the stairwell tried to grasp his clothing but they couldn't get a firm grip. It seemed an eternity before UZ1 hit the concrete floor at the base of the stairs. Those watching back in the operations room couldn't imagine he'd survive such a fall. And what of the glass vial in his top pocket?

Saito issued an order to one of the squad's officers with HAZMAT training waiting outside in an armoured car, already clad in bulky protective clothing. Looking like an astronaut space walker, he moved through the lobby to the stairs leading down into the basement to check out UZ1's twisted and lifeless body.

The steel tube had fallen out of his top pocket and was still intact. When it struck the concrete floor its screw cap had been dislodged. The glass vial had rolled away from UZ1's body, coming to rest on a rubber mat at the door of the hotel's rubbish room. This was comforting news, but not enough for Saito to call a halt to the raid on the top floor.

Two of the elevator squad members had dashed into the Preacher's room before P1 had a chance to close the door. While both were clearly shocked, P1 instinctively went into fighting mode. Neither had time to release their deadly glass vials.

The Preacher seemed to meekly accept his fate as he was manhandled to the floor on his back and body-searched. P1 was sinewy and strong and he resisted. The squad could easily have used a taser to bring him under control, but they feared the electrical charge might burst the vials both were carrying.

P1 was pinned down but still struggling until reinforcements from the stairwell squad arrived and he was forced into submission. A sharp blow to the head with a rifle butt was out of the question: brain damage wouldn't help the interrogators, especially as the elevator squad members assumed that UZ1 had died from his fall.

The door to the twins' room had also been smashed open. They'd been awakened by the commotion outside and in the Preacher's suite but were bleary-eyed from sleep and slow to decide what to do. They offered no resistance and were quickly restrained.

Then the squad checked all three rooms for explosives and extra vials, and all electronic devices were gathered up. These would almost certainly contain vital data.

Back in the operations room, everyone was stunned. Witnessing action like this as it unfolded was hypnotic. Jiro's screens had provided a dazzling array of real-time imagery from the video cameras on the squad members' helmets to the hotel's internal CCTV that he'd hacked in to.

It took more than a moment for the success of the operation to fully register. The usually reserved Saito was beaming from ear to ear, while Matsumoto punched the air over and over. Kim high-fived her colleagues while Jiro, wildly excited, called out, Yatta! Yatta! Yatta! We did it!

Saito signalled to Jiro to bring back online the radio network connecting all of the officers on the street who'd contributed to the exercise. The link was up in a matter of seconds and Saito proceeded to express his gratitude for a professional job very well executed.

Inside one of the surrounding police wagons on the screen those in the operations room could see Bella and Li all smiles and giving the thumbs up to their colleagues. Just then, Saito asked everyone on the network to hold on for a moment while an image of a silent witness to the whole operation was being brought to the main screen in the room.

"I congratulate you all!" Hasegawa said from the National Police Agency HQ in Tokyo. "I have no words to ..." His voice trailed off as he fought to contain his emotions, shaking his head in disbelief.

"I've been watching from Tokyo in awe, awe and admiration," he finally continued. "The professionalism and teamwork you've displayed will have pride of place in the history of our Agency."

A number of officers listening and watching nodded and started to express their thanks for his high praise, but lapsed into silence again when they realised he had more to say.

"We couldn't have done this without the help of Bella from MI6 and Li and his colleagues in Beijing," Hasegawa said quite sincerely.

Bella and Li, still in the police wagon outside the hotel, thanked him for his kind words. While Hasegawa's gesture seemed to come straight from the heart, both instinctively felt there was something contrived about it.

As they glanced at each other, both knew this would be the first thing they'd discuss when the opportunity presented itself.

Chapter 15

Operations Room, Nagasaki
Thursday, 1420 hours

With events at the Uemura Inn now taken care of, Saito turned to other dimensions of the operation. Local and national media had reported a major drug bust in Nagasaki, but had agreed to lay off the story until so-called raids in other parts of Japan had been carried out. This bought Saito and Hasegawa the breathing space they needed. The compliance of the Japanese media, something that had long puzzled Bella, served the national interest well on this occasion.

Kim had assembled all of the surveillance crews in another part of the Police HQ building. Here they would compile individual reports on the operation from their different perspectives. Saito explained that everyone, from Hasegawa down, had something to learn from the way this operation had played out in Nagasaki.

"Our successes can be just as instructive as the lessons we learn from our failures," he said. "Too often we forget this!"

Saito's words were taken as a hearty congratulations to every member of the various surveillance teams, which put them in a good frame of mind for efficient reporting. At the same time, he dexterously steered Yumi onto a different task, fashioned as one of great importance, to flatter her. This would keep her away from her surveillance colleagues and Saito asked Jiro to alert him if she made any attempt to contact anyone by phone, email or text. Yumi was assigned a desk inside the operations room so an eye could be kept on her.

Kim returned to Saito's side, joining Bella, Li and Matsumoto. All were now psychologically prepared to move to the next phase of the operation: interrogations.

"Right!" he said. "Soon, experts will descend on us from all over the country and we'll be up to our knees in briefings. We might have lost two of our targets today but we still have four to work on. We need to fathom the depths of the Preacher's and P1's murky minds, and then there are the twins, of course. Murad, the one with better language skills, may provide valuable insights and information. Meanwhile, their fellow conspirator, P2, is about to be apprehended in Tokyo and we're confident we'll be able to glean something useful from him."

The sooner they got into this final information gathering stage of the operation, the better. Most of the other staffers in the room were busy working on a broad overview of the extraordinary events of the past few days, which Saito would supplement before sending it off to their Tokyo HQ. Hasegawa would draw from it for his formal report to the government, though he was already providing the Prime Minister and a select handful of other ministers with a briefing.

It was still far too early for the government to issue a statement on what had happened. The PM's view was that they should wait until the drug bust story could be overridden by a truthful account of what had actually taken place in Nagasaki, and what that city and Tokyo had been saved from. The PM joked with Hasegawa that politicians so rarely had a break like this where they could bask in the glory of a momentous win achieved by employees of the government no less.

Hasegawa had confided his amusement at this comment to Saito, likening politicians at his briefing to salivating Pavlovs dogs.

While the operations room was still technically in operational mode, the atmosphere inside had changed radically. The flood of visuals on the display screens during the course of the operation had dwindled to a trickle. Just the main screen was still active, though it bore images of only passing importance. The buzzers and flashing lights on the many communication devices in the room were now silent.

However, Jiro, with a cheeky grin, had made a great spectacle of seeking Saito's permission to disobey a direct order to catch up on some sleep. This had drawn a loud laugh from everyone in the room, unaware that it was a ruse cooked up by the pair for Jiro to confide a secret report on Yumi's activities. Saito wanted to get to the bottom of her monitoring of the innovative technology used on the surveillance communications network during the tight operation. He smelled a rat.

Matsumoto had just had contact with the officer in charge of the interrogation cells situated two levels below the building's basement car park. All four – including the twins – were now segregated. There was no way they could pass messages to each other, even by shouting.

Saito wanted them kept in solitary confinement for as long as it took to encourage them to talk. The methods Japanese police customarily used, if required, could be as brutal as anything the Busan Police Chief might have already employed a short time before on the Korean ferry master.

Nevertheless, he'd been impressed by the MI6 success rate as Bella described it to him. He readily agreed to leave the initial, and possibly all, the questioning to her. Perhaps being eyeballed by a foreign woman of unknown origin and background would destabilise and soften up the jihadists, especially P1. Saito regarded him as the toughest nut of all.

"No food, no water," Saito ordered when the detainees were first taken to the cells. "Leave their scratches and bruises untreated, especially P1's, despite any pain he might be in. Give them all an hour alone before starting on P1. And while you're in their presence, be like deaf mutes. No verbal communication and no body language that might indicate empathy."

Matsumoto repeated these orders to the interrogation team, wanting to be sure they understood what Saito had meant by the full treatment.

"Do you want the generator on for that hour?" the team leader asked.

The generator channeled incessant noise and vibration into each of the confinement cells, shattering any possibility of concentration, constructive thinking, or even rest. The effect on most subjects was chronically disorienting.

"Yes, give them a full hour," he replied. "Turn it up high."

"Ablutions? Lighting?" the leader asked.

"No, don't provide them with buckets. Make sure the air-conditioning is off in the cells and keep the cells in complete darkness. Also, strip them naked. Let me know in an hour if they're ready. If not, we'll give them another sixty minutes. P1 prides himself on being a tough cookie, so you might have to throw something extra at him. Keep me posted."

Saito had no quibble with any of Matsumoto's responses. The harsher the treatment, the more an interrogator could offer relief in return for information. He sat back in his chair, gathering his thoughts about about what to tackle next, when Jiro alerted him to a message just in from HQ in Tokyo.

He quickly checked his laptop: P2, otherwise known as Ramsi, the driver of the delivery van who was supposed to detonate the suitcase bomb underneath the Diet Building, had been taken by complete surprise. Now, the highest priority for interrogation in both cities was to discover whether or not there were more cell members in the capital or elsewhere in Japan.

Saito shared this with the others in the room before turning back to Jiro with a quizzical look on his face.

"Anything more coming my way?" he asked. "I could do with some breathing space."

"Nothing yet," Jiro replied. "But there's sure to be something in the next minute or two!"

Those around Saito laughed and he mused that perhaps they were through the worst the operation could throw at them. Perhaps.

Li tapped him on the shoulder. He and Bella had been discussing something urgent with Kim and Matsumoto: what to do about the suitcase? The device had already been taken to a defunct mining site in a rugged, uninhabited coastal area. The NPA and Japanese military used this place for training in explosives and detonations. The crate of brick-sized blocks found in the Preacher's van had been identified as C4, a substance with enormous explosive power. This had to be destroyed, of course, but the suitcase was uppermost in everyone's mind.

"Yes, indeed," Saito said, rolling his eyes. "What do we do with our prized possession? Hasegawa's looked in to it discreetly and apparently there's no one in Japan who knows anything about such devices. Let's face it, there's no precedent for a situation like this."

Bella had already contacted her MI6 colleagues in Tokyo asking them to look into it. Crispin Grenville had advised it was likely to take some time before an expert could first be found and secondly, transferred to the site.

Li flashed Saito a grin. As usual, he had an idea and Saito sensed it was a good one.

Operations Room
Thursday, 1514 hours

Before Bella and Kim headed down to the interrogation cells, Saito invited them to listen to Li's overview of the bomb and its origins.

"Between us," Li started off in uncomplicated Japanese, "when the Soviet Union collapsed, a huge amount of military weaponry and equipment was sold off by Russian commanders stationed in those old underbelly states like Kazakhstan and Uzbekistan. A lot was pilfered there and in the Ukraine, sold on by middle-men to Al Qaeda and a host of organised crime gangs. The situation was completely out of control. Senior members of the newly installed Russian government were even secretly involved in this."

The others were intrigued.

"Now," Li went on, "you may not be aware that China, the United States, Britain, France, Germany and other countries were originally cooperating with Moscow to track down the most lethal of the missing stuff, including quantities of plutonium, chemical weapons and especially, a significant number of nuclear suitcase bombs. The Russians had produced roughly a hundred and thirty of these devices all up, but a quarter of that number vanished into thin air."

No one in the group clustered around Li hearing this had any idea he was so well versed in such matters.

"There's a senior People's Liberation Army general in Beijing who led China's team," he continued.

"He's a nuclear engineer by training and is retired. This man, probably in his early eighties by now, lives in the capital and from what I've heard he's still pretty sharp."

Saito's main concern was ascertaining how dangerous the suitcase bomb was in its present state, and how it could be disposed of.

As if he could read his mind, Li looked at Saito and said, "You could have your military people in Tokyo get onto the Americans about it, but you'd probably just end up right where we are now. Beijing could help."

Saito nodded, realising the import of his comment: that the Chinese were further ahead on this than he'd thought.

"I've actually seen a disarmed suitcase bomb myself," Li revealed, "on one of the training courses I did soon after joining Chinese intelligence. It was an early generation model in an aluminium case significantly larger than the one the Preacher had smuggled in here. It was also clunkier than the device Abu Mukhtar tried to abscond with. The one we now have in our possession is definitely a later model version. The retired general I was telling you about gave us a lecture on these devices, so I've actually met him."

Bella knew that Saito would make a quick political calculation right about now: would Tokyo have qualms about calling on China for direct help in this regard?

"Time is clearly of the essence," Li continued, "so if you wish, I can message my people in Beijing at once. If the general is able to fly over here it might help us understand exactly what we're dealing with."

Saito was clearly of the same mind. "Well, Beijing's certainly much closer than Washington, London or Moscow. It would save valuable time, and furthermore ..."

Hasegawa's image suddenly appeared on the main display, cutting across Saito's train of thought.

"Sorry to interrupt but I've just checked with our military and there's no identifiable body of expertise in Japan on nuclear suitcase bombs."

Hasegawa's appearance reminded the group that the Chief could monitor communications in any of the NPA's regional HQs when operations of this importance were under way.

"I've been listening to what our friend Li proposes," Hasegawa continued, "and I think we should bring the retired gentleman across to Nagasaki as soon as it can be arranged. Do you think he'd be up for it, Li?"

"I don't see why not, Chief. He's a wiry, muscular man who carries his age well. I imagine he'd be keen to help out, and I can't see why the higher-ups in Beijing would oppose it, not that I'm in any position to pre-empt their decision, of course."

Hasegawa smiled slyly and said, "In the meantime, I'll brief the PM on this and get his approval, though I doubt he'll object. Speed and safety in determining the threat is his top priority, as it is ours."

"I'll contact Beijing right away," Li responded. Sitting down at Saito's desk he flipped open his laptop.

In just over a minute, a message was dispatched to Beijing.

Operations Room
Friday, 0615 hours

Less than a day after the targets had been placed in the interrogation cells, everyone was quietly chuffed at how things were progressing. Some interesting information had emerged from the most unexpected quarter.

The interrogation of P1 had ultimately proved highly productive, even if quite tedious at first. He'd baulked at the prospect of being interrogated by a woman, pleading to be given something to wear. He was thrown an old pair of overalls, which was standard practice anyway, though it was positioned to him as a mighty concession – and the last one he could expect. When Bella finally entered the room she addressed him as Yousef and handed him a glass of chilled, crystal clear water.

Valuable information had already been extracted from P2 in Tokyo and speedily relayed to Nagasaki. It gave Bella a decided advantage. She was able to present a very credible face: someone who was already in the know.

When Yousef initially resisted divulging anything about his Uzbek accomplices still in Mindanao, Bella called in four male police interrogators who'd immediately ripped off his overalls. They sat him back down in the chair and remained in the room, standing behind him.

"There's nothing nice about these men," she'd told Yousef sternly in Urdu, glancing at the policemen. "Their intention is to dispatch you to Tokyo where the coercive measures they'll adopt are hardly something a woman should know about, let alone associate herself with. They forced your friend, Ramsi, to open up, so there's no reason to think they won't do the same to you. The three large canisters of the nerve agent you had in your possession were found in his apartment. This provided an incentive for the interrogators to be more brutal than usual."

Yousef remained silent. From what Bella had seen of him during the surveillance she knew he was a highly intelligent man. After a short while, she stood up, offered her hand for Yousef to shake, which he did, then moved towards the door.

As she reached for the handle, Bella turned and said, "I was hoping to help you, Yousef, and to avoid any ugliness. Earlier, I watched the video of Ramsi's interrogation. He talked of the son you've had with a Bangladeshi woman in Tokyo. I was very moved, which any woman and mother (even though I'm not, she thought to herself) naturally would be. That's why I volunteered to come and talk with you. I confess, I can't comprehend how you reconcile in your mind and your heart your affection for little Khalil on the one hand and the vengeance you sought to inflict upon Tokyo and the Japanese, on the other. Your son would have suffered the same fate, destroyed at his father's hand."

Yousef was still silent, his head bowed to avoid making direct eye contact. Instinct told Bella he was ruminating on what she'd just said.

"Nothing will happen to Tokyo now," she continued, "but something will happen to you. If you choose to remain unresponsive you will end up in Tokyo. You'll either be taken there for more, what shall we call it? Treatment? Or you'll end up in prison there. The latter is the more benign of the two. Who knows? If you don't talk, you could well be quietly dispensed with. The system in Tokyo is blocked up enough as it is. No one would be too concerned. However, if you choose to cooperate and share any knowledge you have about your Uzbek compatriot, Ramsi, then you'll only go to prison. The Japanese authorities may even allow visits from Khalil.

"When the Japanese public hears about your plan for the Diet," she continued, "they'll be baying for yours and Ramsi's blood. They'll give you a life sentence if, and only if, you're willing to talk. If you're seen to be helpful and you display an intention to reform yourself, the government can portray that as a plus. Your sentence might even be shortened."

Yousef looked up, studying her face for some time. Bella didn't look away.

"All I can say, Yousef, is I know what I'd do. You should place more value on your own life and redefine it in light of where you find yourself now. If that's what you opt to do, I'll back you."

He said nothing and Bella allowed the silence.

Yousef looked down at his naked body, and then up at Bella. She sensed immediately that he was coming around. Speaking in Japanese, she asked one of the policemen to fetch a fresh pair of overalls and a meal if Yousef wanted it.

"I'll come back in thirty minutes," she said. "They won't touch you while I'm out of the room."

She returned later to find a man not so different from the physical one she'd so far encountered, but vastly different in his attitude. They spoke for more than two hours, during which time he revealed a few unknown dimensions of Islamic State and its jihadi training activities in Mindanao.

That and other intelligence he provided was valuable but, like Ramsi, he was unable to give any useful insights into the Preacher's mind. They knew his line of thinking, as well as the fact that he had contingency plans for every imaginable scenario.

And he was indeed obsessed with contingencies, as his secondary plan to blow up the Sky Tree in Tokyo exemplified, 'just in case we don't take out the Diet building' was how the Preacher put it. But the grandest of all his plans actually resembled a triangle. First, the twins would trigger their suicide bombs in Nagasaki, followed by the Diet building in Tokyo and then the Sky Tree, the latter becoming a culmination rather than a mere contingency.

If the Preacher had other plans, neither Yousef nor Ramsi were aware of them. That was one thing the interrogators in Tokyo and Bella in Nagasaki agreed upon.

She thanked Yousef, telling him the information provided would work in his favour. This had been one of the smoothest interrogations she'd ever been involved in by far. Bella had never believed physical violence or torture were the only effective means of extracting information, though the threat of them had some use. Logic, reason and an appeal to a suspect's values were always what she tried first.

This approach had worked with Yousef, but the Preacher was proving to be a different animal entirely. Every sinew of his being had been distorted by hatred, the extent of which Bella had never before witnessed. His arrogance, ego and self-righteousness were remarkable and impervious to any of the tactics that had worked on Yousef. One session with him and Bella had opted out, leaving him to what she knew would be a much more brutal Japanese interrogation.

The Preacher's craving for retribution seemed to know no bounds and Islam was clearly his vehicle rather than a sincere belief system. The NPA had made it abundantly clear they were more intent on breaking him than they'd been with Yousef.

With her part in the interrogations concluded, Bella was keen to get back to Tokyo and pick up where she'd left off. But her presence in Nagasaki would prove useful one final time before that.

Chapter 16

Operations Room, Nagasaki
Friday, 1025 hours

General Chen Guangying strode into the room with all of the gravitas of a former high-ranking military officer. Tall, ramrod straight and with close-cropped white hair he seemed impressed by the hive of activity and sophisticated technology. Following the successful interrogation of Yousef, the place was once again abuzz with data exchanges between Nagasaki Police and NPA HQ in Tokyo. Jiro's skills were in high demand.

Saito, Bella and Li had greeted the General at the airport and brought him to the police HQ by helicopter. He was not introduced to all inhabitants of the operations room first off. Instead, he huddled with Saito and his command team for a private briefing. What had transpired prior to Chen's departure from Beijing had gone a long way to dispelling the qualms of a few who doubted he could be of much of value on the Russian suitcase bomb problem.

Before agreeing to go to Nagasaki the retired General had asked for professional photographs of the device, taken from a variety of angles, to be sent to him in Beijing. Once the photos had been received he very quickly confirmed that it was indeed a late model device. Images of the bomb's trigger mechanism, found in Yousef's backpack, had also been sent, with the General strongly advising that no attempt be made to open the casing and that the suitcase should be carefully removed to a remote location, protected from humidity and temperature fluctuations. This had already been done and arrangements would be made for General Chen to inspect it there later on.

In the close-knit briefing with Saito's team in Nagasaki the General had expressed concern about the possibility that the device might be armed. From the images he'd scrutinised, the trigger mechanism Yousef had been carrying was incompatible with the device that had been brought into Japan. It was possible that it could belong to another suitcase bomb, the whereabouts of which was unknown.

"Great! Something else to worry about," an exasperated Saito quipped to Li, out of earshot of the visitor.

That possibility had led to further questioning of Yousef and the others, each of them denying any knowledge of the existence of a second device. This was worrying, especially because Chen insisted that the matter required urgent attention. He even volunteered to question Yousef and the Preacher himself.

Saito had no wish to get the General offside, agreeing that he could question Yousef with only Bella present as an interpreter. Saito, Li, Kim and Matsumoto would watch the proceedings on Jiro's screens.

Bella's suspicions were aroused from the start. Yousef was adamant he'd never heard mention of a second bomb. Getting hold of just one had been difficult enough. Chen, who'd been introduced as a retired Chinese scientist, put a number of questions to Yousef, each eliciting a response in the negative.

There's something else at play here, Bella mused, but it's hard to tell what it is exactly. She was inclined to believe Yousef. When they spoke to each other in Urdu, his tone reflected a wish to be helpful. She decided to try a new angle.

Bella said to Chen, "Yousef says he's seen all sorts of boxes and crates being packed and unpacked. If you could describe what a second device might look like, especially if it has a different casing such as copper not aluminium, it might prod his memory."

Chen pondered the matter then stated that all of the casings were aluminium. Only the size differed. That meant little to Yousef.

Chen then asked what it had cost to procure the bomb that had been brought into Japan.

Yousef shrugged. "I heard it was something like five million American dollars, but as I told you, I never handled money transactions."

Chen nodded, which suggested that was a likely price.

"Ask him what he thinks plutonium is going for on the black market," the General said to Bella, "even if it's only a ball-park figure."

In answering Bella's question, Yousef assumed a more deferential form of Urdu. He used terms that were customarily a sign of respect to a woman of high birth. Bella picked up on this straight away, as Yousef assumed she would.

"I don't wish to sound presumptuous," he said,

"but previously you did me the honour of observing that I was an intelligent man. If you would allow me to make an observation of my own, I would say you're just as intelligent as I am, perhaps more so. For that reason, you'll be able to ascertain for yourself what's happening here. You helped me so please don't take offence when I say I'm trying to help you."

Bella immediately knew what he was getting at. She did not believe that a second bomb even existed. Furthermore, instinct told her other facts presented as truths might also be questionable. But for now, she'd bide her time.

Back in the operations room, General Chen was introduced to the staff by Saito. He emphasised that the General's presence fell into the same category as Li's: here but not here. Secrecy came with the territory, so no one had any problem with this.

The General was scheduled to remain in the city for up to three days, with his first task an inspection of the suitcase bomb at the remote abandoned mine. He would be staying at the flashy five-star New Nagasaki Hotel, with the cover story of a retired bureaucrat visiting grandchildren studying in Japan. No one was likely to question that, especially as he was travelling on a standard Chinese citizen's passport that carried no privileges.

On the following day, Saturday, the Japanese Prime Minister would secretly fly to Nagasaki in the company of NPA Chief Hasegawa to meet with Chen privately at Police HQ and to personally thank the team in the operations room. As both Li and the General had done, the Prime Minister would travel from the airport to HQ by helicopter.

Saito was chuffed that his country's political leader was making such a gesture, but Bella and Li viewed the visit in a broader context. If the PM's meeting with Chen went well, they hoped it might pave the way for broaching the China-Japan-Korea science and technology concept. Li had already briefed the General on it and he would also be the only other person in the room during the meeting with the Prime Minister and Hasegawa.

Saito suggested to Bella and Li that while the PM was in town, it might be useful to discuss what if any public announcement he envisaged being made on Operation Nagasaki. How would the Chinese want their contribution to be portrayed? Might they prefer no mention of it at all?

While Li showed the General to the bathroom, Saito, Bella and Kim enjoyed a brief moment of respite.

Saito shook his head and said. "Can you believe what's been achieved here in just a few short days? We've all been in frenzied operations before, but this one takes the cake!"

"You're not wrong there," Kim responded, "but proof of a second bomb or a second jihadist cell could negate all this good work in an instant. You're my model realist, Saito San. I can hardly keep my reservations to myself."

"Point taken," Saito said with a smile. Bella smiled too, though her thoughts were elsewhere.

It is too good to be true, she was thinking. There's definitely another game afoot here and after the most recent exchange with Yousef, I have an inkling of what that might be and who's behind it. When the time's right I'll run it past Saito. He may already have similar suspicions.

Jiro had taken a shine to Bella from the start. It wasn't a crush, nor was it due to the mystique that often surrounds gaijin women with interesting backgrounds. It was more than that. The working relationship the pair had established in the course of the operation had served everybody well. Saito and Matsumoto had commented on it a number of times and Kim had confided to Bella what it was that impressed the young man so much.

"He's never imagined a scenario where foreign spies would labour so hard to protect Japan's interests," Kim said. "He joked that he's never even seen such a thing portrayed in manga, spy novels or movies."

Kim was intrigued but not surprised when she noticed Jiro politely pull Bella aside for a chat. They'd shared a few moments like this previously but on this occasion it seemed more purposeful. What Jiro had to tell Bella in confidence was devastating, not just to her but to everyone involved in the operation.

"I know that technically I should be reporting this to Saito first," he said quietly, "but how this involves you made my decision for me. You'll know how to handle this, but please tell me before you pass it on. I can then report via the proper chain of command."

Bella could see how worried he was, his shaky voice belying the skill of this trained and resilient young police officer.

She listened intently as Jiro told her he'd never intended to record the private conversation in question. It was an accident. Saito had put him on alert, confidentially, at a certain stage in the operation and it was for that reason the listening device that recorded the exchange had been switched on.

"I realised just a while ago that I'd forgotten to switch it off, and that's when I heard them," said Jiro "Though I couldn't understand what they were saying in Chinese, I got the distinct impression General Chen was scoffing at something or someone. It seemed odd to me that they'd have so much to laugh about so soon after the General's arrival, so I ran their dialogue through our translation system to get the gist of it."

Bella was shocked by what Jiro imparted; it turned everything upside-down!

She squeezed his arm and thanked him, before adding quickly, "It's best we're not seen talking for long. Let's stop now and laugh as we part. I'll slap you on the back as though you've just told me a good joke, then we'll casually go back to what we were doing. If anyone asks, just say you told me about the time President Bush senior visited Japan and spewed all over the then Prime Minister at a banquet."

Jiro smiled nervously.

"And don't worry," Bella reassured him. "No one will ever know you've told me but I'll need some time to think about the best way to approach this."

"Fine with me," he said. "I just hope it doesn't mess everything up."

"It won't," she replied, "at least it doesn't have

to. We'll just need to play this much smarter from now on. Wow, we have to be so careful, don't we?"

True to the script, they laughed and Bella slapped Jiro on the back before they went their separate ways.

Chapter 17

Operations Room, Nagasaki
Saturday, 1204 hours

Like most of the others in the room, Saito had managed only minimal sleep during the operation, but he needed to remain sharp for the two meetings about to take place.

Nagasaki Airport Control had just confirmed the arrival of the Prime Minister's aircraft. He, his private secretary and NPA Chief Hasegawa were now enroute to HQ by police helicopter. They had not transited through the terminal and no media representatives had been spotted.

Hasegawa was basking in the glory of the operation's success. On the flight down, Prime Minister Hayashi Kentaro, short, balding and in his late sixties, had been full of praise for the way in which the Agency and everyone involved had acquitted themselves. He'd also commented openly that the nation's intelligence apparatus was in dire need for an upgrade.

"At least we have the British team addressing the problem," he'd said. "Getting ourselves an MI6-type spy service only highlights what we should have been doing overseas years ago. If this operation has taught us anything it's that, without an up-to-date domestic security service working in tandem with a modern international spy service, Japan is just not in the game. We've gone far too long without acknowledging how vulnerable we are. I know you appreciate, Hasegawa San, there's a huge political downside to all of this.'

The PM's commentary warmed the cockles of Hasegawa's heart. All the better, he thought, if the PM needs me to keep this close shave under wraps. It was Hasegawa's dream to see his Agency transformed into a body that could stand proudly alongside Japan's own overseas spy wing as part of the global intelligence community.

"I know you have strong views on the kind of structure we need," the PM continued," and I'll be leaning heavily on you to set our house in order when all this has blown over."

"With you all the way," Hasegawa replied, barely suppressing his joy.

The Prime Minister found this comforting, as bureacratic mistakes and poor performing ministers were the source of most of his problems.

"With the heavy involvement of the British in this operation," the PM mused aloud, "should we simply ask for their help while they're here?"

"Well, yes and no," Hasegawa said slyly.

"Come now, Hasegawa San! Even if we Japanese are renowned for our prevarication, what do you mean?"

"With the utmost respect, Prime Minister," Hasegawa responded, pleased the PM had taken the bait, "what I mean is horses for courses. You see, Britain is a unitary state with everything centralised in London. Scotland Yard and MI5 are a reflection of that. On the other hand, in the United States, the Federal Bureau of Investigation mirrors a very different system of federalism. Now, while Japan is not a federation as such, we do have prefectures, each with its own elected governor and political process. In that sense, our security structure is closer to the American model."

"So what you want is a Japanese FBI with a British-style MI6 international spy set-up standing alongside it?"

"Yes and no again," Hasegawa replied with an unguarded cackle. "What we need is something uniquely Japanese, an over-arching FBI which incorporates the MI6 wing within it."

"Oh, I see," said the PM knowingly. "That certainly makes sense. Given the success of this current operation I can hardly dispute your logic."

Hasegawa took this to mean the PM approved of this proposal, though normally he had scant reason to put faith in the promises of politicians. However, this PM did have enough political clout to drive something like this through. There'd been hardly a whimper from the Diet over the establishment of a proper overseas spy service, so a grander, overarching Japanese FBI concept could piggyback that without much trouble.

It all depends, he mused, on how much we stage-manage informing the public about just how close a terrorist cell came to bringing our country to its knees. That statement will be crucial.

Saito and Matsumoto were at the helipad on top of the building when Prime Minister Hayashi and Hasegawa arrived. Before going down to the operations room, they were briefed on who they'd be meeting. The full complement of officers who had handled surveillance were in attendance. General Chen was, at that moment, engaged in an informal all-staff question and answer session on the future of global terrorism for which Bella and Li were interpreting. The interrogation of targets had been put on hold for the PM's lightning visit.

Arrangements for the PM's private meeting with General Chen were then canvassed, with the PM asking that it be strictly unofficial and informal: no note-takers and not even his private secretary in attendance.

It was agreed that a small room would be used for this meeting and in addition to Chen, only Hasegawa, Saito and Li would be present. To Saito's astonishment Hasegawa proposed that Bella also be included.

"She might be a foreign national," the Chief said, "but she's directly involved in the revamp of our intelligence system, she also speaks Mandarin fluently, and she's been instrumental throughout this entire operation. I feel her presence might add another dimension to this meeting, and a valuable one."

The Prime Minster responded sanguinely by saying, "During the flight down, Chief Hasegawa has extolled the virtues of this Englishwoman, as well as Li from Beijing. It would be negligent of me not to include them in the proceedings."

When the PM walked into the operations room with Hasegawa and the others a spontaneous cheer went up, followed by lengthy applause acknowledging this extraordinary gesture of the country's leader.

The PM easily recognised General Chen standing at the front of the room clapping along with the others. Chen was his first introduction, followed by Bella, Li, Kim, Yumi, Jiro and then each of the other staffers. Bella and Li were singled out for particularly warm handshakes from the PM, graciously received by both, even though Bella was looking for an urgent opportunity to pull Saito aside.

The room fell quiet as the PM readied himself to address them.

Standing beside Chen at the front of the room he said, "An image repeatedly came to my mind of the 9/11 tragedies in New York, Washington and Pennsylvania. I see then-President Bush climbing atop a heap of rubble where the World Trade Centre Towers previously stood. I'm enormously privileged here today, not only as your Prime Minister, but as a plain human being, to be able to congratulate you all on the avoidance of such a catastrophic attack on our country. The professionalism, the coordination, the powers of deduction, the magnificent talents and skills that you've applied over these few days in Nagasaki leave me deeply humbled."

The whole room was enthralled. Prime Minister Hayashi was a respected figure across Japan. The office he held was revered in Japan and Hayashi in particular was respected for his down-to-earth disposition, both privately and as a political leader.

"Very few members of the government in

Tokyo," Hayashi continued, "know what has been achieved here and the unimaginable horrors that were about to befall us. The Japanese public too is, as yet, unaware. I felt it was my duty to come down to Nagasaki to personally meet you and to express my deep appreciation on behalf of the nation before this operation draws to a close."

The PM's voice wavered slightly and he cleared his throat.

"In a moment, I'd like to address each of you individually, but before I do, I have a special duty to perform. It gives me pleasure as your Prime Minister to express my deep gratitude to the Chinese government, and to General Chen and Li Weiming in particular. Put simply, without vital intelligence provided by Beijing, the fate that awaited us could not have been avoided."

The PM pronounced the names of these two men in both Japanese and Mandarin, a most unusual gesture for a Japanese politician that did not go unnoticed.

When Li had interpreted for the General, Chen shook Hayashi's hand firmly and put his arm around his shoulder. As stern as Chen was, he was obviously impressed with the Prime Minister's tribute. It was an image that everyone in the room was unlikely to forget: a tall, dignified Chinese military man embracing a short and somewhat chubby Japanese leader.

As Hayashi began mingling with the staff Hasegawa reminded them that, regrettably, selfies with the PM were out of the question.

Soon after, General Chen and Prime Minister Hayashi found themselves seated at a cozy round table with pots of green tea and an assortment of traditional Japanese delicacies arranged around a bowl of freshly-cut red and fragrant roses.

In an aside with Bella the day before, Chen had mentioned that one of his pastimes these days was growing roses, especially those known as antique of the old British variety. Bella had canvassed the operations room and discovered a policewoman whose grandparents shared the same interest. The elderly couple had provided a bunch of their finest specimens now gracing the meeting room table. In China, there was almost always something behind such thoughtful gestures, as there was in Bella's deliberate act today.

Before the meeting got underway, Bella managed a quick word with Saito: 'Suggest you keep this meeting perfunctory and polite. Reveal nothing meaningful. Fragrant roses also have thorns. Will explain later.'

Saito eyed her curiously but nodded to indicate he knew she was deadly serious.

Chen sat opposite Hayashi. Li interpreted for the General and Bella for Hayashi. Before anyone spoke, Chen pulled out a packet of cigarettes and offered them around. Only Hasegawa accepted, politely moving the large glass ashtray on the table closer to his guest.

Even the non-smokers in the room recognised the distinctive smell of Camel tobacco, a pungent Middle Eastern variety that soon enveloped them.

"This is the sort of get together I really miss," the PM said, addressing the General. "These days my meetings are overwhelmingly about interest groups contesting with each other for a larger slice of the pie. Our system in Japan virtually demands that the government should be all things to all people."

Chen laughed and said, "In my country, it's usually the other way round!"

Hayashi had not expected to see wit and an open disposition in an ex-military Chinese man of high rank. As the discussion unfolded, Chen also displayed a diverse taste in books: history, philosophy, economics, science and literature. His interests seemed boundless.

Bella thought he was as beguiling as any adroit Chinese diplomat, but she knew he must be a wily operator in other ways, one who's no doubt been ruthless in climbing to the top. She speculated to herself that while Chen may think he had Hayashi wrapped around his little finger, the PM could be equally as cunning.

Bella briefly caught Saito's eye and in that instant they both knew they were thinking the same thing. The General was happy to make small talk. After all, he had what he wanted.

"Those of us who work within systems of great discipline and purpose," Chen said, turning to Hasegawa and Saito, "appreciate the enormous amount of energy that goes into an exercise like this. I'm so pleased that we've been able to make a contribution."

Everyone nodded courteously.

Conversation moved onto books, with Chen asking Hayashi which works had influenced him in his formative years. In a deft display of tact and sophistication, the Prime Minister named a number of Chinese classics like Sun Tzu's *Art of War*, then added Adam Smith's *The Wealth of Nations*, Machiavelli's *The Prince*, and the political speeches of Jawaharlal Nehru, India's first Prime Minister.

Bravo! thought Bella.

"What conclusions did you draw from such a broad selection? In the military, I never had the chance to read as widely as you," Chen said affably.

"Well, let me think," Hayashi replied, rubbing his chin for effect. "It would have to be that in any human society consensus never comes easily, certainly not in the political realm."

"A wise answer," Chen responded with a wry smile. "We both know how difficult reaching consensus can be as well as the price we have to pay to achieve it."

Talk of history brought to Saito's mind something that Bella had told him about Li's family background in China. He saw an opportunity to keep the conversation on a platitudinous plane. The meeting would soon draw to a close and this should carry them through to the end.

"I'm intrigued to know," Saito said quizzically, "whether paying heed to the classics assists deep thinkers like yourself and Li to use your intellect to great effect?"

Brilliant! Bella thought.

"You hail from Wenzhou, am I right?" Saito

added, addressing Li. "I understand this area of China has particular significance in this regard, but forgive me, I haven't had a chance to Google it yet."

"Perhaps I can best answer that for my young compatriot," Chen said politely, diverting the question. "When we're overseas, Chinese people always ask each other where they come from. I already know Li was born and raised in Wenzhou, a coastal city in Zhejiang Province, south of Shanghai. It's renowned as the home of modern mathematics in China. Indeed, our first mathematics academy was founded there in 1896 and even today the vast majority of our country's mathematicians either come from that area or received their training at that institution."

Li acknowledged the compliment without adding to Chen's explanation. In truth, he was embarrassed by the smarminess of the General's speech, especially in light of something he'd earlier become aware of. Bella and Li's eyes met and the pair exchanged a great deal in that glance. Bella could see his discomfort and Li got the strong sense that Bella was aware of its cause.

"And I must say," Chen continued to observe, "that young Li here lives up to Wenzhou's heritage eminently well."

This prompted smiles and nods around the table, which gave Hayashi the opportunity to glance at his watch. Chen took the hint.

"Before we break up," he said, "Li has shared an idea with me that apparently originated in Beijing recently. It is for a new and creative relationship, a triumvirate if you will, between China, Japan and Korea."

He used the word Hanguo for Korea, which in Mandarin had connotations of a unified peninsula.

"I only know the bare bones of the idea," Chen went on, "and as you and I both know, Prime Minister, ideas of this nature are frequently still-born or shot down before they get off the ground. But after the events of Nagasaki I do think this time it has merit."

Hayashi smiled and replied, "As some of us gathered here already know, one of our brightest young parliamentarians, Sakamoto Masataka, is the major proponent of this concept in my government. To be frank, I wondered at first how this might work in practical terms. But after seeing what's taken place here in Nagasaki, I'm ready to look into it very seriously."

As they filed out of the room, the General pressed a note into Bella's hand.

"Read this later," he whispered conspiratorially.

She showed the note to Li as soon as Prime Minister Hayashi's helicopter had taken off:

The future is in the hands of fine young people like you and Li. The triumvirate concept is an interesting one that I believe could work well. I will support it in every way possible in Beijing. I hope your friendship with Li lasts through thick and thin. With warm regards, Chen Guangying.

Li read the note and looked Bella in the eye as he handed it back to her. She almost certainly knows how I'm caught between a rock and a hard place, he thought to himself.

Nagasaki Police Cafeteria
Saturday, 1816 hours

The operations room was no longer on 24-hour alert and Saito, Bella, Li and Kim had moved to visitors' accommodation in the HQ's dormitory block. Accompanied by Saito and Li, General Chen would fly out to the mining site by helicopter the next morning to examine the suitcase bomb. He would fly back to China in the evening.

In the cafeteria, Saito and Bella managed to find time alone for a private chat before the others turned up for the evening meal. Li was escorting General Chen back to his hotel and the General had proposed they dine together alone.

"OK, fire away!" Saito said, eager to hear Bella's news.

"Last night in the ops room," she said, "Jiro approached me privately about something he'd unwittingly overheard. I could see straightaway that he was worried but he seems to trust me, and quickly got to the point."

Saito was grinning, which Bella wasn't quite sure how to interpret. Raising an eyebrow, she continued.

"Jiro told me you'd asked him to secretly switch on listening devices in every corner of the ops room and the wider HQ complex, and not to turn them off until after the targets had been brought in for interrogation and the suitcase bomb was in our hands. Jiro thought he'd turned them all off, but when he checked he found the ones in the men's toilet were still on. He overheard Li and General Chen in conversation while they were in there."

Saito smiled, which puzzled Bella even more.

"The General told Li in the strictest confidence, that the suitcase bomb and the trigger mechanism are both duds. And there was never a second suitcase in Mindanao or anywhere else," she coninued undeterred.

"The Preacher and his team believed their bomb was real and they definitely planned to create havoc with it. The bomb now in Japan was a genuine late-model one, but Chinese intelligence had cleverly stripped it of its explosive charge to frustrate the Preacher's operation. That suitcase bomb couldn't even blow its own lid off! The General thought it was a great joke, that the Japanese side, which includes me, could so easily be taken in."

Bella suddenly realised that Saito's sardonic smile meant he already knew this.

"My dear friend," he said, reaching out and clasping her hand theatrically."Jiro did switch those devices off, but I turned the ones in the men's toilet back on before the General arrived. While it's undoubtedly true that the General is China's expert on Russian nuclear suitcase bombs, I'm pretty sure he's also the one Chinese intelligence consulted when their operatives stumbled across the Preacher's plot in the first place.

"Also, I'm willing to bet that the suitcase bomb we now have safely stashed in our abandoned mine was supplied to Islamic State in Uzbekistan by local agents working for Chinese intelligence there. It may even have been General Chen himself who suggested the plot to blow up the Diet Building."

"Well, that certainly fits in with the oblque tip-off I got from Yousef during his unoffical interrogation," Bella said. "Having met the General now, I can see how all this might fall into place. Bastard!"

The look on her face told Saito what must be going through her mind. He squeezed Bella's hand and said gravely, "Unfortunately, its entirely possible that Li's been in on this from the start."

Chapter 18

Operations Room, Nagasaki
Sunday, 1417 hours

Saito returned to the operations room from the mining site where the General had inspected the suitcase bomb. Bella was helping Matsumoto and Kim compile a confidential report on the operation that would go to Hasegawa in Tokyo and then be passed onto the government.

He pulled up a chair and beckoned to the group and Jiro, still busy at his control panel, to join them. Li, Saito explained, was flat out accompanying the General on a sightseeing tour in a chauffered Police patrol car suitably rigged with listening devices and cam-corders, of course.

Out of respect to Bella, his tone was anything but jocular, but before Saito uttered a word, everyone in the huddle knew that something must have gone exceedingly well.

"First up," he asked Bella, "have you listened to the toilet tape? Jiro knows you and I have spoken about it and we agree that Li sounded genuinely shocked when General Chen gave him the news. What do you think?"

Bella nodded, saying, "I only needed to hear the recording once to know that Li wasn't in on it. I think he was actually quite taken aback by the General's boasting. Clearly, Chen wasn't concerned about the rest of us involved in this operation. Despite knowing that Li and I are friends from way back, I was appalled when I heard him scoff that we're all just collateral damage."

Bella paused for a second then said, "Li's silence told me how deeply offended he was by that. He might be a clever spy, but he's not a deceitful person by nature. I bet you anything he thinks Beijing's antics are pretty shabby to put it mildy. Anyhow, as soon as I get a chance I'll raise it with him."

"I'm so pleased to hear you say that, Bella, and I agree," Saito responded. "I've told young Jiro here that I totally support his decision to tell you first. Let's face it, this operation has had cross-cultural fault lines running through it from the start, something that you in particular have handled beautifully. I can't imagine where we'd all be without you and I'm proud Jiro had the smarts to approach you first."

Bella leaned over and gave Jiro a hug, the young policeman beaming from ear to ear.

"Come on then," she said to Saito, spiritedly. "We're all keen to hear what happened out at the mine site."

"I thought you'd never ask," said Saito with a laugh. "General Chen was adamant that once he'd checked the suitcase and made sure it was safe, he wanted to take it back with him to Beijing for further examination. Of course, I knew his highest priority would be to get the device out of our hands, to remove the evidence of their skullduggery. You should have seen the way he handled it, scrupulously, as though an errant fart might trigger it off! It was pretty funny."

Saito smiled and shook his head while everyone else laughed heartily. It was a much-needed circuit-breaker to the pent up emotions of the past few days.

"When he'd finished and declared it safe, I told him Japan's top nuclear experts would arrive tomorrow to dismantle the bomb. He wasn't happy with that at all, but quit protesting when he realised we planned to, what's that phrase? Stick to our guns. Li just went along with it. He must know that we know.

"By insisting that the bomb must remain in Japan," Saito explained, "I emphasised that as China had saved us from a dreadful fate we were obliged to dispose of the wretched thing. If a radiation leak were to occur, it would be on Japanese soil, not in China. Of course, I have very different plans for our suitcase, to which we have all become greatly attached, I'm sure. Police officers aren't customarily sentimental, but I've decided on this singular occasion we're entitled to be. Therefore, I'll be taking the dreadful suitcase bomb back to Tokyo with me to be installed as a prize exhibit in our NPA museum!"

That gave rise to another round of laughter.

Nagasaki Airport
Sunday, 2048 hours

General Chen waved before stepping into the cabin of his government jet. Saito, Bella and Li had escorted him to the airport on the police helicopter, landing in a restricted area close to the plane. As the pilot fired up its engines, they stood together savouring the mild evening breeze wafting in from the sea.

All three had a great deal to think about in light of what had transpired over the past forty-eight hours. They lingered on the apron in silence, knowing that as soon as they boarded the helicopter they would re-enter their operational world, its parameters now significantly changed.

Bella was thinking that Saito's suggestion was best. I can't see any other way, she mused. This situation had to be confronted head-on and quickly. Li wouldn't want it any other way. He might have picked up on a hint of suspicion when his new-found colleague and friend Saito insisted the suitcase bomb should stay in Japan.

Then there's my friendship with Li, she thought. In those few fleeting exchanges we had when Chen was in the crowded ops room he seemed different. Although he's a past master at covering up his emotions, I can always tell when something's off kilter. The question now is how do I broach this with him — alone, which is Saito's recommendation, or when the three of us are together as professionals?

She turned back towards the helicopter in silence. Whatever we do, she thought, we're going to have to inform Hasegawa ASAP. He'll then be obliged to brief the Prime Minister immediately. And what about Masataka? He'll be furious! He has so much political capital tied up in this.

PART 3

Chapter 19

Prime Minister's Office, Tokyo
Monday, 1727 hours

Chief Cabinet Secretary Ozawa stood before a forest of TV cameras and microphones to present the government's statement on recent events in Nagasaki.

Ozawa had long been considered an approachable government figure for the local media. As was his practice, he'd already provided a private briefing for senior journalists, suggesting questions they might like to ask and outlining the no-go areas.

Surprisingly, there'd been no leaks to the media about Prime Minister Hayashi's lightning visit nor the fact that NPA Chief Hasegawa had accompanied him. Blocking electronic communications in the immediate vicinity of the Uemura Inn over that critical thirty-six-hour period had proved effective. However, the media had clearly cottoned on to the fact that something much bigger than a drug bust had taken place in Nagasaki.

Ozawa signalled that the clicking of cameras and other devices should stop: he was ready to speak.

"I am now able to inform you," he said, in an authoritative voice, "that over the last few days, government agencies have been involved in a major anti-terror operation focused in Nagasaki City and adjacent areas. This was not a drill, although the training our forces regularly undergo definitely stood every officer involved in very good stead."

The journalists who had not received a prior briefing busily took notes, while those who had already spoken to Ozawa looked decidedly relaxed. Everyone knew how this game was played and that nothing was to be gained by bucking it. Media conferences like these were carefully controlled and the journalists who attended them were little more than government publicists. This had never sat well with Bella: why have a free press in a liberal democracy if it wasn't actually free?

Ozawa continued, "A group of Islamic State jihadists, operating initially out of Uzbekistan and more recently from a base in Southeast Asia, attempted to smuggle a cache of deadly weapons and explosives into Japan. With vital assistance from our counterpart agencies in both China and South Korea, we were able to apprehend the jihadists together with their cache of arms. The government is deeply grateful for the cooperation rendered to us by Beijing and by Seoul, and especially from Busan. There has been an outstanding degree of coordination between our three countries and the government hopes this can be reflected in other areas in the future."

What a pity, some of the journalists were thinking, that we won't be given details of this three-way operation. Must have been a big deal to bring something like that on!

Ozawa made no specific reference to the involvement of Li Weiming, General Chen, or Bella, but he did say, "The government also wishes to express its deep appreciation for the skilled assistance kindly afforded to us by the British government. This assistance was vital to the success of the recent operation and is testimony to the wisdom and experience of Britain's foreign agencies that have a much richer heritage than our own."

This sent some of the less-experienced journalists present into a tailspin. How could Britain possibly be part of this Nagasaki thing? Those in the know however, understood that Ozawa was buttering up the British.

"Now, I have an important request to make of you," he went on. "Because of the clandestine nature of this operation, which continues on a number of fronts, the government asks the media to desist from pressuring the agencies concerned for information. The same goes for the citizens of Nagasaki who may have witnessed certain events there. The government's priority at this stage is to cut this terrorist cancer out to the fullest possible extent. The safety and well-being of all Japanese and our country is paramount at this time."

Ozawa bowed slightly to indicate the conclusion of his statement.

"Might you answer a few questions, Cabinet Secretary?" asked a journalist from a major newspaper.

Ozawa nodded his assent.

"Was the operation restricted to the Nagasaki city area alone?"

"No, it extended to Tokyo, but the planned attacks were effectively thwarted quite early on."

"Will terrorist activity have any impact on the 2020 Summer Olympics?" another journalist asked, one who'd actually been pre-briefed.

Ozawa frowned slightly, then said, "The short answer is no, but we're now much better informed about where terrorists think our vulnerabilities are."

Ozawa bowed and quickly left the dais. His statement had been cleared with Beijing, Seoul and London, the Chinese carefully crafting a request for one minor change: that mention of Britain be left until last. Tokyo had been obliging on that point, and the Cabinet Secretary breathed a sigh of relief that no questions had been asked on it.

Li was now working with Saito and Masataka on a detailed chronological report of what had occurred, an edited version of which would be released in two to three weeks. The Busan Police Chief and a senior member of the Korean government were also in Tokyo working on that draft. Bella was only partially involved, due to the fact that Sir Crispin Grenville was keen to have her return full-time to the MI6 team working on a new overseas spy service for Japan.

Saito had informed Hasegawa about the suitcase scam, who in turn had briefed the Prime Minister. At the PM's request, only the Chief Cabinet Secretary and the Defence Minister were made aware of the manner in which China had attempted to exploit Operation Nagasaki. Much hung on a secret meeting due to take place just before midnight where Masataka, the main proponent of the triumvirate concept would be informed of China's antics.

Office of the Chief, NPA HQ, Tokyo
Monday, 2317 hours

Hasegawa and Li occupied a large meeting room adjacent to the chief's office. They sat alone at one end of the long, antique keyaki-wood table that had belonged to Japan's first police commissioner in the Meiji Period. They had only been together for a few minutes when there was a jaunty knock on the door. Saito had arrived with the others and by the sound of his knock, things were going well. Nothing to worry about, was the clear message it conveyed.

Saito entered with Bella and Masataka, who was the only person in the room not in the know.

"Take a seat," a confident Hasegawa said, gesturing to them. "I won't be staying. I've already explained to Li that while this room is extensively wired, the system is not switched on at the moment."

That drew a laugh from everyone. Bella was relieved to see the Chinese chicanery now out in the open and dealt with in a light-hearted way in Li's presence.

"He's graciously chosen to take me at my word," Hasegawa went on, giving Li an avuncular slap on the shoulder. "Let's face it, the only way to tie up all these loose ends is to trust each other. It's only trust that brought Operation Nagasaki to a satisfactory conclusion."

He then tapped Masataka warmly on the arm, something he'd never done before, and said, "Fear not, my friend. Overall, this is a wonderful story of friendship, professionalism, mutual cooperation and goodwill. Despite the efforts of some to heap shit on this wonderful collaboration, nothing can ever tarnish what we've achieved in the past week. It's absolutely extraordinary!"

With that, Hasegawa left the room, closing the door quietly behind him.

Masataka cast his eyes over the faces at the table and pleaded, partly in jest. "Put me out of my misery. What is this all about and who was heaping the shit?"

Li glanced at Bella, then they both looked at Saito.

"Would you prefer me to start?" he asked.

"Yes please, Saito San," Li replied. "I trust you implicitly."

Saito got straight down to business. "Masataka San, we're meeting here at this late hour because Li believes he may be under surveillance. He probably isn't, but just in case and because he's already in this building, we thought it would be best if you came to meet us here."

Masataka noticed a slightly embarrassed look in Li's eye.

"You'll recall those strictly Top Secret intelligence reports kindly provided by Li's agency? Well, they were instrumental to us blocking a jihadist attempt to attack both Nagasaki and Tokyo. The terror plan was real and the intelligence was real. It's all been a great success and we couldn't have pieced everything together without Li's help. Along the way the higher-ups in his organization, in their infinite wisdom, chose to add another layer to this already complicated exercise. Through an intermediary, they provided the Islamic State terror group in Uzbekistan with a late-model Russian nuclear suitcase bomb."

Masataka nodded. He was already acquainted with the detail, which didn't surprise the others.

"These IS Uzbeks also believed the device to be real, paying a high price for it. They managed to get it to Mindanao and it was smuggled into Japan via Busan. Li and Bella can tell you more about that later, but suffice it to say, we were all led to believe by the Chinese that this device was real and very dangerous. Someone in Beijing must have thought this would be a good way to maximise the value of the favour they were seen to be doing us."

Masataka shook his head, though not in a way that was hostile to Li. Masataka was not an angry man by nature, but Bella knew that insincerity on this scale made him burn.

"Now, Li was never aware that the suitcase bomb we'd been led to believe was real, was in fact a dud," Saito continued. "But a retired Chinese general who kindly came to Nagasaki to help us handle the bomb, let the cat out of the bag. In a private aside in the men's toilet, which we had bugged, he let Li in on the scam."

Masataka shot Li a sympathetic look.

"That's the story in a nutshell," Saito said. "Now, before I leave, let me sum up the current state of play. Li's pretty sure that the people he reports to don't know that we know. He would've been hauled back to Beijing if they did. General Chen also tried his hardest to take the suitcase with him, but I managed to hang on to it, with the full knowledge and approval of Hasegawa and the PM. Only two other cabinet ministers know about this and the PM wants to keep it that way for as long as possible."

Masataka nodded in agreement.

"So, can you three take it from here?" Saito asked tentatively. He would have stayed if they'd invited him to, but the strain of the last few days was starting to take its toll.

"We most certainly can," Masataka replied.

A tired Saito then opened the door and backed out of the room bowing, as was the custom when deferring to more senior people. It was a warm, almost theatrical gesture, which made them all laugh, including Saito himself. Masataka was astonished. Saito, an inveterate tech-head, had clearly been transformed. It was something to behold.

He turned to Li and said in Japanese, "Zenzen heiki yo: I'm completely at ease with this."

"And, it's getting late," he said, looking at his watch. "We could all do with a good night's sleep, especially you two. Bella tells me you're staying in Tokyo until the end of the week. Let's have dinner tomorrow night – just the three of us. Would that work for you?"

Li smiled broadly.

Chapter 20

Tokyo Club
Tuesday, 1215 hours

"Look, Hasegawa, we've known each other for many years," Nakamura Keita, a rightwing politician from the House of Representatives said with an air of disappointment and puzzlement. "What did those confounded Chinese put in your tea down there in Nagasaki?"

Hasegawa gazed out of the floor-to-ceiling window on to the soothing vista of a walled Japanese garden. He felt intensely frustrated, and Nakamura had a bad habit of raising his voice.

The exclusive club, since the 1880s, had been the only gentlemen's establishment in Tokyo modelled on its London counterparts. Now housed in an ultra-modern, though quintessentially Japanese building near the American Embassy, members customarily spoke in hushed tones.

If Nakamura dares to speak loudly in here, Hasegawa thought, someone might tip off an opposition member who'd be only too eager to raise his indiscretions on the floor of the House. That wouldn't auger well for his ambition to become more involved in national security matters. People with loud voices simply couldn't be trusted with such matters. He recalled Bella saying something along the lines of 'spies avoid loud-mouths like the plague'.

"Listen to what I'm saying and you'll understand," Hasegawa said in a polite but serious tone. "Fundamentally, nothing's changed. It's just that recent events have taught me much more about China and the threat it poses to us. To put it simply, my friend, we have to equip ourselves to play the Chinese more effectively at their own game."

Nakamura grunted in response. He was built like a battering ram and had been a star rugby player before entering politics.

"I hear you," he replied, a look of disdain on his face, "but I can't see how we can ever trust them."

The waiter took their order and removed the wine glasses. Neither wanted alcohol at this time of day, nor did they have time to dilly dally. Nakamura was a notoriously slow eater.

Once the waiter had left, Hasegawa leaned forward and said quietly, "I understand why you say that and I don't disagree. But we have to be realistic. The problem with the Chinese is detecting the angles they're playing in any dealings you have with them. There's always more than one dimension to any scenario. Sometimes there are several. And, OK, we do that too. Who doesn't? But the Chinese have elevated game-playing to an art form, and nowadays they have much greater clout and are able to enforce their own will."

Nakamura grunted again. He was renowned for his doggedness, his gravelly voice like sandpaper. But he was politically astute and highly influential.

"I wish I could be more specific about what happened in Nagasaki," Hasegawa said, lowering his tone for effect, "but I can't. It's better you don't know at this stage. Hardly anyone does, and please don't go sniffing around trying to find out. That'll only make matters worse."

Hasegawa thought to himself that even a half-confidence shared with Nakamura would be better than none. It would keep him onside.

"Suffice it to say, the Chinese played us. Even though they'd helped us enormously, they just couldn't resist a sting in the tail. In a way, I almost admire them for their clever and devious tactics. But I cannot abide their dirty attempt to take the mickey out of us on matters of great importance to Japan. They always have to have the upper hand. What they've done sticks in my craw."

Nakamura warmed to this private insight.

"In my office last night," Hasegawa continued, "I caught a few seconds of your parliamentary colleague, Fujii, on TV. He was frothing at the mouth about the very idea of Japan, South Korea and China signing a trade deal. I accept we need to think that one through carefully, but the way Fujii goes at it reminds me of a cranky terrier that just won't let go of your trouser cuff."

This time Nakamura's grunt signalled begrudging agreement, which spurred Hasegawa to push harder. He had his own plans and ambitions, and to realise them he had to get the anti-China hawks in the Japanese parliament to tone down their rhetoric.

"While I concede Fujii does make some interesting points," he continued, "his irrational pack mentality troubles me. He's against any deal of any description with China and he utilises the worst form of nationalistic jingoism to support his argument. He comes across as a bigot, mouthing the same old anti-China lines endlessly. That won't get us anywhere."

Hasegawa hoped that he'd at least put Nakamura into neutral gear, which was no mean achievement. Persuading him to move ahead in a more positive way would be the trick.

"Look Nakamura, the old guard in China that you and I know so well, is still there but it's morphed into something much slicker, more lethal, more street-wise on the international stage and more willing than ever to use its strength and position to get what it wants. We ain't seen nothing yet!"

Nakamura sat back in his chair and scowled at Hasegawa, but said nothing. Hasegawa was on a roll.

"Our friend Fujii," he said, waving his hand dismissively, "even called China the Nazi Germany of the 21st century. OK, you and I might agree with that in many ways, but where does it get us? Where does that sort of talk get Japan? Replaying the Second World War or re-heating Cold War slogans won't achieve anything. Moreover, I now realise how it alienates a younger generation of Chinese coming through the system: gifted young people who can possibly act as, how should I put it? ... intermediaries, who understand the value of meeting us halfway."

Nakamura was nodding now, though ever so slightly. Hasegawa took this as a positive sign. Knowing how the man's mind worked, he sensed that he'd found an in where none had existed before.

"We have to be slicker too," he continued. "We have to change our rhetoric, change the face we present to the Chinese, play them at their own game. There's no other way for us to survive. My offsider, Kuroda, told me this morning he'd heard the PM distancing himself from Fujii. Apparently, when asked what he thought of that kind of rhetoric Hayashi said it simply didn't meet the high standards expected of all government members, that he didn't condone it."

A gust of wind outside bent the stands of bamboo in the garden, as though reinforcing what the Prime Minister had said.

"Now, why do you reckon he said that?" Hasegawa continued. "It's not just because he has to as PM. I'll tell you why. Truth is, he's shocked at how the Chinese tried to toy with us, like a cat monstering a mouse. Hayashi and I know exactly what happened in Nagasaki and we don't like it one bit. It's galling! But we also know that jumping up and down like recalcitrant children isn't going to get us anywhere."

Now Hasegawa could see he'd managed to penetrate Nakamura's thick skin. While the man chewed his food in silence, he readied to deliver the final blow.

"I want to leave you with two thoughts," Hasegawa said in a hushed tone. "Firstly, Hayashi's fully onside with my idea of creating a Japanese FBI. I plan to vacuum up those piss ant appendages like the Public Security Intelligence Agency and dissolve them into this wider structure. Furthermore, I'm determined to have this new MI6-

style spy service that the British are helping us set up lodged under my umbrella too. I'll call it the Homeland Security Agency."

"Oh, I like that!" Nakamura responded, the most animated he'd been all luncheon.

"Well, if you play your cards right," Hasegawa said with an obsequious smile, "you could find yourself chairman of the parliamentary committee that oversees it."

Nakamura's smirk indicated the appeal of that suggestion.

"And what was the second thought you wanted to leave with me?" he asked.

Hasegawa paused for effect before leaning forward and growling, "Tone down your rhetoric and get Fujii and his bunch to do the same."

Prime Minister's Office
Tuesday, 1527 hours

Sakamoto Masataka was the last to join them. The Gaimusho, Japan's Foreign Ministry, which regarded him as an annoying gadfly, had not been advised of the meeting, let alone of his attendance. To have alerted them would have given rise to outrage, the last thing the Prime Minister needed now.

"Ah, our mystery guest arrives!" Hayashi said, greeting Masataka. Their warm handshake showed how close the two were.

Bella and Sir Crispin Grenville were already there, not in the PM's usual meeting room for visitors, but in a much smaller more intimate area that had no table and just four comfortable armchairs.

"Another clandestine huddle, eh?" Masataka observed in English, drawing a laugh from the others.

"Indeed," Hayashi agreed, his own English at a near comparable level. "The last few weeks have seen a flurry of activity, the likes of which I've never experienced in this office. My Prime Ministerial duties have precluded me from focusing on the Nagasaki Operation as much as I'd have liked. But it's clearly been in the hands of very capable people and we've achieved a positive outcome – despite the crude antics of our Chinese friends. For that, I'm most grateful."

He gestured towards Bella and bowed his head in a display of appreciation.

"Your role in all this, Miss Butterfield, defies easy description," he continued. "You do your Service proud."

Bella thanked him with a similar considered inclination of her head. Grenville, sitting alongside her, was beaming. She was well aware of the significance the success of this operation had for him. It boosted MI6's stocks enormously.

"Now, let's get down to business," the PM said. "I've invited you here today for this strictly unofficial meeting – much like my visit to Nagasaki that never happened."

But this meeting certainly was happening, and it had put the British ambassador's nose quite out of joint. He demanded to be included, only desisting when Sir Crispin threatened to take the matter up directly with Downing Street. MI6's task in Japan was far more important than the ambassador's preoccupation with diplomatic protocol. And besides, to all intents and purposes, this meeting was strictly off the books: no one in the Japanese bureaucratic system knew anything about it.

Hayashi checked his watch. "I have a full hour," he said, "and I'd appreciate your independent and candid view on a number of matters. It's extremely difficult for me to get that here, as you can appreciate. Luckily, Masataka and I think along the same lines, but the issues I'm wrestling with now will impact greatly on Japan's well-being. I have to get this right, so please be frank."

This posed no challenge for Bella. She'd never been unnerved by seniority or high political office.

"Let me start with the Chinese," Hayashi continued. "I don't plan any overt nor covert reaction or retaliation against them over the suitcase bomb stunt. If my dealings with them over the years are anything to go by, I'd say the Chinese are just being Chinese. That's what they do. Throwing a tantrum won't change anything and will make Japan look bad. We have to be far more cunning and sharper-witted in managing our relations with China, just as Saito was in Nagasaki."

He gestured to Grenville, the most senior in years of the four at the gathering.

"Precisely, Mr Prime Minister," the Englishman replied, with a touch of formality due to the nature of their discussion. "I gather no information about the suitcase bomb has seeped out to your parliamentary colleagues nor the media?"

"So far, no," Hayashi said. "You can imagine Fujii and his co-conspirators having a field day if they had the slightest inkling. No word has yet reached the Gaimusho either, nor have I confided anything to our incumbent Foreign Minister, whom I intend to replace soon with Masataka."

Masataka glanced at Bella, raising an eyebrow. He seemed in no way surprised and she marvelled at the matter-of-fact way in which Hayashi had imparted that momentous piece of information.

Grenville picked up the theme without skipping a beat saying, "The key thing about this recent encounter is that Saito managed to hold onto the suitcase. It didn't go back to China with General Chen. This will be a source of great displeasure for them, knowing as they do now that they've been beaten at their own game. The Chinese know you'll pass it onto the Americans, a very galling prospect indeed.

"In my humble opinion, Mr Prime Minister, Saito's adamant stance will have earned him great respect, and by extension Japan. You've scored a noteworthy run, to use cricketing parlance, and I agree, you don't need to consider retaliation of any kind," Grenville concluded.

"How about Li's status in all this?" PM Hayashi asked. "I already know Bella and Masataka agree that he wasn't privy to any of this nonsense." Grenville deferred to Bella who addressed the issue head on.

"That is correct, Prime Minister. Masataka and I feel there's nothing to be concerned about on this score. If Li's Chinese masters didn't trust him they would not have allowed him to come up to Tokyo to assist us with the final report. Of course, he's still their man, and will be debriefed later on who he met and what he did in Tokyo et cetera. But he'll play down his relationship with Masataka whom he met in Beijing at my introduction before Nagasaki, and me, as he's always done. When he returns to Beijing at the end of the week, Masataka will maintain contact with him on the three-way cooperation concept as far as it relates to the science and technology spheres. That way, a line can be drawn under the Nagasaki incident."

Hayashi expressed satisfaction with that approach then said, "This leads me to something crucial to my government right now. Our NPA Chief, Hasegawa, is endlessly in my ear about establishing a new FBI set-up. I actually think such a body could serve Japan very well, bundling together a number of loose ends in our system at present and bringing them all under one roof." Everyone nodded their agreement before stopping short at what the PM said next.

"But I don't want Hasegawa to run it. I'm afraid I just don't trust him. His ambitions and ideas I can handle, but not his fluctuating stances. Before Nagasaki happened he was a thinly disguised anti-China hawk, closely associated with the likes of Nakamura and that loud-mouthed Fujii. Then, in the blink of an eye, he suddenly changed his tune on the Chinese, thanks no doubt to Li's brilliance and the way he and Saito worked together so effectively. And let's not forget that this was your introduction,

Miss Butterfield," the PM said gravely. How true, Bella mused to herself. A short time ago I was the Butter Bitch and now I'm Saint Isabella!

"While he's unamused by the suitcase issue," the PM continued, "Hasegawa no doubt believes he can beat the Chinese at their own game. I sincerely hope we're able to do that, but I don't see him as the appropiate person to captain the team. My duty is to put someone in charge who's stable and reliable and whom I can trust implicity."

Bella stirred in her seat, which caught Hayashi's eye. "You have concerns?" he asked. "Not in the least," Bella said. "It's just that Sir Crispin and I would rather hear Masataka's view before we presume to offer an opinion that is in any way useful."

"How I wish I could be so deferential in English!" Hayashi said, smiling, before returning to the point. "Let me tell you something, Bella and Sir Crispin. Masataka's aware of this, but I propose to place this new security organisation in the hands of Saito. He's already agreed to take on the job and he wants Kim as his deputy, along with Kuroda, currently Hasegawa's right-hand-man. Kuroda's long been my man, how might you English say it? … my fly on the wall at the NPA. He's balanced, professional and gets on well with Saito. The three of them will make a formidable team, I believe."

While there was no dissent on that score, there was one big question hanging over their heads: how would Hasegawa react to this plan to unseat him? It was then that Hayashi revealed something highly disturbing.

Chapter 21

Shibuya Ward, Tokyo
Wednesday, 0021 hours

It was late when Kuroda arrived at Saito's home. Neither looked forward to the task they had to perform. But it boiled down to a matter of duty and to the security of Japan.

Saito's wife and children were asleep so the pair crept into the kitchen at the back of the house and closed the door quietly. Sitting at the table, Saito switched on his laptop as Kuroda produced the USBs he'd been asked to bring.

The pair had recently discovered that Chief Hasegawa had established a direct channel of communication with the FBI, one that wasn't routed through the NPA's standard network. It had been a complicated process but Saito had finally worked out how they could access this private channel, while remaining undetected. There were certain passwords that he knew and others he could figure out that would probably give them access. It was the sort of circuitous route that only Saito could map out. Kuroda's job was to download the data Saito had designated.

"You're a wizard," Kuroda quipped as Saito downloaded, cross-referenced files, then keyed in various passwords.

Kuroda was in his mid-forties with a pleasing

and confident manner. He was also exceptionally bright, which had a lot to do with why they were friends.

"My daughter's made a tray of sushi for us," Saito mumbled, pointing to the refrigerator while his eyes remained fixed on the screen, "and there's a huge bowl of your favourite gobo in there too. Leave some for me."

Kuroda found the food, placed it on the table and turned to a draw where he knew they kept the chopsticks. He sat down again and pushed the gobo closer to Saito, who nibbled on it as he often did when in deep concentration.

Some twenty minutes passed before Saito had his light bulb moment.

"We're in!" he declared.

Kuroda pulled his chair closer and watched the first document come up on the screen.

Addressee Eyes Only.
From Singleton,
Chief, FBI Division 4.

Soon after your Filipino preacher Roberto Cruz instructed other Uzbek jihadists to remain in Mindanao and not travel to Japan, Beijing used contact in office of President of Philippines to get approval for China to launch clandestine raid in Mindanao. Beijing could have acted alone but sought approval to curry favour. This is of great concern because it cuts across longstanding and extensive anti-terror work United States is engaged in with Phil/ Gov in Mindanao.

Targets were apprehended by Chinese operatives and removed by Zodiac to CH/naval vessel where they were extensively interrogated. Our NSA intercepts indicate resulting intelligence was not transferred to main Beijing database, which explains why CH operative assisting you in Nagasaki didn't know about it. CIA and other reports on this operative indicate he's an independent thinker, a maverick tolerated because of rare analytical and other abilities. Can provide further reporting if required.

Regards, Singleton.

Saito and Kuroda's worst suspicions had been confirmed. Hasegawa had not shared this additional intelligence with the operation in Nagasaki, a professionally unconscionable act. Saito opened the next document in the chain, a repeat of an earlier transmission that had been received then deleted. Hasegawa had clearly not replied.

Addressee Eyes Only.
From Singleton,
Chief, FBI Division 4.

Received no response to earlier message so repeating herewith. Assume you're pre-occupied with events in Nagasaki.

Report of Filipino sleeper cell operating in Tokyo confirmed. Cover is Cruz's Christian activities in Tokyo. NSA intercepts reveal three Filipino Muslims involved have had no detectable contact with two Pakistani jihadists you now have in custody, which probably explains why your interrogation did not uncover this.

Filipino threesome live under assumed names and false documentation in house in Setagaya Ward rented in Cruz's name. Cover is shelter for Filipinos resident in Japan engaged in spreading word of Christian Gospel. With such status, group receives rent supplement from Japanese government under program to assist South East Asian nationals under age of 35 either studying or engaged in cultural or non-commercial activities in Japan.

Threesome appeared to panic following Cruz's failure to contact them at pre-arranged time during his trip by van from Nagasaki to Tokyo. They didn't try his cell phone, clearly on strict instructions not to. Having been

informed by Cruz's sister that she
had no idea of his whereabouts or
what he was doing, they also called
HADRIAN, another Californian
resident and known Islamic State
supporter. Aged 42, and a former US
Marine, he is currently undergoing
interrogation by us in LA. Looks
like a goldmine. Do you want full
transcript or summary? Will await
your response.

Regards, Singleton.

"How could he not tell us this?" Kuroda said in a low but angry voice.

Saito was dumbfounded, saying, "And none of this has so far cropped up in our interrogations of the Preacher. If we'd been informed of this we'd have gone in hard again on him. Well, we'll certainly begin doing that now. There's no other way to put it, we've been betrayed."

Saito's face was pale and tired. He'd even lost interest in the gobo.

"But why?" he said, almost to himself. He checked the time, then turned to Kuroda and said, "Let's read a few more before sending a surveillance squad to that so-called shelter in Setagaya."

As Saito brought the next document up, both wondered if the other was thinking the same thing.

*****

Setagaya Ward
Wednesday, 0154 hours

Hasegawa walked the short distance from his home to a nearby childrens' playground. He'd put on a raincoat because of the drizzle and was smoking a cigarette, the first from a fresh pack.

The central light in the playground had been out for weeks and, on a night like this, there was no one around. He spotted his contact beyond the low hedge of azaleas before reaching the open gate. They exchanged no greetings and remained standing.

"We nabbed the first of them late yesterday evening," Hasegawa's contact reported, "and press ganged him into calling the other two on his phone. They were already at home. He told them he'd bumped into someone he wanted them to meet and they should come to this playground."

Hasegawa was relieved to hear this.

"His two mates suspected nothing and were here within five minutes," the contact continued. "We had a small delivery truck parked outside the other gate over there. All three of them were lured into the back without any trouble, on the promise of quantities of drugs with a high street value. After we'd rendered them permanently useless, if you know what I mean, we took their house-keys and went to search their place."

Hasegawa remained silent. At least that's the three Filipinos out of the way, he was thinking with relief.

"We gathered up laptops and a few electronic

devices, plus we found their passports and other documents as well, things that shouldn't be left lying around. We packed it all up in three suitcases with some of their clothes and a few other sentimental items and then left. It will look like they cleared off."

Hasegawa drew heavily on his cigarette, then tossed it on the ground and screwed the butt out with the heel of his shoe. The contact offered him a fresh one and lit it for him.

"You OK?"

"I'm fine," Hasegawa replied, "just glad you've gotten rid of that evidence. Thanks."

"Don't mention it. It's what friends are for."

Hasegawa simply nodded. It was good to have friends, but some were better than others — and different, too. Some friends also came at a high price.

"We'll have someone drop into the estate agents later this morning," the contact added. "We can say the lads had to move to northern Japan urgently to look after a church whose pastor has been taken ill suddenly. The lease will need to be paid out. That will settle things."

"Hopefully," said Hasegawa.

"Don't worry," his contact said, consolingly. "We'll fix it and anyway, you should be applying your mind to much more than housekeeping matters like these, eh?"

"Yes, I suppose," Hasegawa replied, with a nervous laugh. "I'm just relieved, so very relieved. I've been dreading front-page headlines like, Filipino Jihadists Found Living Near NPA Chief's House!"

"Not a good look," his contact said with a

snort, "especially when they were posing as trainee Christian missionaries."

This was far from a laughing matter for Hasegawa who was, at that moment, in much deeper trouble than he could ever have imagined.

Shibuya Ward
Wednesday, 0214 hours

Saito and Kuroda were less than a quarter of the way through Hasegawa's secret communications trove. They were tired but resolved to read one more FBI report before calling it a night.

```
Addressee Eyes Only.
From Singleton,
Chief, FBI Division 4.

Interrogation      of      HADRIAN,
the   American   IS   supporter   in
California,   still   under   way.
Herewith  overview  at  this  early
stage  for  your  consumption:
As  a  US  Marine,  he  served  in  a
number  of  war  zones  in  Islamic
countries. When NSA analysed his
comms traffic an incredibly complex
network  emerged.  Not  only  has  he
been  proselytising  as  an  Islamic
State   sympathiser   with   serving
and  former  soldiers  in  the  US, but
also  with  those  serving  overseas.
Both  us  and  NSA  agree  HADRIAN's
been  remarkably  clever  in  covering
```

his tracks, to the extent that this is first time he's come up on our radar. Of immediate concern to you in Japan will be fact that some of those Muslim soldiers are serving in US forces there and in South Korea. They too have been promoting IS cause. This whole scenario is rapidly becoming big and ugly. Fasten your seatbelt. Will revert ASAP.

Regards, Singleton.

"Another storm front like Nagasaki," Kuroda speculated, shaking his head. "How much deeper does this go?"

"This could very quickly turn into the perfect storm Nagasaki might have been if the suitcase bomb had turned out to be real! It reminds me of the Aum Shinrikyo doomsday cult that had followers in the most unexpected parts of the government system, including the Self-Defence Forces and beyond. Let's pray our agency isn't infected in the same way. The interface between US Forces here and in Korea is, as Deng Xiaoping put it years ago, as close as lips and teeth."

"And the Chief's done nothing about it," Kuroda added.

"No, he hasn't," Saito replied thoughtfully, "which brings us back to the question of why. This will have to be taken up directly with the PM, and that'll be delicate. Hayashi's a trustworthy man who,

I believe, has the country's best interests at heart. But we can't ignore the pressure all this will put on his government."

Kuroda nodded, thinking that politics is like a firestorm that burns everyone in its path, with no concessions for decency and honour.

"But before we approach Hayashi," Saito added decisively, "there's something else we should do. What I have in mind is unorthodox in the extreme and probably the most dangerous and extraordinary thing we'll ever do in this job."

Chapter 22

Hibiya Park, Opposite the Imperial Hotel, Tokyo
Wednesday, 0735 hours

It was a gusty morning with low cloud and a chill in the air. They found a bench slightly removed from the streams of office workers taking a short cut through the park.

Saito and Kuroda had made contact with Bella and Li, and they'd readily agreed to meet. No questions were asked, but both understood it must be a matter of the highest priority.

Bella said in Japanese, "Two senior officers from the National Police Agency, a Chinese and a British spy all looking chummy on a park bench in the centre of Tokyo. You don't see that every day!"

They all laughed, after which Saito got straight down to business.

He looked at Li and said, "After Nagasaki, Kuroda and I trust you and Bella implicitly. Right now, we need to plug into this braintrust to help Japan out of a very threatening situation. In effect, we're asking you and Bella to step back from your respective agencies and nationalities and to, how can I put it? ... go neutral for a moment."

The expression on Saito's and Kuroda's faces spoke volumes for the seriousness of the request. Bella glanced at Li then back at Saito.

"Early this morning, Kuroda and I managed

to break into a secret comms line that Haseagawa's been running for some time. Up until a few hours ago, this line has only been accessible to him," Saito said, allowing himself a fleeting congratulatory smile. "Our Chief's been in direct contact with a senior FBI manager in New York about everything we grappled with in Nagasaki. Reading these secret emails, we've discovered extra dimensions to that saga that Hasegawa never shared with us during or since Operation Nagasaki."

Bella and Li nodded in unison as Saito revealed the content of the FBI cables, particularly those dealing with fundamentalist infiltration of US military forces in Japan and South Korea.

I reckon I know what's coming, Bella thought, and I'd be surprised if it's not the same thing the PM was alluding to at our meeting with Masataka and Sir Crispin yesterday afternoon.

"There's a stack of material we haven't had time to wade through yet," continued Saito, "but from what we've already seen in the early hours of this morning we think Hasegawa must have been holding back for a reason. We just can't figure out why. Doing so didn't help Operation Nagasaki, and it doesn't help our Agency nor even Hasegawa as its Chief. It certainly hasn't helped Japan's national security. So the question remains: why? Kuroda and I have our suspicions."

Bella and Li exchanged a knowing glance.

"We're all on the same wavelength, I think," Bella said. "When behaviour like what you've discovered about Hasegawa is irrational and inexplicable to senior officers like you two, who've worked alongside him for years, there's usually only one reason, and it's an utterly distasteful one – treachery. Perhaps he's being blackmailed over something in his private or professional life? Possibly, he's just a puppet, obliged to respond to whoever's pulling the strings, to save himself from whatever predicament he's gotten himself into."

She hesitated briefly before imparting what the Prime Minister had said.

"As I'm sure you know, Masataka and Grenville and I met with Hayashi briefly yesterday afternoon. He raised the issue of Hasegawa's recent behaviour, singling out his staunchly anti-China stance before Nagasaki, and decidedly pro stance after, as an example. The PM told us that some time ago he and Fujii were talking about the spy service we're helping Japan set up and Hasegawa's name had been mentioned. Apparently, in an oblique aside, Fujii warned him to be wary of Hasegawa, that he may well prove to be someone else's man. Hayashi assumed the comment meant Hasegawa might be too cosy with a rival faction in his government's ranks or perhaps he might even be courting members of the opposition. That set us thinking, though we kept our suspicions to ourselves."

She looked at Li, who immediately reacted, saying, "That's fascinating. From what you've told us Saito San, I'm assuming the nature of your's and Kuroda's suspicions are the same as Bella's and mine. We both get the distinct impression Hasegawa's been turned, that he's working for other interests.

And it sounds as though he's in really deep."

"That's what Saito and I are worried about," Kuroda said. "It's an unthinkable situation to find ourselves in. Our own Chief is a traitor."

"But for whom is the real question," said Li. "Let's start at the top of the pyramid of possibilities and work our way down. Hasegawa's unlikely to have been turned by the yakuza, so it has to be a foreign spy service. That's probably what we're dealing with here, wouldn't you agree, Bella?"

"Agreed," she said, picking up on Li's inclusive language. This was now a problem that belonged to all four of them. They'd have to come up with a joint solution.

Li said, "Let me tell you first up, that I don't think he's being run by my service. Of course, after the events of Nagasaki, it's possible he is one of ours and I've not been told, but that's most unlikely. If it were the case, I'd have been briefed on how to protect such a sensitive relationship and maybe even charged with the task of enhancing it while I'm in Japan. I think we can categorically rule that out."

Bella nodded. This is Weiming in top gear, she mused affectionately.

"Of course, we need to consider the Americans," he continued. "Why, knowing what the FBI knows, would they have let a thing like this run on? Maybe the FBI are still trying to work out what Hasegawa's up to and aren't ready to act yet. If they were, they could easily invite him to visit the United States for consultations on something sensitive, take him into custody there, then confront the Japanese government with his treachery via back channels. He'd be quietly returned to Tokyo and handed over to the Japanese authorities for processing."

No one disagreed with Li's logic. He turned to Bella, who was nodding and then said, "That leaves one very likely candidate. The Russians."

"That's what Kuroda and I think," Saito said, in a way that told the others this gelled with their suspicions.

"Assuming it is the Russians who've recruited him," Bella said, "let's look at what they'd want from him. A dead giveaway for me is Hasegawa's determination to establish a broad-reaching FBI-type agency, with Japan's brand new overseas spy service under the same umbrella."

Saito and Kuroda were all ears. Getting this sort of perspective was what they'd been hoping for.

"That would be a coup of the first order for Vladimir Putin," Bella continued, "having a man in Moscow's pay sitting at the very top of Japan's new spy apparatus, giving Russia direct access to shared British and particularly American intelligence. It would also provide indirect access to the Five Eyes Intelligence club, encompassing Australia, Canada and New Zealand."

Li chipped in here, saying his colleagues in Beijing referred to the 'Five Eyes' as the most powerful intelligence network in the world. Saito looked at Li and smiled. They both knew China wanted access to that network just as much as Russia, if not more.

"I'm sure there'd be something else in Putin's mind too," Kuroda proffered, "and that's the Richard

Sorge case here in wartime Tokyo. As an ex-KGB man, Putin would be only too aware of how that German journalist worked as a spy for the Soviet Union in the early 1940s. Via his contacts in the German Embassy in Tokyo, Sorge gained access to vital Nazi intelligence. He was able to warn Stalin that Hitler wasn't planning to attack with Japan in the east. This allowed Moscow to pull back the many army divisions in Siberia, a huge help in the defence of the motherland against German advances from the west. Now that's what you call an intelligence coup."

Bella nodded and said, "Let's not dismiss the significance of possible Islamic State penetration of US forces in Japan. Putin would want nothing more than to see US, Japanese and South Korean forces weakened in this part of the world in such a substantive way."

"And," Li interrupted, "another win for Putin would be to have Islamic State smuggle nerve agents into Japan for release into the subway system, or worse, at the Opening Ceremony of the Olympic Games. The Games would be cancelled – a major blow to Japan as the host nation."

There was a momentary silence before Saito checked his watch.

"We've only been together twenty-odd minutes," he said, "and you've helped us enormously. There are other Russian matters that Kuroda and I have encountered that more or less confirm this, but there's no time to go into that now."

As they all stood to go, Saito shared one final

thing with Bella and Li.

"I already have a surveillance squad I can trust," he said, "tailing Hasegawa night and day. They're keeping to the shadows and Kuroda and I are keeping tabs on his comms as well."

"Good luck with all this," Bella said. "Feel free to run checks via me and Grenville with MI6 and MI5 if you need."

*****

As Li headed for Haneda Airport in a Chinese Embassy car he excused himself to the driver, with whom he'd been chatting, and opened the letter from Bella that he'd had no time to read.

Her hand-written note was in English, on plain paper, with a cigarette drawn at the top of the first page. Between them, that meant burn after reading.

My dearest Weiming,

Just a few lines to let you know that PM Hayashi is going ahead, though warily, with the China-Japan-South Korea joint research triumvirate concept. He'll announce it further down the track once the air has cleared. Let's face it, he has a lot on his plate at the moment, and General Chen's trickery over the suitcase bomb has done irreparable damage. It makes China look untrustworthy at the very moment it's trying to draw Japan and South Korea into a new and creative relationship.

Hayashi will commit $US1 billion to a trilateral long-term relationship, but to assuage the anti-China *hawks in the Japanese parliament, the funds will be released over time in four separate instalments. The first $US250 million will be the initial announcement, covering a number of medical research projects that Japan and South Korea are already involved in, but packaged as a threeway arrangement. The PM has spoken to the Koreans about it. He didn't let on about the fake suitcase bomb, however he intimated that he's more than pissed off with Beijing's recent cavalier behaviour. The Koreans agree that China should be very closely monitored during the first part of this threeway collaboration.*

The Koreans even joked that all China has achieved is to bring Japan and Korea closer together, which let's face it, is no mean feat!

Masataka's OK with that and has been given overall control of the intiative. But he's still cranky about what's happened. It's going to be a long haul for China to win back his trust. The challenge for China will be to match that undertaking and things will roll on from there. I hope the overall plan does ultimately get off the ground, but as you and I appreciate, there's a powerful urge not to trust China too readily on the intellectual property rights and industrial espionage fronts particularly. Unfortunate, but realistic.

Now to matters personal. We still didn't have a chance to talk about our own future, through no fault of our own!

The scene you described of us fishing on a lake, with a cottage that we share up on the hill behind us, set me thinking. I see roses growing over our front porch, a vegetable patch we would tend together and

I can almost smell the mountain air.

Weiming, I'm no longer concerned about my biological clock. I don't feel that pressure in our relationship any more. Of course, it would have been nice to have children together. But I don't think that's ever really been a necessary part of our friendship, at least not for me.

As we've discussed many times, there's no point in one of us resigning from our respective service to be with the other. That scenario would never be accepted by either side. There would always be grave suspicion about whether you or me had really left the game behind.

What we may well do in the future, though, hopefully long before we're in our dotage, is to both resign and set about writing quirky spy novels together. Imagine them featuring a cross-cultural couple trapped in professional Catch 22 situations – damned if they did, and damned if they didn't.

Didn't your father used to say that the best decision a person ever makes is to decide not to decide right now, but to set a time up ahead when that decision can be reviewed?

I think that's what we should do, at least until we know the time for any decision is right.

None of this changes the fact that we are kindred spirits who have chosen to travel the path of life together. That is such a great gift, one that I'm grateful for every day.

With much love and affection, as always,

Bella

PS: Saito got Hayashi's permission to request MI6 runs a check with the NSA in the US on Hasegawa's secret comms line. Turns out, that FBI chap, Singleton, had smelt something fishy and reported it to the NSA already. They found Hasegawa was using that line for all sorts of shady activity, including illicit fund-raising for government members hoping to topple Hayashi. Grenville got London to put our own GCHQ on it and they discovered that some time ago, the Russians managed to hack into Hasegawa's secret comms line and have been blackmailing him ever since. It seems he started off in a small way, but before he knew it was caught up in all sorts of shonky deals and was way out of his depth. He should have stuck to police work and stayed away from the world of spies and politicians!

Postscript

The Preacher, along with Yousef and Ramsi, were dispatched to an interrogation centre within a federal penitentiary in the United States. He was subjected to more persistent questioning and despite his effete manner, he proved much tougher than anyone had imagined. The Japanese government was pleased to see all of them leave the country, where they would have been an embarrassment in the local prison system.

Ramsi's fate was uncertain, but Yousef's was more promising. Bella formally recommended, via the MI6 chief in London, that he be considered as a possible instructor for the American de-radicalisation program.

Yumi in Nagasaki had been exposed as an informant in Hasegawa's network, established to collect information and intelligence for his Russian masters. She had been tasked by Hasegawa to monitor and report on Saito's innovative technology used in the NPA's surveillance communication system. The traitor's network was revealed to have spread across all four main islands of Japan.

Hasegawa himself was remarkably forthcoming under interrogation, incentivised no doubt by a government guarantee that he would not face criminal prosecution. Soon after Operation Nagasaki drew to a formal close, he agreed to retire on medical grounds. Though this was a complete fabrication, that's what was publicly announced. A rumour was also deliberately spread that Hasegawa was suffering from lung cancer which fitted neatly with his notorious smoking habit.

Saito, the new head of the NPA, with his trusted colleagues Kim and Kuroda, pushed for annual polygraph testing for all NPA employees, as well as all staff appointed to Japan's new overseas spy service.

AUTHOR'S NOTE

When Japan opened up to the West in the mid-19th century it quickly realised how much it had to learn about the world it had closed itself away from for some 250 years. Emperor Meiji was restored to the throne in 1868 to sit at the pinnacle of a new German-style parliamentary system – from which the word Diet is derived. 'Sons of Meiji', the brightest young men of the time, were dispatched overseas to study such things as engineering, railways, shipbuilding, medicine and law.

When this writer arrived in Japan in the 1970s to study, the Japanese doctor I consulted wrote his prescription for medication in German, a practice that continued for many years before the switch to Japanese was finally made. All Japanese medical practitioners and pharmacists were well versed in German technical language though few ever learnt how to speak the language itself.

The Sons of Meiji didn't just study and train overseas. They were obliged to compile reports in their native tongue on everything they saw and experienced. These reports were widely disseminated back in Japan and this well-orchestrated process was, in effect, a massive intelligence gathering exercise. It helped the country industrialise and generate wealth for its citizens.

Japan emulated the West in creating colonies of its own in Korea and Formosa (present-day Taiwan).

By 1931, when it invaded Manchuria, it was firmly set on a nationalist-militarist path. It drove deeper into China, and ultimately challenged the United States by attacking Pearl Harbour, resulting in the Pacific War. The brutal legacy of that period dogs Japan to this day.

With the end of that war in 1945, Japan quickly set about rebuilding its devastated industrial machine. Once again, large numbers of businessmen were dispatched overseas to scour the globe for the knowledge and resources the country needed. They established a new intelligence gathering system, this time with Japanese trading companies in the vanguard, followed by banks and a wide variety of manufacturers, carmakers and exporters of consumer products.

Once the reports generated by these overseas operations were received at their corporate headquarters, many were passed on to the Japanese government. While this was a makeshift intelligence system in many ways, it worked magnificently while Japan's economic model was in the ascent. The 'Asian Tigers' – South Korea, Taiwan, Singapore and even China – all followed suit.

But then there was a shift in the global economic and trading paradigm that had served Japan so well. The country was unable to adjust its existing model to accommodate these new realities and it sank into a funk that lasted for some decades. Meanwhile, across on the Asian mainland, China continued to develop at a rapid pace, flexing its muscles in all sorts of ways.

Japan's previous intelligence gathering processes simply weren't up to scratch and proved relatively useless in helping the nation avoid being drawn into China's burgeoning gravitational orbit.

That's when the Japanese realised they needed a new overseas spy service, one that could gather intelligence in much the same way as Britain's MI6. The British agreed to help, as did other members of the 'Five Eyes' intelligence group comprising the United States, Britain, Canada, Australia and New Zealand.

However, all of this masked a much grander historical development now well under way: the challenge the East poses to the West. It appears that the epicentre of global power may be returning to Asia. Bear in mind that until as recently as 1820, China was the world's leading industrial giant.

This doesn't mean the West is a spent force. Rather, it obliges Westerners, like never before, to understand the subtle nuances of not only culture, civilisation and language but how power is exercised by China. The West also needs to observe and understand the responses of China's neighbours to that country's continued rise – hedging their bets and struggling to maintain as much of their independence as possible. This process is gargantuan in scale but often invisible and excruciatingly slow. Unfortunately, there is no multi-lingual guide book and map in this instance.

Spy services around the world, by their very nature, operate largely along the fault lines of great change. That's where most economic, geo-political, technological and scientific developments take place. These new paradigms in turn force major governmental, bureaucratic and corporate systems to change their ways. Many individuals in those systems find it difficult if not impossible to adapt. But spies are already trained and equipped to handle such things. They have traditionally danced along these fault lines to gather the secret intelligence that their governments desperately need. Crossing cultural borders, operating effectively in foreign languages, grappling with vastly different thought patterns are all commonplace to a spy.

And then there's the vital role of trust in the secret intelligence game. A spy's personal security and operational safety depend upon the relationships of trust that the spy creates and nurtures with his or her stable of traitors. Only spies who have done this successfully know the pivotal importance of weaving a silk cocoon of protection around each individual informant. Trust is the thread by which everything hangs.

If they are deft at doing this, spies can work wonders in the oddest of circumstances, coping with contradictions and ironies that would flummox most people. It is a form of agility and resilience unique to the craft. The roles that Bella and Li play in *An Elephant on Your Nose* exemplify those qualities, and the results, at their finest.

ACKNOWLEDGEMENTS

When authors, publishers, editors and cover designers work smoothly together – each understanding where the others are coming from – the creative process hums like a Rolls Royce engine. That's what it's like working with Jen McDonald, Dave Burton and the team at For Pity Sake – my thanks to everyone involved. I am grateful too, to Jim Fallows, Ross Coulthart, Richard McGregor and Mike Kennedy for being so generous in providing their views on this book.

I also owe a debt of ongoing gratitude to a group of close friends who kindly read the first draft of anything I write and provide candid views, without pulling punches. Richard Pyvis, my old school mate Dr Humphrey Elliott and Barbara Zuegg go to great trouble to ensure that the story line flows naturally. I deeply appreciate the valuable time they kind-heartedly devote to this process. Dr Christopher Ward, Nic Vardakis and John Ballantyne also help in this regard.

I take this opportunity to thank Robert and Yvonne Steinberg, my sister, Roma Hill, Julian Pedersen and my erstwhile colleague, Dr Jenny Minter, for their unwavering support over many years and on many fronts to clear the path for creative pursuits like this book.

Warren Reed
August 2018

ABOUT THE AUTHOR

Warren Reed is a former Australian Secret Intelligence Service (ASIS) agent who currently advises businesses on the geopolitics of globalisation with specific emphasis on Australia and the Asian region.

A regular media commentator on espionage and terrorism, Reed is often sought out to comment on the human side of spying.

Born in Tasmania, Reed undertook two years National Service in the Australian Army before completing a degree in Political Science and Business Administration from the University of Tasmania. In 1973, he was admitted to the Law Faculty of the University of Tokyo as an Australia-Japan Business Cooperation Committee Scholar.

On his return to Australia, Reed consulted for a major Japanese trading house before being recruited by ASIS and trained by the British Secret Intelligence Service (MI6) in London. His ten-year career in clandestine work focused on Asia and the Middle East, and he has lived and worked in Tokyo, Cairo and New Delhi.

Reed left ASIS in 1987 and subsequently held the position of Chief Operating Officer for CEDA.

Fluent in written and spoken Japanese, Warren Reed's other language studies include Mandarin, Bahasa Indonesian and Arabic.

PREVIOUS WORKS BY WARREN REED

1989 - *The Confucian Renaissance*, co-authored with Reg Little, published in Australia by The Federation Press, translated into Japanese and Chinese.

1992 - *Australia and Japan: Grappling with a Changing Asian World*, published in Japanese by Chuo Koron, Tokyo.

1997 - *The Tyranny of Fortune: Australia's Asian Destiny*, co-authored with Reg Little, published by Business & Professional Publishing, Sydney.

2004 - *Code Cicada*, published in Australia by HarperCollins with a Chinese translation published in China by the People's Publishing House, Beijing, in 2014.

2005 - *Plunging Point: Intelligence Failures, Cover-Ups and Consequences*, co-authored with Lance Collins, published by HarperCollins in Australia.

2013 - *Hidden Scorpion*, self-published via Amazon.

2016 - *Ethics and the Future of Spying: Technology, National Security and Intelligence Collection*, co-edited with Jai Galliott, published by Routledge in London.

2018 - *An Elephant On Your Nose* is the first Warren Reed novel to be published by For Pity Sake Publishing.

So you've written a manuscript.
What now?

Printed in Australia
AUOW01n0845121018
303821AU00002B/2

9 780648 283973